Praise for Harry Mathews

"Harry Mathews is a writer of immense elegance and skill."
—*New York Review of Books*

"Harry Mathews has few, if any, equals in modern fiction."
—*San Diego Union*

"Harry Mathews is the only American author I know whose utter origi-
nality does not erode his heart and his content."—Ned Rorem

"In his inventiveness and erudition he is like Pynchon, Barth, and
William Gaddis."—Granville Hicks, *Saturday Review*

"Mathews is a delightful original."—*Times Literary Supplement*

"Like Roubaud and Perec, Mathews engineers a funhouse labyrinth in
which guise defigures guise and the logic that reigns is that of represen-
tation."—*Village Voice Literary Supplement*

Works by Harry Mathews

Fiction

The Conversions
Tlooth
Country Cooking and Other Stories
The Sinking of the Odradek Stadium
Cigarettes
The American Experience
Singular Pleasures
The Journalist

Poetry

The Ring
The Planisphere
Trial Impressions
Le Savoir des rois
Armenian Papers: Poems 1954-1984
Out of Bounds
A Mid-Season Sky: Poems 1954-1991

Miscellanies

Selected Declarations of Dependence
The Way Home: Collected Longer Prose
Ecrits Français

Nonfiction and Criticism

The Orchard: A Remembrance of Georges Perec
20 Lines a Day
Immeasurable Distances: The Collected Essays
Fiandomenico Tiepolo

THE SINKING OF THE ODRADEK STADIUM

Harry Mathews

Dalkey Archive Press

Library of Congress Cataloging-in-Publication Data

Mathews, Harry, 1930-
        The sinking of the Odradek Stadium / Harry Mathews. — 1st Dalkey Archive ed.
            p.   cm.
        ISBN 1-56478-207-7 (pa. : alk. paper)
            1. Eccentrics and eccentricites Fiction. 2. Married people Fiction. 3.
Treasure-trove Fiction. 4. Ex-convicts Fiction. 5. Revenge Fiction 6. Revenge Fiction.
I. Title.
    PS3563.A8359S56   1999
    813'. 54—dc21   99-35094
                                                                        CIP

This publication is partially supported by grants from the Lannan Foundation, the
Illinois Arts Council, a state agency, and the National Endowment for the Arts, a
federal agency.

Dalkey Archive Press
Illinois State University
Campus Box 4241
Normal, IL 61790-4241

Visit our website at: www.dalkeyarchive.com

THE SINKING OF THE
ODRADEK STADIUM

Some people assume that in addition to the great original betrayal a small particular betrayal has been contrived in every case exclusively for them, that, in other words, when a love drama is being performed on the stage the leading actress has not only a pretended smile for her lover, but also a special crafty smile for one particular spectator at the back of the gallery. This is going too far.

Kafka, "Reflections on Sin, Pain, Hope, and the True Way"

Part One

I

...confidence in words, Twang. I suck my tongue for your chervil-and-lavender flavor.

This afternoon I went to the Beach to see a new hotel, the Brissy St. Jouin. It has been described as the "Naples ultra" of Miami splendor. There is teak sawdust in the Oyster Bar, where I began my tour with a screwdriver ; the lobby is decked with much gold. That was all I saw. La Nosherie, the Mannikin Pis rumpus room, and the Jupiter Seaside Fungus Collection had to wait for another visit.

What arrested me, ankle-deep in peacock feathers, was a battery of television sets assembled for the inauguration as a "monument to intercontinental awareness." Above the lobby fountain, seven sets rose vertically from a spray-shrouded base. On either side of the midmost screen, three others were horizontally aligned, hung by transparent cords from the distant ceiling. No sound from the construction reached the naked ear; but telephones, each equipped with a panel of buttons, connected viewers to the various programs. Stopping to sample this profusion of "light inscribed by light," I stayed until I had exhausted the repertory.

From the top of the vertical rank, the highest set showed a program from Paris, a children's spelling bee. A little boy carefully chalked the word *batrimoine* across the blackboard of a classroom where a dozen schoolmates, mainly girls, sat watching him. They laughed at his mistake. The West is mad. I could not live without your words, no matter how you spell them.

A documentary emanating from Indonesia appeared on the set beneath. The subject was a celebrated Balinese *gamelan*. There were close-ups of the instruments demonstrating their use, then a series of stills of the entire orchestra: taken over eighty years, the photographs faded each into the next to form an animated historical image. Throughout it the instruments neither moved nor changed, while the performers aged steadily and from time to time were suddenly replaced. Shots of the current fighting followed. I thought of the *kuchi* playing for us their reedy serenades, as we ate your delicate slop-rice.

At the end of the left-hand arm of the assemblage I tuned into an advertisement featuring the Indians, a baseball team. Players were seen on the field, then in a kitchen eating "Mateotti's pizzas." Baseball is like *zem*, except that a ball is used.

To the right of this I watched an American film broadcast from Hawaii. The sound track was dead. A man in nineteenth-century dress was seated at a table, eating from a bowl of pears. After a while he pushed the fruit away, used a finger-bowl to wet his lips and forehead, then took up a quill pen and began writing on a rough-edged page. The camera followed his hand as it traced the words, O *say, can you see...* I passed the consulate today. The Cow of Plenty was snapping prettily in the breeze.

On the adjacent set I briefly switched on a popular mathematics congress in Florence. The subject was psychic topology, so rapidly discussed I could not even follow the English translation. By Florence I mean Florence, Italy.

Russia held the place of honor at the crossing of the vertical and horizontal ranks. I witnessed part of a biological experiment. For ten minutes the screen was filled with the front-face close-up of a cat. Every few seconds a white arc momentarily quivered between the tips of its moustache. A mild hum accompanied the toy lightning. The cat lay quiet, shifting its eyes from side to side. *Amour, amour, quand tu nous tiens...*

To the right a local quiz program was being transmitted. It took place by the swimming pool of some Beach hotel, perhaps the Brissy St. Jouin itself. I listened to one exchange. "In what year did Captain Kidd begin his career of piracy?" "Uh... he turned out in 1697." "Correct!" The contestant was thrown into the pool. The weather has been chilly these past days, with the north wind.

Next to this came an advertisement illustrated by flights of the eagle owl swooping on its prey. (I want nothing, except one thing.)

At the right of the horizontal rank, I watched an Indian movie about the tribulations of a lamb lost in Calcutta. The lamb's innocence so touches those it encounters that butchers and starving men befriend it. The film made me hungry.

Switching to the set underneath the electrical cat, I viewed a performance by the Peking Opera of *Russlan and Ludmilla*. I waited until the end of the canon for Ludmilla's father. How is Bamma Deng?

The screen below was blank, glowing with creamy light. The program was supposed to be from Pretoria. A flat voice recited a love poem.

Below, an English documentary enlightened with X-rays the murky functionings of the womb, including partheno-genesis. The colors were scrumptious.

Finally, the lowest set showed a program from Cairo. Presented against a background of local music and dance, its subject was the circular bread of Egypt. We learned of its usefulness when fractioned in making sandwiches, even with soup.

An old man standing nearby engaged me in conversation when I set down my earphone. He wore blinding beach attire and carried a basket of comb shells on one arm. Under the other an unfamiliar receptacle caught my notice. The old man answered my stare with the words, "This is a pilgrim's flask, such as was carried by those who journeyed to Santiago de Compostela." Turning back to the television assemblage he pointed out to me, at its very apex, the blue-and-white figure of a cherub. "Do you think it's one of the della Robbia gang?" The cherub leaned winsomely on a cittern that had been tilted to one side, and held aloft a triangular plectrum. We chatted long enough to exchange names; then I decided to go home. I was getting dizzy from the six thousand dozen roses banked against the lobby walls.

Miami looks so vertical and unimaginative after the dusky lateral circular something of your village—it was like a shiny wooden nut dish. I have been quiet, mostly. Dan had a party to celebrate the end of Lent. He gave it early—on Good Friday—because it was to be "different." It wasn't. Such occasions leave me feeling like a beaten mark. I come to them filled with high spirits that are quickly and indifferently taken from me. It doesn't matter. My hopes are unquenchable. I feel that I stand on the brink of lofty exchanges that will make the ills of life ridiculous. After each respite, even a nap, we can all meet each other as gods. I have entrusted my life to expectation, as if the bud would surely blossom. I can only live this way.

Have sent the money you need. Isn't it lucky that you were born in an Italian colony?

I was right: the name figures in the "hypothetical lists" of the Donation.

II

April 6

Pan persns knwo base bal. The giappan-like trade-for mishn play with it in our capatal any times. To morrow to work be gin. It's cleen eccepts for the talk. The in-habits live in draems. To raed this has need, not idees but a tenshn (to-trans-late of Twang): "After a land-like giourney a yuong man-Pan a rive deep in a rest hwere the her of his choise was live in a mall she has make. Green aster hang, man re-sieve no to-

greet, re-turn to his ghest—there is no re-plies. Rael Zen he
is to can make to get a-tention; the stud go to a nother art of
rest and biuld his-self yeers. Later, new as-to-weep-like fall
leeves, he 's line. He then drop. Every thing run throuh the
rest to teech and say, Thank you." Here, is Rome. Your to-
write with baeutifl discovery of Miami is a preziate to no
end. You are write a bout name—good—then have you
found-ed map? Or, are you to can found it? and how do
you dou? The one-most inter-lohutor of Twang in Rome is
a boy-child whowho say in playce of my way, but, in italian,
"Dont stop me, I giust raech 6,523,281" and go on to count,
sit-ed on the steppes of the Graet Squaer. So brothr, my
mynd hargo of love seek you one-most in one deriction, then
in a second derection, then in a 3rd derexion, then in a forth
direction, like wise up ward, dwon ward, and all-round, the
sence of to-love-like minde in-fusion all thing with no limit,
no narrow, no to-hate, no ill desire. You care for mor Zen
storys. It 's un-easy to write them, with this dificint langu-
ague, and they so pleyn; yet here is one. And I sey, "Good-
bye, *neng* of Twang."

III

April 11

Divine testimony is the best, and your letters bristle with
Eleusinian truths. By them I know I exist, even if I would
rather you proved it by digging your nails into my palms, or
your toe into my flank. So I believe you blindly—I believe
you when you say I am a *neng*; but you must step out of the
holy fire to tell me why.

That old man I met at the Brissy St. Jouin called three days
ago. Would I join his party on a visit to Panoramus? Next
morning we gathered into two cars for the drive. It was nice,
in a dismal way. Our highways are now paved with a material
that when warmed by the sun emits a smell of fresh bread;
the worthy effect is destroyed by a nostalgia for neighborhood
bakeries. The ugliness of the state of Florida also depressed
me. It appeared concave rather than flat, and the mean

age of the inhabitants glimpsed by the roadside was at least
seventy-one. Panoramus was no different. It is the shelling
capital of the universe, its beaches are lined with old, avid
hobbyists stooping endlessly. My host came over to ask if I
was glad to be there and then attached himself to me for the
day, whisking me along the beach, leaving me not the smal-
lest chance for a drink. The shore was messy. A wealth of
mostly broken shells was diversified with fish skulls, medusa
carcasses, and used containers. We searched for new-moon
shells and picked beach roses and violets. Then, although the
mercury was low, I went for a swim. The salty water stung
like fire and I didn't stay in long; just long enough to open
one foot on a can. We proceeded to the Shell Museum cafeteria for a lunch of roast lamb, beans, and leaf-and-fruit salad.
(That's how the dishes were listed. A blind man would have
had difficulty naming them, since they were as odorless as if
frozen, which they partly were.) At the end of the meal a
black girl, moving in an ethereal or at least ether-like cloud
of vetiver, arrived to guide us through the museum. "You
shall be the two millionth visitor of our conchological col-
lections," she sweetly said to me, ending a vague hope that I
might cop a heel. I know I sound ungrateful, but I kept my
feelings to myself. (And O my dearest, I cannot look at anything, even a collection of shells, without turning my
thoughts towards you. My time is never wasted. Thanks to
the serene passion within me, and the ministry of the post
office, there is nothing in the world that does not commem-
orate you—girls who are beautiful and black because you are
beautiful and lemony, the smell of the sea because of your
landlocked mother's broths, greyhounds at the track because
of your sister's hands at her shuttle, the pavements of roads
because I wish they led me to you. Even garbage helps me
recall, although of course it is too tame to match, the fumy
litter of your markets.) Smiling, she took me by the hand
and led me through the museum, where we inspected bearded
conchs; shells used to make purple dyes; an Indian shell shield
from pre-Columbian times; shell sculptures by local artists
(e.g. "Nessus abducting Dejanira.") Afterwards we went back

to the beach. I watched a greyhound bitch sniffing after wristwatch-size brown crabs that kept sidling off into the wavelets, leaving her unseeing and perplexed. There was lightning out to sea. On the drive home I had a talk with Mr. Dexter Hodge, a very class person whom I have met once before. He told me that he had been accosted outside the cafeteria by a guitar-strumming lad who proposed taking us to a cockfight.

As to your questions: I do not have the map and it is not certain that I shall find it. The Donation I mentioned is a collection of 19,000 old maps smuggled over in 1966 from the Maestranza in Havana. The object of the theft was to exploit the treasure-hunting craze by selling the maps, but the State of Florida impounded them and deposited them for safekeeping in the University of Miami library. They have never been catalogued, but lists of possible origins have been compiled. A number of maps came to Havana from Santa Catalina, after the fort there was dismantled; and since the archives of the fort record our captain's hanging in 1537 and the seizure of his effects, his name appears on one of the lists. This means only that *if* he had a copy of the map, it *may* be here.

It's the season when worms start spinning cocoons, in the north the crows are leaving the woods, the snows of the past melt and the eyes of men become unstuck. I go on blinking in your perpetual spring light. You have made the eyes I look through. Abstract convergent lines orient the fractions of my world to a point beyond the horizon that may well be your navel. I may not sense this at every moment, any more than I smell the hairs inside my nose, but at the end of each minute or day I remember happily that it is so. Only occasionally do I think of you in a distracted way (longing), and the milk on the hob boils over.

IV

April 15

Amortonelli have-make be fore crime-like hystery, a satir a gaints Pope-most *Clement VII* (Medici). Be fore, there was any thing to find out from a bibliotheck near. That man is truth-like to you in to-tell the briggand ave the end-most days in Rome. It was can for Twang to find a paper near 1600 whiwhich say: *of-Amortonelly* to-wrotes in Vatihan bibliotec. And is can look soon at its. Years, and *G. A. Medici* is re-turn and *Pius For.* He awllays buy penshn to Amor-tonelli, lest perpaps his verse buyt him. So, hwen my not-to-exist grub-like flesh pass, there is fear lest one late-er be book worm bluynd and dark. Yet is to-fire a stic or few of in sense be in-sureance to proteck me lest cruel re birth? Once, yess, a lama-most munk of Tibett, whowho have-eat cheazes with graet love, and he in deth be then a chease worm. Onemost, *neng* have sense nose, that wish to say, nose to have thought on when one squatt and moove a way thouhgt; then, Buddha's nose. O yass, there be my puprose to learn like, in a dark roome, the lihgt of lamp with to-shatter obscurety, with to-give and to-scatter ligt, so that discovery then there will pomp a way the shaddw of darks-nesses and schatter the ligth of to-know, and like too, the lihtg of our re-lation with the advance in to the darkmosts of this world, things one after one light until all are glod. The crime-full poet has come here soone after in-Italy, and stay until dead 1561, eccept wen his *Hardinal Giovonni Ongelo Medici* is ex pulse by *Paol 4.* The nose of Buddha is beatiful and *neng* a rive to sense beautifl thing—you. Any time we say *neng* and non *vin* (cadavar) to make confort to the hadavers.

V

April 20

I have lately felt as though I were wading through a desert-ed desert. I know it's only a little while that I haven't seen you, and again in a little while I shall see you... meanwhile my mind's mouth has been dry. The research is discouraging, there are so many maps, full of flattened bugs and dust, each to be laboriously unfolded, then refolded. Our captain's career has rubbed off on none of them, and my only "fact" is still this: the name given to me by the Red Arrow man (I'm sure of it because I wrote it down) is identical with one on the Donation list. The work is also slow, since it has to be done after office hours. My colleagues started complaining that I was becoming "withdrawn." They mustn't guess the truth.

Then this afternoon, walking toward my bus-stop, I had a brush with Nemesis. I was passing a tidy speckled-egg bungalow when I saw beyond its Moorish patio, raised above the low wall of a terrace, the peroxide head of my sister Diana. I called to her; the head looked up, and looked away. I crossed the patio for a closer view. The person, who was not my sister, was stretched out beneath the unflattering sun on a pneumatic deck, naked except for a pair of sungoggles. I turned back, too late. "Eve!" she yelled. A tawny watchcat, fierce as a lion and as big as a schnauzer, rose from her side as if winged. Striking my right elbow, its claws only nicked my arm, since the fury of its leap unseamed my coat-sleeve and dropped the beast to the ground. But as you know, I cannot run very fast, and another jump fastened the cat to my shoulders, where it opened six parallel slits in the cloth and flesh of my back, before abandoning me at the patio gate. I ran on, expecting further assault, but only the womanly cry of "Stay away, maniac!" pursued me down the sidewalk.

Can an evil spirit open blind men's eyes? Even as I stood sobbing in the street, and later, while the druggist cleansed and dressed my lacerations, I became aware that I had been brought back to life. My frightful sensations had lifted me above habit into a conscious emptiness where I could begin feeling again. For days I had wallowed in dreams, forgetting what you have made me, charmed by phantasms of my loneliness and its childish yearnings to be soothed—as if we deserved nothing better than to be instantly locked into an everlasting ice cream parlor! Scandal and pain wrenched me awake: then you became absolutely present to me, not for long, but in that time your bodily presence would not have made you more real. I felt your fingers on my face, which was like a blind man's face under their touch.

It's late now. I'm in my office, ringed in maps. To the east a new moon is rising, in the sky I crossed not long ago to have a stranger transfigure my life in the unlikely shrine of the Bangkok airport. Soon this exile will end.

VI

It 's cruel to be-weep for those dayze and nights, not
minites when your to-write come but one time with out end
of 2 weeks-long. To be lock to gether in forever lasting ice
craem is not as bad a thougt. (I vow, to treatmeant my
english!) To-put "we" close "*tharaï*" is all ways hanromy in
Pan, in every way—*tharaï* "with no to-end".

The papers of *Amortonelli* are-give in to the Vatican but not long,
be cause *Hosimo de' Medici* whowho will-be soon Gran Duc of Tos-
cany I, take them 4–6 months after the brigan dead. G. A. *Medici* is
be come Pope but he 's but a north-most Medici, he has a dett to
Cosimo for to-say he is cousins and all-most a graet tuscan Medici.
How full the wish even to see you once mor, see if some marks
life give in your face after last we meat each othr. How many
dusts to lift to discover that I discover! So many, the small
Monsignor Latten, a shortness with jewls, descend from heigths to see
and say me more, that in those dayse there is a talk, so: said in the
next year daid of paludism, the sons of *Cosimo* kill themself in to-
fight a bout the paper of the thief; and this musts mien it is not but
sattires? As we mieet it then is un-clear there is some great tendency, you musts put in my hart to to remembem a bout the
Banghok air port and the Mister Red Arrow. And do the
man-mother of the beests no help your hope with other tells of
the tresure, how did he say exatcly? The feeling is, my English
not whatwhat it would be—force, be cause all-day takking
italian. The litle Paple ociffer say, it 's part of an age-most
story.

VII

April 29

Since you again ask, this is how it began. On my way east,
after Rome, I was seated next to Mr. Zonder Tittel, a friendly
Canadian working for the International Red Arrow, the
conservation society. Mr. Tittel was traveling to Indo-China
to capture specimens of a wild cow called the coubou, or
kubu. Have you ever seen one? It roams the plateaus of south-

ern Laos in small herds; its only food is the bark of the native apple, which is being girdled into extinction, taking the coubou with it. Until recently no one cared, since the coubou was thought to be only a domestic breed gone wild. Mr. Tittel himself learned otherwise when he examined one animal: "I got a crowbar between its teeth and prised its goddam jaws apart, and there was a mouth two million years old."

Mr. Tittel then asked what had brought me to the Orient. I gave him a short course in Pan history. He was not very interested in the early missionaries or in my plans to microfilm their records in Pan-Nam. But when I mentioned working at the Miami U. library he perked up and began discussing treasure troves. He had heard about the maps from the Maestranza and asked if any of them had proved valuable. I said I had nothing to do with the maps, and that I knew little about buried treasure. He then started telling me about the "craziest" chest of gold in the Caribbean. If only I had listened more attentively! Here are the main facts of his story. I know how remote they must have seemed in those giddy days.

The treasure was hidden, probably in the Florida keys, by the Catalan Jesus María Cabot, captain of *El Paráclito*, and his associate Amortonelli, a Florentine. The ship sailed from Barcelona early in the 1500's, bound for Mexico. Blown off course by a hurricane, it was wrecked on the Florida coast. The partners salvaged and buried a large coffer not far from the wreck, with the help of two members of the crew. When the survivors of *El Paráclito* were rescued, one of the sailors denounced Cabot and Amortonelli; later, however, he failed to identify the hiding-place. The captain and the Italian were arrested, and the former hanged. Amortonelli escaped and is supposed to have returned to Italy.

This is all I "know." It is reasonable to assume that each partner drew a map of the treasure's location. That is why I asked you to look for the map in Italy while I search here. (I have written to the Red Arrow man for a complete account; apparently he is still harrying the Laotian bush.)

At Bangkok we prepared to go our ways; but Mr. Tittel

had more to teach me. He had hinted at a moon of riches. Now he was to reveal the sun and earth. Spying your *phrap* across the airport lobby, he led me toward you. He said that you were "typically Pan," that you would probably be on my plane, and that you could "help me off to a friendly start. They're such an easygoing people, she won't mind our accosting her. You'll see." He started to address you in the twinkling cadence of your language. You listened patiently, without indifference or interest. I was already collapsing. I tried to be a cliff but sank like swirling pebbles. Your eyes did not move yet swept tides of confusion through me. Then, when you turned to me, your first words ("Hello baby") plunged me into melancholy. I could neither leave, nor believe. If you had noticed that "great tendency" you might have been kind. If you had been kind, the world of dreams would have reclaimed me and ended all hope. It was enough to walk with you to the plane, and sit by you, a glimmer of folded silks.

My first alarm was soon over. I felt that our proximity was now like that of two actors when, after a performance, they drop their masks and resume a spontaneous friendship. But since I had worn a mask all my life, I didn't know how not to act. And you, who had never put on a mask because you are truth itself, could not see that my face was nude. If you had thought about me at all, you would have taken me for an idiot. But you did not seem particularly aware of me until, in Sah Leh Khot next morning, wishing me well, you told me the way to your village.

Meanwhile you abandoned me for the night to the distractions of the *Deuam phap* fair, through which I rode on the emerging whale of my desire. Everything seemed beautiful, if sometimes unfathomable, in the glamor of a race that included you.

I entered the fairgrounds through a gate resembling a huge white N whose left apex has been broken off. On its uprights primitive guns, relinquished by visiting tribesmen, were strung on brass chains. Beyond, a movie billboard announced Ava Gardner in *The Joan Crawford Story*.

Drifting through the flashing lanterns and loudspeakers, I stopped at a little cinder track where preparations for a foot-race were under way. As I approached the group of runners and their handlers, I nearly tripped over a boy who was scurrying on all fours through the crowd. He looked up at me, raised a forefinger to one eye, and pinched my shoe. I glanced around me: six feet away an unlaced boot lay on its side. I picked it up and gave it to the boy. Sidling over to the track, he cunningly substituted it for a similar boot that rested on the starting-line among a dozen others. The boot I had found weighed at least five pounds—it was plainly "loaded." I kept an eye on it, until it was finally put on by a runner wearing the number four. I pushed into the thick of the crowd, where I rightly guessed that bets were being taken, and learned that "four" was the favorite. While I wondered what runner to back, I saw the boy who had changed the boot placing a few *khrot* on "six," and I followed his example. The race started; number four won easily; number six finished last. Pan runners surely do not race with weighted shoes. I had been made to "find the leather," and I paid duly for my greed.

I next stopped to watch a kind of dance, performed on a small wooden platform by a husky old man. The dancer lay on his back or side and applied his legs to his head and shoulders, or his arms to his legs and hips, in slow lurching gestures punctuated by swipes of fist, foot, or knee. Except for the groans of the performer, there was no accompaniment.

Farther on I joined the audience of a shadow play, where willowy puppets moved behind screens of colored silk. The action began with a horde of demon-like figures shrieking around a solitary hut. When the demons withdraw, a venerable man steps out of the hut and sings gently for a while. The leader of the demons approaches him disguised as a beggar. Soon, at his bidding, a vision of viand-laden tables appears. The old man drives the beggar off with a few roars. The demon then returns as a beautiful woman and conjures up another vision, this time of girls dancing. The demon is again repulsed. Then all the demons, chanting in evil chorus, attack and steal the old man's pig. As they decamp, a grotesque but benevolent genie rises from the ground, scatters them, and returns the pig.

Did the Italians bring this story to Pan-Nam?

Passing a field where moonlight *zem* was played, I thought I glimpsed you in the crowd, a wishful hallucination. Staring after your shadow I could see no one's features right, and when I tried to paint your face against the gloom, the colors were faint, and troubled by the hollow masks that the night mixed among the living.

Nearby, families of blue-turbaned Nau were selling their traditional comforters, embroidered with tennis rackets, those colonial relics; various roots, of which I bought a sampling; and of course their stinking sea-salt cakes.

Towards the western gate, I observed a native wall-and-ball game. The wall was of soft clay, straight and thick. Equipped with six-foot, spoonlike bamboo bats, two players in turn hurled a wiremesh sphere against the wall, whence it had to be dug out. What is the point of this game? Another couple played against the far side.

My last halt was for the monkey kites. Eight of them, with their busy passengers, were sailing about fifty yards from the ground in agitated proximity. I presume the monkeys have been trained to strike the other kites. Their exasperated cries followed me to the hotel, where I slept fitfully. I was shaken with the memory and anticipation of you; also I couldn't figure how to turn off the light.

In the earliest morning I met you as you were boarding your bus. I could not discover whether inclination or courtesy made you glow in that manner. In irreproachably noncommittal tones you said I might visit you. By then my feelings were clear; when you departed I let myself float into them. As I savored this joy, I felt the miseries of my life crowding down like angry beggars. They did not make me run away, because for the first time I knew I could satisfy them.

(There were other beggars as well, your orange-toga'd monks, cadging their breakfast. This practice seems degrading to us westerners. How can it be thought holy?)

You wonder if the fight over Amortonelli's papers does not prove them to be other than literary. Remember, literature was then a dreaded weapon. The first Cosimo had Il Burchiello murdered for his sonnets. Not that you are wrong. How could I ever think that you are wrong?

Don't forget to date your letters.

As they say in Pannam: *Duvaï maï*

VIII

May 3

Monsignor Latten say, it-all mixt with the hystory of—then his word fall out from my aer. A gain: *"Quella vecchia storia delle tosature."* But, wholding the words, I be leave they are italian idiotism, like Amerihans say "trim any body". One moom-time I account my 32 nature-like parts with resbonsipil to-breathe and I get a yas, there is can to be ohter censes. Mons. Latten is not hear, he 's in Luang Pra Bang for the synod. Yet the vocabaruly sur-render the idea for *tosare* "to hlip" that is "clip coins", so *tosature* "clippins"—a per-hap conenction with some traesure? I gioin my to-trouble-book-shelfs to this impusle.

You writ assid, brothr, of *Deuam phap* fair. Pans have ever bronz in ther shoes for to-run. Whowho is quikc-est, put on the haevy est shoose. Nor the old man-Pan on a bed have some need for the musical, be caus he 's in war no dance, one hlaf of man with otter half, a long fihgt. You have say *duvaï maï* but we are not to can say this all-thoug it will-be treu, *duvaï* is fair-well for the long-time, or even deth, it is rwong with *maï* that is now and for-this-moment. You will-say *tharaï* "for-ever" with *duvaï*. Not say-so to Twang! Not tenis raguets are on Nau hovers. They are wulwas.

You have see my gold bonzes "degarding" and you are worng. They have the ful contenpt for materialistist sotiety, to-beg make them free from the strusture. The bal-gaems are to gether a game, one grup here, one group here, the desire is to-get one ball through the wall. In that teatre the old man is the crule man-mother of the sky whowho will non give rain (pig). The heros make grate atcs to have it from, but you

have-see the hate of the bittr dead get up to give us no thing.
When you wait you did-can to see after how they get the
pig. The sky-most monekeys have-not-kut the kites but one
other. When a monekey is been-kill he homes down. A
string is on to the him and not to the kite, and that hite go a
way and have no triunf.

I've the memry of your to-come in my town. Our dog in
the under-house likes you, he make the strange woof of
tendernes and sensure—then, I have interest in you. And hiss.
Do not put a way your memery of the litlte money you will
send. Do not think, the of-Nau things be roots, they are
tirds, yet are OK if you aet only little. I & you; harmnony;
peace.

IX

May 8

Good news: yesterday I was given access to a university
computer. This should speed up the map work. Lester P.
Greek did the favor, during a chance meeting on the library
steps. He holds the Finnegans Wake chair in our Comp. Lit.
department, runs the municipal television trust, and is supposed to be on the big con.

Don't you think you may be wasting your time in Rome?
Amortonelli's papers are certainly in Florence. Why labor
after will-o'-the-wisps?

Thank you for correcting my Pan usage. May I point out
a similar mistake of your own? In one letter you wrote
"forever lasting." One can say "forever" or "everlasting"
but not "forever lasting."

It was interesting to learn about the fair.

The bank will forward your money, which I hadn't forgotten. Do you know the amount is exactly what I paid for
you, not counting the exemption from field labor? How I
miss your village, its lanes of teak and bamboo houses, quiet
under the silk-cotton trees! And your house, or Bamma
Deng's, the dark cool house by which I often stood, watching
the lizards slide over its posts, so unlike my street of blind
doors. Even in the shade, the pounding of my blood would

burst out in horrible sweating, as I waited for a hand...

Could you help reconstruct the events of our wedding day? It's hard for me, because I was so drunk. I don't feel remorse about this: such events are not to be piously hoarded.

By ten in the morning I was already teetering. I remember handing out countless cigarettes to the smiling groups around the stands, decked for the feast with streamers, green candles, and rice brandy.

At some point I spoke to you, or tried to, but you were taken away. I looked into a mirror and saw my face.

There came a slow gathering of people from every direction, like battalions drawing together before battle, or pilgrims at the consecration of a shrine, all eating dried squid and smoking my cigarettes. The alcohol began to ignite my skin; I felt as though I were being flayed. Boys led me to a carpeted area in front of the house, where your mother and aunts were arrayed. A long dialogue began, I think in verse, between your mother and a gnome who had been chosen to speak for me. Did you know him? I understood that he manufactured sundials. It was terrible to fall asleep during this exchange, when I was supposed to be begging for your hand, yet no one seemed to mind. The women's laughter woke me. They weren't laughing at me—what was it they were laughing about? Finally, the gnome left, with whispered words that sounded like "Beware of green wolves!" A bowl of cuprous liquid was set before the women, into which they dropped thistle-like tufts that dissolved in smoke. The chief bonze, who with other monks had chanted drowsily through the morning hours, rose I gathered to assert that the marriage was now proclaimed, received, professed, undergone, and enacted. But the ceremony went on. You were brought down, a small mat was set between us, and there you placed a handful of winter rice shoots, and I a dollar bill. That was the sign that everyone could return to his feasting.

I remember much better, a few days earlier, going up to see you in the opium fields. I had woken early. For a time I tried to read *Birth, Breath, Breast* by Norman O. Brown, but a shrike was singing, so I went over to your father's house to ask for your hand. You had already left. The basin where you had washed (publicly but modestly, no doubt, with your *phrap* raised about your ears) glowed in the near-light like a little milky sea. Bamma Deng was sitting on his verandah. I addressed him directly, pleading devotion and honesty against my ignorance of Pan ways. He answered readily and at length, displaying that perfect Italian of his that, down to the charming dissonance of his hard c's, aspirated in the Tuscan manner, suggests rather a lifetime in Florence than a few years' study in a Far Eastern *liceo*. He called me his son, admonished me in sententious periods to trust in God, informed me of the customary rites and obligations, and accepted my proposal. When I told him I had not yet spoken to you, he warned me that his agreement depended on yours. I had hopes of your willingness, and such an abundance of desire that I felt that you could not help sharing it; so I hurried off to find you, stumping up the rooted, gullied path that led to the crown of the hill. Rubbery leaves swatted my sweat- and tear-glazed face. Once I halted to recover my breath and gazed unperceiving over the pulse fields below, gray in the first light. I resumed my ascent at a slower pace, but my feelings banged on within me. I tried to distract myself by naming the innumerable trees that towered confusingly about me over the ferns and wild deutzia bordering my path. Liquidambar, magnolia, padauk, varnish tree... the effort was useless, I was obsessed with your smell and skin. I must have come into the clearing like a slavering lunatic. It was tranquil there. The sun was a yellowish ball in the eastern haze. In its aquarial light you all appeared in dwarfish silhouette, erect or bent as you spooned the droplets oozing from the cropped shoots. At first I could not distinguish you. Your familiar laugh brought me to you. I said that I had spoken to your father and that he was willing that we should marry. Because I could imperfectly make out your features, and you did not at once reply, I was shaken with doubt, and all the intensity of my hope and lust careered toward bitterness. Then you cast away your spoon, and with a soundless flutter dropped to the ground to embrace my feet.

X

May 12

Listn! I have, how ever, find: coin clippings are-can to be a treazure.
1391 the papa *Bonifacio IX* sell this emty abbazy of Montpelas, that is
neighbr-like to Avignon on a edge of of-Antipopoes land. The buy-
man is Messer *Todao*, he 's a fiorentine who have a hous in Mont
Pelier. He for-get to pay, the pope take his propriety in Florence, of-
it is a part a box of gold-most-hlippins with a worht of 37,000 florini!
The mother of Twang and the interlocutor of the mother of
Twang were-laugh be cause they sing fun-y things to the
other. Firts they are to-make a musick-full list of every thing
that is like 2 lovrs can not be separate

> dust & watter
> nale & fingre
> oil & carpet
> flower & name of-flower
> wacks & fire

tehn wehn she have let a end of her to-question:

> The ivery pins, the iorn kneedles
> —have you brougt them a long?
> The umbrellow of parrot-like feather, the *phrap*
>   of gold-like cloth
> —have you brought them a long?
> The rynocerous buttr, the of-Japan appels,
> —have you brought them a long?

and so otter hard debts, and he answer

> We bring a long the ivry pins, the iren neadles &c.,

my mother aks

> Muts I give her to you? do you vow to-want-her
>   even if she   ug-ly?
>   even if she   more I 's than teeth?
>   even if she   mmore tethe than hairs:
>   even if she   so pale as the Eureups?
>   even if she   crooket as *bukhaï?* (kind of brush)
>   even if she   drunk in the mournins?
>   even if she   your emeny is her lovr?

and he ansser

Yas we want her even all-though she be ugl-y &c. and they are-laugh to gether while this be cause I have great respett for I 'm pritty, chaste, and sobre.

My eyes are bend-ed from the to-see old hand scritts and prints and still, I found not *storia delle tosature* with *Amortonelli,* or *Medici.*

My family have all great rispect for much quality, much beauty, and the man-mother and the mother of Twang have no punish-meant from heavn, but it be-stow on these genitors comfrots in lovly symytry, 3 gerls, 3 boys, a gerl, a boy, five gerls, five boys, then a boï and a gerl that is Twang. No one baby die, and we are poor yet we are live in harmony with heaven and under heven. May be you are co-rect, that I maek the end to work here. But there is so much other mathers of your to-write a little, in your most-deer be cause most-new letter—there are so much things hwere I have the same to-feel with a eletricly dellicate clear-ness so I all most have no brath to make my voice strong that the current not be break, and my thought be ex-change only in a part, and your ex-sistence that now is write ovre me so passed mine farthar and nop stop. *Weï weï lemö slop.* Wo-woe the mysyry of love, we say. But it has no so bad a soun be-cause *weï* is "a-las" and "sad-ness", OK, but all-so "to-laugh". You shall for-ever rememer *lemu* be cause it is, "love".

XI

May 17

If Lester Greek runs for Congress he'll have my vote. There is new material at last, thanks to Les's computer. It checked the names of Amortonelli and the captain against one million nine hundred and seventy-two thousand items of information, obtaining one positive response. The document indicated was in San Juan de Puerto Rico. I have already received a copy of it, unfortunately in translation.

Here is the text. Clearly it is part of a letter addressed to the captain on the eve of his sailing from Barcelona. It says nothing of the treasure's location but confirms its presence on *El Paráclito.* The opening is lost.

...to Lyon in the company of the Aretine, whose name

was Gherucci. On the second day, when I had been
crossing the city in her pursuit it thus happened: the
watery element, as if it had been drunk up and con-
tained too long, poured down so emphatically that I
was forced to creep along like one afraid of the watch
close under the overhangs, where the cellar door of a
money changer's house being unbarred on the under
side, I fell into it head over heels, like a blind man who
in an earthquake comes tap-tapping with his cane and
falls straight into hell. I fell on straw, that is into silence,
such that I heard my own blood. To be brief, I was in a
Jew's house, unasked and unperceived. A grave conversation dropped thinly down from a room over me,
and I was moved (O destiny) to hear it plainer, and
slunk up a stair more ladder than stair, old and ill-fitted
so that it would have squeaked my undoing but for the
essential dampness of the place, and brought me, light-
footed as the lover who treads to a husband's snores,
close to the ceiling, that was their floor. Two were
speaking, one much, the other no more than as if to
nod his head. The first told how he had been sent to
inquire about a chest of silk that his master, the Abbot
of Montpelas, had discovered unaccountably abandoned,
nay hidden even, in a dark corner of the abbey. There
was a great quantity of silk in it, taffeta, with a piece of
brocade that at one end was embroidered with six crow-
like figures, and on the lid of the chest were crudely
carved three fish. Diverse and sundry tropes were introduced by the narrator to piece out these few mean
facts, and well I knew why, it was wiliness to prick the
Jew's interest, for getting money or knowledge out of
him I did not understand, and I would not wait either
to hear more or to sneeze because my own inquisitive-
ness was inflamed: I had been thoroughly taught the fame
of that treasure that today I told you of; so like a trout
climbing a waterfall I wished my body after my soul up
through the cellar door, found Gherucci, and that
night we made for Montpelas.

There we stopped little, because the chest was gone. Three sunless crowns slipped into the hand of a fornicating monk found out that it was dispatched to be sold in Barcelona, in the company of two friars less covetous. We followed them, and caught them not until Narbonne. Toward Beziers they progressed and took Fontfroide in their way, although it was clean out of their way, to stay with the Cistercians. They thought it their haven yet it was ours. They must when they left lead their horse and their wagon (drawn by two pumicegray asses) up a narrow valley where we could fall on them; and so we did, and doing lost all our itching doubts, which as we rode along the sands of Languedoc had like their whining myriad mosquitoes sung in our ears, Is it gold? For the monks answered our threats bravely. They used such unspeakable vehemence a man would have thought them the only well-bent men under heaven. Would they defend taffeta so? Their righteous unbudgingness would have forced us soon enough to arms, when one of them lifted the long brass cross that hung below one hip and struck Gherucci, who had dismounted, so great a blow his head opened and he fell agonizing to the ground, sprawling and turning on the stained grass like a fish newly plucked from the stream, and we thus came to arms even sooner, I mean too soon. I knocked the other of them from his horse and leaped down on him, whereupon he cleverly slit my thigh with a poniard from under his skirt, as he rose. I thought, "Mark the end," and killed him after he had run a few steps. He fell into a shrub of flowering thyme so that he died sweetly. Not a moment lost, but I got to my horse to detach my arbalest: the first monk was away, and the cart with him, I armed, sighted, shot, and caught him fair, yea and so fair that had he not been impelled by the greatness of his goods he would have stayed. He went out of my sight with the quarrel protruding from his shoulder, like a brown pear stuck with a clove. Will men suffer thus for taffeta? No more than for hearthwood or cider apples, then they give up their little store and live, as the beaver pursued bites off his stones for the hunter to gather up, and lives quiet. Heavens bear witness with me it is so (but heavens will not always answer when they are called.) The uncocking of the shaft had given our horses a mind for exercise. I could not follow, and meditated upon my bloody thigh to devise what kind of death it might be, to be let blood until a man die. It is the same as if a man shall die pissing, with this thought I muffled my wound with cloth, got after my horse, and set out to catch the stalwart monk. Gherucci I left unburied, in his clotted hair.

Slowly with my leaden ache, hardily with my golden desire, I journeyed five days through a country full of shrill-breasted birds but empty of traveling monks, though one left a plain trace. I saw his corpse at the convent here. They had sold the chest, but gave me no aid to find it: at last I came to your ship, where it is buried, like Christ among the common bones, under a load of corn.

That the treasure must lie where it is, I readily admit, for the hours are too few to bring it up without setting every beggar and the Count of Barcelona on our necks. Yet I will not abandon it finally, but beg that you take me on your ship. We shall be partners in ambition and glory, your capital is your captaincy and that the gold will be under your absolute sea sway; mine is telling you so, and telling no one else. The account, which I have delivered to you part spoken and part in this letter, will (I trust) have sufficed to convince you that I do not talk of wax-and-parchment proposals. Should you ask, why do they send such wealth to the new world, I believe its notoriety is too vicious to bring it into daylight without there being knowledge of it, and danger and blame to the church; but the fables of Mexican gold will be accounted an honorable womb for its rebirth, when it has there been melted and fashioned into new bodies.

Alas, that the coffer lies under such a night-storm darkness of grain, you cannot see it (nor touch nor take nor spend). To have faith without sight is hard, but you must have it. Why should I mislead you? If my words are empty, you will toss me naked to the fish, or hang me in pieces on an Indian palm. You will learn that I speak the truth: when the wheat is emptied, you will see what is to be seen—as the sails are raised on your masts, the veil of your understanding will lift; when the wind fills them smooth and white like a groaning wife's belly, your joy will swell like them. Your risk is nothing, taking me aboard will cost you little. Yet think of the rewards. *Experientia longa malorum* has taught me that greatness is given only to the mettlesome. What are your hopes? It is said that you are evilly in debt. There remains no way for you to climb suddenly but by doing some rare stratagem, the like not before heard of: and at this time fit occasion is offered. I have told you the gold's worth. Is not this to be struck bravely for (though we shall risk dancing in a hempen circle)?

I do not trust my life to a fool or a coward, I spare to such a few words of disdain: you seem a hardy honest man. That you left me at your lady's bidding (for *en amour hastive point son cueur ne trouve contentement,* her voice chimed so winningly I hear her yet) is no matter, because the god called Love will not be worshipped by leaden brains. For myself, exactly how well or ill I have done, I am ignorant (the eye sees round itself, sees not into itself): but I am not altogether Fame's outcast; truly she has feasted me with the vigorous nutriment of commendation by those whose Virtue is strong in the world. You have seen I was wounded, and recovered in a week. I have been thrown into rivers and risen drier than my pursuers. I have handled snakes and drunk deadly poison and come to no harm. In this, fortune has not made me reckless. I do not esteem the pox a pimple, I do not provoke swords when I want toothpicks. As for my honesty, you know I do not set my cap over my eyebrows like a politician, and nod and keep my secrets to myself; nor as the eagle casts dust in the eyes of crows, delude you lest you delve into my subtleties. Openly have I presented my words and myself, to be seen and allowed.

Now my fame and fortune rest with you. They are become leaves on the tree of your honor; you will choose to shake them off scornfully as wormeaten and worthless, or preserve and nourish them, for the harvest you shall find.

AMORTONELLI

2 Aug. A.D. 1537 (=*May 11*)

And so the captain took Amortonelli with him. I suppose that the silk in the chest signified gold because a famous treasure was known to have been concealed in it.

The next day I had a disturbing encounter with Dexter Hodge—do you remember, I saw him in Panoramus? I had driven out to the Firestone depot through the vacant town (Miami is puzzlingly unpeopled in this season, and unkempt too, with blackened fronds of low centaury still littering the gutters) to replace my front tires, and there was Hodge. He was ordering an extraordinary quantity of rubber-covered maritime gear—oars, keels, cables.

"I have decided to go into the treasure-hunting racket," he announced to me grandly. "Our first hunting grounds are to be the waters around Stork Island. Have you heard of its friendly dolphins? They play with visiting boats. We're afraid that unless we rubberize our protrusions, the dolphins will injure themselves, bleed, and attract sharks."

During this explanation the clerk, a short spaniel-faced man, stared at Hodge as though he were raving. Hodge took no notice and went on, to my consternation, to ask me to join his group and "turn out on a big game." After this he resumed his business without another word to me.

How should I have responded, or now respond, to this proposal? It is perhaps unimportant.

It's surprising that you also should have found an Abbot of Montpelas. One would enjoy a connection, but the gap between them is so vast. Are you sure your date wasn't 1491?

At present my thoughts turn elsewhere. I gaze into my gin-and-tonic, where a last shrinking ice cube drifts among de-accelerating bubbles. Fancy has decided that this translucent, no-longer-cubic cube is a herald from the East. As it melts, it will release your essence to be drunk up. Afterwards, I'll reread your letter. Its words touched me beyond imagining. To find such pleasure sustained by such innocence is a satisfaction transcending the present conditions of human life.

XII

May 21

Twang can not know when death will-come, or wher or how, but as brath heave in and from my lung, so the smell of Zachary through my brane.

The Mister Hodge—why not? Go near him, yet tell no thing, and with to-listen hear may be gold-like fax for real gold; and all ways of look into earth and see.

The *abott of Montpelas* get the abby in 13 (thirteen) 91. This is a sure, I find the of-pope grant in Vatican Library. Too it 's-publish by Wal-cower in Anals of Banking, 1970, No. 3. And now, how doe I? Lorn more a bout Misser *Todao* and his stoff or go to Florenze (Italy)?

My freind of here at-last make in-visitation to her home for dindins. This is one very large *bouffé* meel. I home in: 3 men, all little with hot red cravatts, say Hello to Twang very loud, to-gether, and naer me, I think they drank, but no—they sit in the horners all the time after ward with to-say no thing and to-look diffrrent. I say to my frend a litle, yet I listne much. The tlak of many man is ful of division for them, for me new systyms. I think, I will-rememmer a part, I wrote it write after:

1: "When I say, *slab*, I maen, *slab*."

2: "But whut do you dou with the *signifiant?* A road sign say, Miami 82 mile. What re-ality do this indicate? Miami?

The distans be-tween the sing and the sity? The location of
the sign? The semi-ottic (?) re-ality, the mmediate realita,
posit a structsure..."

3: "I like Miami—of coarse it *is* infect-ed with Amerihans."

4: "Why strutcher it though? The elemens of the consep
'sign' thath you naem, and othrs giust as importort, are grasp
by our outerd consciouscnesce in a kine of frifloatin jazz con-
tinume, so when I see the in for-mation containt, the so call
content, I all so *feel* the grainy-ness of the would or flaky-ness
of the pent, which ar part of the so-call form, in factt I can
feel too the in-formation at any rat it's only one hork of many
bob-ing in the opent see of simultanity..."

1: "You're re-moving fenomema from the realn of linguage and so of thoughth. Langua must rehognies diacrony
as-wel-as sincrony. When a man go-in to a forest to cuddown
a tree, trim it, and gaze at this felt, mutilatet tree, the conseppt
'tree' do non dis-appear until he have huttitup in to severel
peaces. How ever, as soon as he look at it once it be peeces,
the conceptt 'tree' dis-appere and is re-place by the honsept
'bored' and later 'sign'. Nore do he think, 'I've-paint a tree'
or, 'A forest point to ward Miami...'"

I love this takl, be cause it is a bout Miami, and so, full of
youre skinn. The sense of to-rub was not a ware, onely to
me, yet so near, so near, my *tharaï lemu*—my for ever love.

The man that cut tree, so small, more-short than Mons.
Latten, tak to me: "How go your re-cerches in the vatican?"
I say, no thing.

XIII

May 26

Synchrony is one man's crony, and diachrony is another
man's crony...

It will not be easy to "go near" Hodge. His name is an
essential local power.

He is active in the expansive manner of old tycoons. He
spends here the money he makes elsewhere, mainly I think

in Victory Oil, contributing it to civic projects, advancing the cause of urban planning, and providing directly or indirectly many jobs in the Greater Miami area. He attends concerts and lectures, is a director of our Revival of Reading chapter, and from time to time publishes a sonnet in *Sewanee Review*. He may frequently be seen taking walks around the town, without gun or bodyguard. Every afternoon he visits his friend Silex Jewcett, who has spent half his long life in prison but is revered by the people of Florida as a saint. Hodge arrives at the municipal jail with a chamber band of thirteen sarrusophones playing spirituals, chats a while with Jewcett in the visitors' room, and leaves to the invariable strains of "Praise God from Whom all blessings flow." Earlier in the day he can often be found at the Emerald Diamond coaching rookies of all ages, for he is a great sportsman. He has sponsored several swift milers, his *sepak raga* team—this should surprise you—boasts the fastest elbows in the West, and he is the source, guide, and goalie of the soccer team.

All this has brought Hodge prominence. Pictures of his squidlike face frequently appear in the *Sun-Times*, once even in *Time*. His less praiseworthy ventures are overlooked; apparently more for fun than profit, he has collaborated in some dubious undertakings. He directs one establishment called the Egyptian Temple, a "psychic gymnasium" whose activities are secret. Its members undergo an initiation that includes some form of baptism. They are an uneasy lot: track addicts, ward heelers, and other worrisome types; few seem to benefit from the "mysteries." None of them, however, complains.

A more reputable building for which Hodge is responsible is the New Wars Shrine. The monument is built entirely out of weapons. The columns are rocket casings. The altar is made from the illuminated instrument panels of heavy bombers. The wall of the apse consists of two thousand steel helmets stacked on their sides, their rims facing outwards: the exterior has been transformed into a giant memorial hive. Hodge pays the salary of the former Marine sergeant who serves as beadsman, a title that circumstances have altered to "beesman."

Hodge's own house, although small, is a jewel of classic modern. It is built in the shape of a sundial and faced on all sides with malachite. Its one stark ornament is a high relief over the front door representing two wolves seated face to face, and between them a slender candle burning with a perpetual gas flame. The flower arrangements around the house are very sure.

Do you understand why I'm nervous about soliciting Hodge? The invitation to join his group of treasure-hunters was casual and never renewed. Any reminder might well be thought impertinent. I hesitate to tell him of my own plans (*our* plans), or to lure his interest with prospects of another treasure. He's too sharp for that. He is also not a person to whom one makes a gift to receive a gift in return; at least, not openly. Yet I'm impelled to follow your advice, and not just to learn more about treasure-hunting. I would, frankly, love to move in that world. In fact if I take up his offer my sincere "yes" will submerge my scheming "yes." But what can I say when I accost him—"I'm on Tom Tiddler's ground, picking up gold and silver"?

I forgot to say that Hodge is popularly known as the Invisible Jesuit. Perhaps this refers to the Temple.

My own life is pale. It is always the same here. This neighborhood is so utterly without significance. I suppose to wouldbe boxers in Mauritius or Nome, Fifth Street has some significance, but I do not count it among the significant neighborhoods. There was another party at Dan's last night. It was so boring that after ten minutes I said I was tired, lay down in the bedroom to feign sleep, and was indeed soon asleep. When I awoke the place was deserted. I walked home through streets wet with May dew, glistening in the smaragdine dawn. I skirted an ocean of spilt milk where a tanker truck had exploded. Afterwards I made a snack, wishing hard you were making it for me. I would like to be assured that you will always be with me, and that I shall soon "come home." Enough complaining—things aren't so bad. After all, I've passed the worst of the vernal insomnia season, the rose fever season is almost over, and if Decoration Day weren't just around the corner it would be clear sailing.

I think you should go to Florence. Meanwhile I'll write the university in Montpellier to find out more about the Abbots.

XIV

May 30

Hwile your answer was come I have a to-meet with a man strogn in know-lege, and help, the name of him is de Roover, whowho say he 'll give the ex-perience of the hard appuratus of the Archivio segreto del Vatihano. Mr de Roover and tell of clippin-for honditions in the middle age: it is a tomb crime. How han clippins be maked in to money? Delicate, and more-so, be cause he 's cert this graet a amount can be one-ly one: of *Otto di Guardia*.

There 's the nwes of the tresor a lttle after that it is come to the popope. Then, the clippins are give to *Giovanni di Bicci de' Medici*—he late-er put a start to the grate bank. This, was to do pay-meant of a dept that Pop *Bonofazio* have have with *Vieri di Cambio*, who come be fore *Giovanni*, and a round 1393 *Giovanni* over-take his lie-abilities & acids. (Ho—my firs english joke!) So *Giov. di B.* a gree to do sell of clippins, he 'll-have his money and 'll-put the balance to the popal a hount.

The *Otto*, a stickcy misre, is come to Florence with *Farinata degli Uberti* and his Glibelhines. In a so safetyfull posizion, he hlips florins while the Ghibelines are in top (until to 1266) and make bucats of gold. Be cause of him (hate), Florence give the order of *fiorini di sug-gello* that have the sense "in seal bags".

And then, I con-tunue with my to-look for a treasure of clippins, chiefly in a shelves of name Introitus et exitus ca-merae apostolicae.

Hwat is to-persieve and to-think? That i've reflects per-ceptions in this material-suttle world, oh such are no thing when I go-in even to the firts absorbtion. *Naï sheen-am*—"so I in-dure (?)"—the daze, for the nihgt can not be in dure but is to die in teers and sleep. I make my las ricerch to day, to morrow I'll say, *Duvaï Roma*.

And: godl florens are in busunuss on-ly after twelfifty, per-hap many-man have small ex-perienze of them, and so it is safe-er for *Otto*. What give me pleasor in you, I han not know hwy, it is my memorease. So this gold sting like death fishes. Crime, potilics, make the stingma, and it go to no money, tradaded a cross years until *Giovanni*.

XV

June 4

Otto di Guardia's hoard makes an enthralling tale, but... Best of all who ever were loved in dreams, allow me one "but." Bypaths are an extravagance we cannot afford, and surely Otto is one. If the Medici have anything to do with our treasure, it was long after Giovanni di Bicci.

I had no sooner written you about Dexter Hodge than my relations with him abruptly changed. One morning he appeared at my door to ask "if he might drive me to work"! I have seen him twice since then. The last time furnished emphatic proof of his new opinion of me: I was given a private tour of the Egyptian Temple.

Hodge's interest seems unnatural and I am upset by it.

One enters the Temple grounds at 14 St. Luke's Lane, a posh little street in the new residential section. The gate opened at the approach of Mr. Hodge's limousine. We nosed through it and turned into an alley of yews leading to a graveled parking area. There we continued on foot.

About twenty acres of land surround the Temple: park, garden, and pasture. A group of barn-like buildings stands at one end of the grounds, and towards it we directed our steps. "Here," said Mr. Hodge, "is my sacred zoo." We passed enclosed fields where zebras, buffaloes, and gazelles grazed, a mud pool whose surface was swollen with an ellipse of hippopotamus, a stretch of sand occupied by a camel and swarms of blond hares, an eighty-foot-high aviary of glistening wire. The buildings housed reptiles, fish, and insects.

After we had visited the menagerie, Mr. Hodge, gazing about his domain, explained: "In the practices of our Temple we implement man's ancient belief in the *ka*, or double.

Every animal you have seen belongs to a member of our congregation, not only as his property, but as a visible and objective symbol of his inner life. Through their appearance, the state of their health, the nature of their diet, and a host of lesser omens, these creatures manifest the hidden truth of the man. When assailed by spiritual doubt, by anxiety over the influences of the world, or by curiosity as to what the future holds in store, a member has only to visit his animal doubles to find illumination."

Mr. Hodge chuckled. "That's the pitch. It's a fascinating business, but then the meeting of two cultures is always exciting."

Having admired the zoo, charming in its Ludwig der Zweite way, I expressed my amazement that it could be run at a profit. How could the Temple clientele, known to be less than prosperous, buy and keep the animals?

"Once they believe, they find the money; and once they're initiated, they believe."

We had reached the Temple proper. As we mounted its steps, bells pealed quietly about us. Draped in a weighty rust-colored robe that matched his beard, a Catonian figure stood in the portal.

"Wherefore, child, wishest thou to ascend..." he began, his voice cracking sleepily.

"Can it, Johnny," Mr. Hodge interrupted. "I'm just taking a friend through."

Bowing us in, the attendant murmured, "Thank *you*, Mr. Hodge."

As we entered the building Hodge said, "The main rule of the initiation is not to play the hinge. If a novice looks back, he has to start over. There's no significance in this, but after a while he wonders what's creeping up on him from behind.

"When he has crossed the threshold he strips and gives his clothes to Ramsama," Mr. Hodge went on, indicating the bearded man. "He is led through this door into the first chamber. In the vast room, as if to emphasize the pettiness of the individual in the Great Mystery, the novice is confined in this pyrex cell. Lights in its ceiling illuminate the silvered walls and floor, which mirror the novice grotesquely. He is left alone, standing by that little pyramid of green marbles. Sooner or later he touches them, starting a mechanism that releases and ignites a flow of propane gas around the base of the walls. The lights go out. Blue fire fills the cell with a whoosh. The flames singe a few body hairs, and the mirrors refract great heat. The novice is in quite a lather when we let him out.

"He descends the stairs to this corridor, which is even dimmer than now. Attendants seize him and wrap him in three sheets of translucent black polythene, zipping them together. Hermetically enclosed, he is left to work himself free. This should be easy, since the zippers can be opened from within; but the novice is hot and anxious, batteries of strobe lights flash darkly over him, and before long he starts to suffocate. His gasping face at last appears. The lights steady to an agreeable shade of green; cool air is wafted over him; ladies disengage him from his shroud, and rub him with soothing oil. His hopes rise.

"The male attendants reappear, however, to hurl him down another flight of steps (safely padded with foam rubber.) He lands in a blacker cellar, a real dungeon. He is taken and thrust upside down through an elastic aperture lined with hog bristles into a tiny compartment in which he fits barely and cannot move at all. Wait a sec, I'll turn on the lights. The hole is made of obsidian, hard, smooth, and opaque. A woman's voice announces that the novice is to remain there twelve hours, with the passage of each hour to be signaled by a gong. In fact the 'hour' is rung every ten minutes—in his terror the novice loses all sense of time, and two hours is enough for the required effect. There is no light, little air, except for the gong the silence is complete, the oil with which he was rubbed is spiked with Tabasco, and every so often a bone-and-leather claw presses against his chest. I tell you, when he comes out of there he's a new man.

"I forgot to mention that until this last confinement, a deafening recording of the *Turangalila Symphony* has accom-

panied the initiate through his trials. The music now resumes
more softly. Following the faint signs of daylight, the novice
emerges onto the terrace. Here the ladies wash him, wrap
him in a linen tunic, and seat him at this table, where a basket
of grapes and cherries has been placed. By now he is so dis-
couraged that no matter how hungry he is, he will not
touch the fruit for a long time. Finally he must. He eats a bit:
there are no surprises. I make my entrance. Attendants remove
the fruit and replace it with a pile of marbles, like the one in
the pyrex cell. I then pluck away the feather awning that
shades the terrace, marking the end of the ceremony and the
novice's admission."

Mr. Hodge is known to perform this gesture with *panache*;
it is often cited as an example of his old-world charm.

"I now begin indoctrinating the novice, who is weak with
exhaustion and relief. A capacious chair is brought out for me,
into which I settle luxuriously; and, while I give my lecture,
I quaff champagne and dip an occasional crisp into a bowl
of caviar.

"I start by declaring that there is only one road to happiness in our universe: abnegation and love of one's brother.
The first step must be the lessening of one's attachment to
base things. One must learn to be poor; and while true poverty is of course a spiritual essence, it can be approached
through material acts. Therefore the novice's money will not
be returned with his clothing. Anticipating complaints, I
warn that love is a stern master.

"I then describe the *kas*. I explain how useful animal
doubles can be in ordering one's spiritual life: how, for instance, it is easier to love one's brother through his double
(with the corollary 'He who hates his brother's double is a
murderer'); how one learns from the *kas* to open the bowels
of compassion; how, with one's private world made visible,
self-understanding becomes easy, and through it universal
knowledge."

Here I broke in with a question that I had meant to ask
earlier. Were the initiations into Miami's exclusive Knights
of the Spindle conducted on similar lines? "But," Mr. Hodge

answered incredulously, "those people are the pure quill!"
He resumed his account:

"Usually the novice accepts my theory. I put this acceptance to a harsh test. I confront him with the obligation of
founding a psychic menagerie.

"A complete system of *kas* comprises fourteen traditional
categories, which should ideally be represented by different
animals. These categories are strength, power, honor, prosperity, food, long life, influence, brilliance, glory, knowledge, magic, creative will power, sight, and hearing. A
correct psychic menagerie might consist of an elephant, a
lion, a horse, a bee, an ant, a turtle, a pilot fish, a peacock, an
eagle, a seal, a viper, a monkey, an owl, and a bat. To perfect
it, you would then pair your *kas* with anti-*kas*, so as to polar-
ize your spiritual qualities in the most revealing way possible.
Each *ka* would then cohabit with a creature that was its cate-
gorical opposite. You could match the elephant with a caterpillar, the lion with a chicken, the horse with a parrot, the
bee with a coyote, the ant with a grasshopper, the turtle with
a butterfly, the pilot fish with a giraffe, the peacock with a
buzzard, the eagle with a rat, the seal with a sheep, the viper
with a camel, the monkey with an earwig, the owl with a
mole, and the bat with an eel. Of course some combinations
are impossible: how could one prevent the elephant from
walking on the caterpillar, or the lion from eating the chicken,
or the earwig from entering the monkey's ear? In any event
the collection is too grand for our customers, who settle for
much less ambitious, that is less expensive solutions.

"We permit them to buy one animal to fill several categories. The elephant is probably the best example of spiritual
versatility since he can, with the possible exception of brilliance, cover the field. The two elephants you saw are here
for that very purpose. Even with local animals one can manage: a bear, a sponge, a !ynx, an alligator, a puma, a manatee,
and a duck satisfy all the requirements aside from honor and
creative will power, two virtues in small demand.

"So after the novice has admitted the desirability of a
menagerie, and after I have shaken him with an appraisal of

various kinds of whale, I turn to cheaper beasts, which I pick with a good idea of how much money my client can be persuaded to spend. He jumps at the chance. He promises to buy, say, a horse, a mina bird, and a small shark. You must remember that he is hungry, thirsty, tired, confused, naked, and trapped. He'll pledge me his bottom dollar to get home, and I have a book of open checks ready to forestall backsliding.

"After their initiation, most members return to the Temple only to consult their *kas*. We attempted communal activities, but the clients are such a suspicious lot that it was hard getting them under one roof. Now we just field a baseball team.

"A new member often stays away at first, suspecting that he's been swindled. But when he learns that his *kas* have arrived, sooner or later he wants to see them. They usually delight him; not because of any affection for animals, but because the *kas* represent money, and he transfers his love of money to them.

"The work of fostering the member's belief in the *ka* devolves on the zoo keepers. For the time being I fade out, bearing the load of initial resentment, and not reappearing until it has been forgotten. The keepers expertly secure the member by furnishing likely material for the demonstration of *ka* theory. They submit elaborate reports of each menagerie's diet, excretions, pulse rate, and temperature, which are supplemented with affectionate accounts of its daily behavior. The keeper's experience and the member's credulity, without which the Temple would never have attracted him in the first place, gradually bind him to his animals. And as soon as a single correspondance occurs between an animal's life and his own, and chance brings this about as often as calculation, his enthusiasm alone is enough to perpetuate the phenomenon. He is so delighted by access to supernatural power that he will make his life conform to his *kas* to preserve it. If, for instance, he finds his prosperity-*ka* ailing before a poker game, he will either be too worried to play well or unconsciously lose money to prove the *ka* right. And when a *ka's* condition is favorable, members will surpass themselves to achieve success. At the last elections one party hack delivered the toughest ward in the city after his gorilla ate an extra five pounds of bananas."

"Maybe your theory works," I suggested.

Mr. Hodge looked into the distance.

"Professor Stedman Cinques of Columbia University has proved... No, no," he laughed, "don't make me go through that. It *is* true that the human may sometimes function as the animal's *ka*—but that's a delicate subject."

He paused to light a cigar. "We've had one unforeseen problem. Some members, after growing very fond of their animals, turn equally suspicious of them. I couldn't understand why until I realized that having radically identified themselves with their *kas*, they come to mistrust the animals as they mistrusted themselves. We've had to provide various types of inanimate scrying for them—haruspication, visions in pools of mercury, palpating the umbones of Venus shells. One remedy is to slaughter the *kas* and investigate their entrails, in the Roman manner. Another menagerie can then be started."

I asked if *kas* were consulted about sexual problems.

"Of course. That sort of divination is called shadowing."

"Do you see the members often?"

"Every day. I have to. You see, since 'the universalism of the Temple allows of no restriction,' our assembly is a bunch of mediocrities, misfits, and cowards. They never stop complaining, about themselves, about the world, and worst of all about the mystical universe. Why do you think I know the Vedas and the Book of the Dead almost by heart? It's the long hours I spend meditating with my miserable customers."

We were once again at the parking area. Mr. Hodge instructed his chauffeur to take me home. He concluded our visit with a pre-Socratic remark: "The games grow old, but the marks are always new."

Since then I have returned to my monotonous schedule. I've had enough of this sad world that spins forever in its greater and lesser dreams.

Do you think it prudent to involve the de Roover person in your research?

XVI

Giune 8

When 1/2 the erth sciscors us, my all-earth is *slop* (misiry), such misyry *me wun lucr-em vin*, I 'm similir I am eating a horpse. This is deep Pan re-act to wo—more-creul than to-be death and ate.

A gainst memory I out-leave the signifiant detell. The tresure took by Pop *Bonifaze* has the name de tribus serranis, whiwhich have the italian to-mean dei tre sciarrani, "of 3 see perches". In the lettr to the of-ship captain, that has-be in your lettre to me, *Amortonelli* ear the man with full-er voice say, "on lid of chesst were-carve crewdly 3 fishs." I'm so mist up by different moneys in the '400, are you can say how this have worth of that?

My mind is in-certn why Mr Hodge 'll-have no interest in you, be cause you "upsets". Is he not can harmony-inpulse to you, as you're sweet? Ana-way I clime the train to Florenza to night. I have the idea, it is your 2 scales of years? But I do n't see this like tru.

Now we have 3 chains from of-Mr-*Todao* clippings and the hord of *Amortonelli*. One, the fammily of *i Medici*, two, the *abbott of Montpelas*, and three fish. I tell to you, I miss you dear-ly. I love you yet more. The to-be in bed with Inglish Grammr of Jespesen is not very fun-y, mon ami.

XVII

June 13

How vividly I see you! So near I can imagine touching you. But I want to touch more than your wraith. Twang, can this scheming after gold justify the decay of contentment that separation imposes? If only I could detach my hope of riches from the thought of your eyes! It's as though looking into them had ignited a passion for difficult glories. But without you I sag; without you, I could believe that the soul and the body are not one.

It must be getting hot in Italy. Do you have summer clothes, and enough? Nothing, I suppose, could be cooler than a loosely ordered *phrap*.

Dexter Hodge continues attentive. Yesterday he mentioned events of the summer season (*the* season in Miami now) to
which he will take me. This was a relief. During the previous
week he had talked of nothing except his desire to have me
play in some baseball games he is sponsoring.

I think my worries about him were fantasy. There is certainly no age problem between us.

You've seen baseball. Can you imagine me playing? Mr.
Hodge left me no choice. One afternoon, after a few gulps of
rum, I drove over to the diamond for the first time, expecting sure humiliation.

Mr. Hodge welcomed me and introduced me to his team,
the Sovereigns, who represent the Egyptian Temple.

The Sovereigns wore uniforms of bright orange mohair
into which cabbalistic emblems in green and purple had been
knitted. They belied Mr. Hodge's description of Temple
members, and seemed to be true gentlemen-sportsmen. Some
had nicknames behind which I discerned Miami celebrities,
a fact that I kept to myself, addressing them by their chosen
monickers: the Calcium Nut, the Locus Solus Kid, Christ
Tracy, Mushnick the Second, Cortisone Moonface, Omnibus
Hesed (the pitcher).

Mr. Hodge wanted me to catch. It was obvious that I
could play no other position. I insisted that my arm was
weak, and so became an umpire. I can't throw, or catch, or
run, or hit—I can only love! Mr. Hodge felt it was sad to be
an umpire so young. He decided to play catcher himself:
"I'll manage the team just as well from a squat."

The Sovereign's opponents were the Class Cannons. After
two games their team is still wholly mysterious to me. Its
members have remained nameless and almost wordless. They
do not speak unless circumstances force them to. None has
ever admitted his identity to me, or replied to my advances
other than with flashing gestures of the hands.

At three o'clock Mr. Hodge told me to start the game. I
asked the manager of the Cannons if he was ready. He responded by taking from a square box next to the bat rack a
golden hunting horn, which he raised to his lips. The Can-

nons assembled behind him. The manager blew three short
pure notes, then tucked the horn under his arm.

The Sovereigns had meanwhile lined up in front of their
dugout. As soon as the horn call ended, they began to sing.
The music was homely, the performance smooth:

> The Lord knocks over the proud man, but never hurts
> the humble.
> Throw yourself down, He'll lift you up, no matter how
> low you tumble.
> Curse the Devil and he'll depart, spurn him who'd work
> your ruin,
> But bless the Lord, draw near to Him, and He will take
> you to Him.

> The Lord knocks over the proud man, but never hurts
> the humble.
> Throw yourself down, He'll lift you up, no matter how
> low you tumble.
> Curse the Devil and he'll depart, spurn him who'd
> work your ruin,
> But bless the Lord, draw near to Him, and He will take
> you to Him.

> The Lord knocks over, &c.

As they repeated the stanza, irritation, mute and irrestible,
gripped the Cannons. At last their shortstop climaxed a
pantomime of swelling fury by forcing out, in a hiss of thril-
ling sibilance, the word "Cease!" The teams broke ranks, the
Cannons scattering over the field, the Sovereigns returning
to their dugout. I waited behind the plate (its pentagonal
whiteness unspotted by any cleat) while the Cannon battery
warmed up. I noticed that the right fielder, a slender youth
with shoulder-length golden hair, was straightening his flow-
ing locks with long strokes of his comb.

The pitcher nodded his readiness. I waved my arm and
called out, inexplicably forgetting what game was being

played, "Serve!" I at once altered the command to the correct "Play ball!" as a soundless snigger enlivened the infield. This was my only mistake.

The Cannons dominated the game. In defense their speed and deftness controlled the ball completely. In fact on the rare occasions when a decision went against them, they managed somehow to make the ball disappear, thus stopping the game and creating a most unnerving confusion. Usually, to get the game started again, the adverse decision had to be reversed, compromised, or cancelled; sometimes Mr. Hodge would successfully plead with the Cannons to restore the missing ball. His tactic was to express intense compassion for the fielders, while arguing that it was in the general interest to resume the game. The ball would then reappear as mysteriously as it had vanished, perhaps bouncing nonchalantly in the pitcher's glove.

Once even Mr. Hodge's patience was surpassed. In the seventh inning the Cannons had narrowly missed a double play—both runners were safe on first and second. The base-ball disappeared. Mr. Hodge walked out to the shortstop and began his plea. The shortstop pointed down the road, to a spot where Mr. Hodge had parked his aged jeep. It was now gone.

Mr. Hodge lost his temper. "By God, I'll take you to court for this. I know I can't expect you bastards to know right from wrong, but at least you can tell the difference between a baseball and a jeep!"

The shortstop silently held up the ball in his ungloved hand. Mr. Hodge took the ball, cocked his right leg and, like a Thai boxer, swatted the shortstop across the ear with his foot, knocking him to the ground. The Cannon got up with a mimic snarl; but neither he nor his teammates complained. Mr. Hodge turned away, tossed the ball to the pitcher, and was walking off the field when from behind the Sovereign dugout the Cannon bat boy rolled the jeep into view.

I observed all this distractedly. The batter waiting his turn had been whistling "Lover, come back to me," and I had been shaken by the song's nonexistent pathos.—There was a time when my attachment to you naturally found its words. Now separation has worn a chasm within me, words are engulfed by it. If you do not know how desperately I love you I shall never be able to tell you.

Forgive me for thrusting these after all useless emotions on you. That stupid song!

So play started again. Having two men on base did the Sovereigns no good. Neither then nor in any other inning were they able to score. On the other hand, the Cannons wasted none of their seven hits.

In the second inning, after a walk and a single had put two men on base, the Cannon manager with a certain ostentation planted a six-foot high cane in the ground in front of his dugout. The right fielder, the long-haired blond, was at bat. The Sovereign infield razzed him loudly—"Hey, sweetie, the Youth and Beauty Pageant's tomorrow"—but he took no notice and doubled in both runners. Two innings later, with a man at first, the Cannon manager stood a stiff-backed wooden chair next to the cane. The batter hit a home run. Finally in the sixth inning, with Cannon runners on second and third, the hunting horn used at the start of the game was set bell downward between cane and chair. One batter fouled out, but the next hit a long single. Watching the sixth run score, the Sovereign catcher (Mr. Hodge) cussed, "Damned Hebraic parallelism!"

I performed my role satisfactorily. The Sovereigns were friendly, in spite of their weak play. The Cannons were unrelentingly distant. Only once did any of them react to my presence. As the fourth inning commenced, their catcher approached bearing a Ry-vita smeared with cottage cheese. He handed it to me without a word as he settled behind the plate.

I hope you like cottage cheese as much as I do. There is, however, nothing like it among Pan dairy products.

When I arrived home late in the afternoon I found that my pockets had been emptied of their contents—bills, small change, bloat pills, everything! I had left my keys in the car, so at least I could get into my own apartment.

Next day the Sovereigns won, 1–0. They scored their run in the eleventh inning on a walk, a stolen base, and two sacrifice bunts. They are not a great hitting team. The Cannons were shut out by a new pitcher, a wiry chap named Peter Jeigh. Mr. Hodge introduced him to me with the comment, "As a Sovereign he may be a mite snider, but watch him pitch." He *was* good, although he had only one arm. He had lost the other "blowing the chase," whatever that means.

Peter Jeigh was almost as silent as the Cannons. I heard him speak only once. Shortly before the game, I found him gazing into the palm of his glove, which he was massaging with neat's-foot oil. He murmured, more to himself than to me, "I shall attain sympathy with inanimate things."

Between innings I told Mr. Hodge about my missing possessions. He immediately went to speak to the Cannon manager. Returning, he promised that the matter would be cleared up. Nothing was apparently done, but when the game was over my missing belongings were back in my pockets!

I wrote to the University of Montpellier for help with the Abbots of Montpelas. I referred in passing to a consignment of silk that may have figured in certain transactions...

As you say, the three perches do plausibly link the clippings with our treasure. Your flair is incredible.

You ask about the currencies of the time. The question is not as difficult as it might appear. The first thing to get straight is the Florentine florin, or rather florins. The gold florin that was called "sealed florin" for the reasons you mention was soon debased, so that in the fifteenth century a new coin had to be created to replace it, the "large florin." It was worth a tenth and later a fifth more than the sealed florin. Actually "replace" isn't accurate since the two florins coexisted for a time until the older one was abolished, in 1471, but for simplicity's sake think of the matter as a replacement. In any case these are the two florins to remember—however, see below. Next you must consider a third Florentine money in use during the fourteenth and fifteenth centuries, the pound, more precisely the "affiorino pound." Let me say at once that this was not real money, there was no pound coin it was just a money of account. It was divided into twenty affiorino shillings and the shilling subdivided into twelve affiorino pence. These smaller units were also imaginary— perhaps imaginary isn't the exact word—oh, I forgot to mention that the florin was also divided into shillings, into twenty shillings in fact, like the pound, and also into two hundred and forty pence. The reason I forgot is that these shillings and pence are also imaginary, but of course the florin was not imaginary—there was a real florin coin (I mean naturally two coins, as explained.) Well, matters became simpler after the introduction of the large pound, no, no—the large *florin*, because the habit arose of accounting for fractions of the florin in terms of the divisions of the affiorino pound, according to which the florin was equal to twenty-nine affiorino shillings and three hundred and forty-eight affiorino pence. So remember that both the large florin and the pound were made up of the same shillings, twenty in the latter and twenty-nine in the former, and that in both cases the shilling was in turn divided into twelve pence, so that there were two hundred and forty affiorino pence to the pound and three hundred and forty-eight affiorino pence to the florin (large). Still, you should not forget that earlier the florin was also divided into its own shillings and pence, twenty and two hundred and forty respectively. In other words, a pound can be reckoned as twenty twenty-ninths of a later florin.—You may ask, if all these small moneys were imaginary, how did people pay for a sack of potatoes (I realize that there were as yet no potatoes.) You see, parallel to these gold systems there was another system based on silver, and it was used for such transactions. The main unit here was, as a matter of fact, also a pound, the "lesser" pound, and like the other pound it was divided into twenty lesser shillings and two hundred and forty lesser pence, but you must not let the equivalence of the names suggest equivalences of value—the values were absolutely separate. The trouble is that there was no legal ratio between gold and silver, so it's hard to say *what* the relation between the two, or three, systems was. However, this is only a little cloud in a generally sunny sky. Let's return to the first pound. This affiorino pound linked Florence to the pound system that was common to much of Europe during the Middle Ages. I don't mean to imply that the pounds of the various countries (which weren't really countries, I know, I only call them that for convenience)—that the various pounds were interchangeable. Far from it. But at least they had the same idea behind them. In England there was the pound sterling still current today, in Flanders the pound groat, so called because it was based on the groat, a small silver coin. That these pounds were silver did not prevent them from belonging to the international system that included the gold Florentine florin. Incidentally, you must not confuse the Flemish pound groat with the Venetian pound groat, the latter being based on a gold coin, the ducat, rather than on a silver coin the groat. (The pound in Milan was based on a silver coin as well, the imperial, which was constantly depreciating, so that the Milanese pound was always becoming smaller than the other pounds. Still, it was a pound.) In Geneva the situation differed in that the pound was *not* the main accounting unit, but the crown or rather crowns plural, since there were two, one being sixty-four to the mark and the other sixty-six—the mark was gold— forget about it. This system went to Lyons with the Geneva fairs, so that the Lyons branch of the Medici bank reckoned in crowns (at sixty-four to the mark) whereas in Avignon they did their accounting in "pitetti" florins. This florin is the other kind I referred to while defining the properly Florentine ones. It was lighter than the sealed florin, or at any rate lighter than the sealed florin before it was debased: consequently it was divided into twenty-four and not twenty shillings and two hundred and eighty-eight as opposed to two hundred and forty pence. The word "consequently" in the preceding sentence somehow does not ring true. Finally, there was one last other florin, imaginary in the way I have used "imaginary" in connection with these currencies, which was found in Genoa in quotations of money rates and held equal to twenty-*five* Genoese shillings. But generally merchants in Genoa used the Genoese pound, just as they used the Barcelonese pound in Barcelona.

Does this clear matters up?

XVIII

Theu is "us". I say this werd a gain, and again, to me. *Ticbaï stheu, theu ticbaï stheu.* O, yes. I'm tire *wuc vin*, like a deadboby. Trip is done, with no-sleep. This time I write only, I'm here. Any gown is enough evne ruff and old. You will-have no fear, for my close. The hope come to me, to see out and a round in summer time and winter time, with free glanse, from a mountn, hwile my eys re-volve in a Khmer slime of heal'th—I to be nature with loooks in to nature with some ease-like sym-pathey like the blue-eye gras of meadows have a look in to the face of the sky.

Part Two

XIX

June 22

They have caught the sulfuric acid fiend, whose last target was our drinking fountains.

There is, for me, even better news. ("Black oxen cannot tread on my feet forever.") Mr. Hodge has proposed me for the Knights of the Spindle.

The Knights are the most exclusive club in Florida, with an unvarying membership of sixty-six. It is extraordinary proof of Mr. Hodge's influence to have secured my nomination. When he told me of it, I protested that I did not deserve it; he refused to listen. "You can't knock me. You're a good man." My protests weren't entirely honest—he might have been playing a painful joke. But he confirmed my eligibility by presenting me with an angel-noble of ruddy luster, suggesting that I cure my stye in time for the initiation.

Did you see that a new six-pointed star was discovered at the Miami observatory? Appropriately, it lies within the confines of Moses' Basket.

Today, as I walked along a street in the faubourgs, a van came squealing round the corner, the sun blazing on its windshield and I suppose in the driver's eyes. It was an apple van, full of "manducation apples." Have I told you about them? They are a fruit of resilient texture, specially developed to teach infants how to chew, and they've boomed. One cannot visit the supermarket without hearing a number of mothers, any number of grandmothers, and innumerable great-grandmothers raving about them. But no one remembers that the practice was originally Pannamese. I've forgotten your fruit—doesn't it mean "bone mango"?

This happened around noon. It must be noon in Florence —no, midnight. Twang, when shall we once again watch chameleons puffing on a sunny tree? Dan is throwing a party here this evening. He wasn't able to use his own place because he's in flight from his next-to-last twist (I never met her.) There is no peace for me here. My walls are gauze-thin, the roar of wassail penetrates them as if they were imaginary. Perhaps my last sentences give the impression that the party has already begun. It's a pleasant idea. I would like to be writing you in solitude while my friends and others wildly celebrate a room-and-a-half away. And when the party does start I may not actively participate. My recent high life has exacted its price, diarrhea, so tonight perhaps I'll withdraw to this desk, and gazing under my bright little lamp at your last, tender, undated letter, commune with you over rice and tea. My loveliest one, let us always be shrines to each other, consecrated to faith and confidence! Thanks to you, I count myself among the "little remainder" of the saved. Damn this party and this life of waiting! Cleaning up will be the worst. I remember that after one of Dan's revels the scraps filled seven garbage baskets, bodies excluded. Speaking of which, Grace has a date with "someone new" tonight and plans to bring him. She'll go on carping about you none-theless.

I can't send you money with this letter because my check-book is all stubs, but Monday I'll get a new one. Oops—the debit and credit columns are exactly even. But that's all right. Mr. Hodge today gave me some tips on the hounds, and since bookmakers know no Sundays, I'll collect to-morrow.

I forgot about the apple van. Not that it was interesting, only scary. I had gone out to Dalmanutha to see the green lion, famous to readers of "Believe it or not." As I said, the fellow was dazzled as he rounded the corner, and he veered onto the sidewalk, missing me by one micro-inch. Limp with shock, I sat down on the pavement. The anxious driver jumped from the cab. It was the long-haired right fielder of the Cannon team. I assured him between wheezes that I was unharmed. He trembled silently, then declared, laboring each syllable, "My name is Hyperion Scarparo," and gave me an apple.

XX

June 26

I have the wish of to-say in my last latter, yet fatique did not can. Gold is no fool-like dreem, in all place in all time that's worth-full. Tell you to Bamma Deng you not be-lieve so, he say, Forth! (Twang shall n't ever say it.) I thikn all-so empire is honormost post in the sport. But you 're tacit, a bout, who win the threemost game?

Atr-am, wey nob mau Lao, that signify: I think aï, to have-be a Laotion! For they are ever board in of-love bussness, and guiet after, yet Twang do-tell to you. At late-er that mid-niht of hlock, I mont the train to Florence. I de-vide the room with 2 man-Italian. One to left speaks english, and he 's the thought, I 'm his reel friend. One hquench the light for sleep, I do n't enter sleep, for the "friend" lie on me, all-so after I stroke him hard-ly. I think, that is absurb to be-come wiled. The man who do n't say english or any thing go down in Terni, Umbria. The fiend have be-gin agin, I want you, I do a-long fiht for ours til to Firenze. I 'm strong, but he 's top, and un-wieldly, just be fore the stazion I have-braek two of my best naels on him. It's pael dawn as he con-docts me to a hostel. Well, it is a nough for to day.

XXI *

July 1

Jesus! When for once I was ahead, your letter came and set me back a week of Sundays. I try to improve my feelings but it's no use. The spirit of sacrifice is beyond my compass. Don't *you* be reconciled to such a sacrifice. If you can bear it I cannot, the thought of you being in the coils of that worm annihilates me. It's bad enough staggering down the dark avenue of my imagination, seeing your shawl soiled and your necklace shedding pearls about the train. But those words "conducts me to a hotel"—at any price ransom those words from the well of despair where they lie chained, tell me what they mean. The greasy scum, to pick a jewel when the streets are full of mudkickers! Beloved, tell me exactly what happened, because reliving the scene, extrapolated from your prose and deformed in the convex mirror of anguish, is hourly kneading my brain into new folds. I'm too nervous to work. (But Montpellier promises to help.) Twang, only a frail miracle joins us, a silky cocoon that we precariously spun, to be clung to until the later time. I would commit murder to protect it. The only pleasure I've had since this morning is imagining that man beaten like a snake, or strapped across the muzzle of a howitzer. You didn't eat with him? He don't deserve to lap cold tea from your saucer.

XXII

July 3

Yet how, gives Montpellier the help (who's he)? Have-pass 3 months since I write a zen story as you in-joy, hear is a other to extratract you from angger: "A yuong man a range his stance so he have can to a distant land to study a certan Master Three. At an end of three, with to-feel of no sense, he 've-present to the Master his de-parture. The Master say,

* Special delivery

'You 've-be three, why more?' 'A greed.' But he stil feell he have-do no advance. He tolded the Master, that he was the Master, say, 'Look, Three and Three.' 'Stay Three.' He did but with sucsecs. He have-tell the Master that have-happen, the Master said, 'You 've-be tears, moths, sands, the end of time. You have-*hate* in-lighten-meant. Hommit suisise.' The end of the dent was in lighten." I have-donde this trans-lation giust as I come to west, so it 's clumbsy.

That poor man-italian is a poor one. Oh I say it to you, he 's full to his hairs (not-many) with shaem and sorror. As he make those events he 's dronk, as the 3-dollar skunk. At the dawn he vommit over the piazza del duomo, and mingle his tears to-it (like the zen youht.) I have-telled him, now it's addio. He said, I mean arrivederci, but I say, no, for-ever, I ex-plane the to-mean of *duvaï*. This is then he vomitt. Have I give the Pan word of I vommitt, *uüax-m*, it 's so otomato-poetic I beleve? He raise and fall any times on the cobbler stones, he wax eloquence, and he does an aoth on the hat of his mamma he 'll-be ubediant to Twang, and good, so it is all rite, and what more, I all-so my in tire love, my *stheu lemu*, Twang rise an neel at your foot and beg to obeg you. I 've not eat nether love with him, on-ly scratsh, and we all two have a litle pain (I, my bustit nails) and this, is a muilde bound.

XXIII

July 7

You have half drawn that arrow from my bowels, but I still cannot dispel the vision of what may have happened. Scouring my thoughts with the bristles of reason has not banished the possibility that you consented, no matter how little, in the desires of that odious man. You must know that even a passive surrender to impureness begets moral anarchy in general and insomnia in particular. Lord, lord, the noose tightens and I choke—at this moment he may be taking advantage of your generous nature! I tell you, bad fruit means a bad tree, and such trees should be cut down and burnt. Why don't you stick him in the can for a while?

Yesterday the preparatives for my initiation began. I visited the Knights' official tailor, Mr. Zone, to be fitted for my robes. He followed a ritual procedure: purple-red cloth, worked with random crescents of silver, was wrapped around me and shaped with a large razor.

As Mr. Zone began his task, I was joined by Dexter Hodge (my sponsor), and two Knights who were to examine me. Greeting me in a stiff, kind way, they declared me fit for Spindle candidacy: competent persons had seen me leave the Egyptian Temple "under the awning of accepted novices." I turned toward Mr. Hodge, who lowered his head to mutter, "Don't bobble them. It's O.K."

Masked with spangled cloth, three framed pictures hung on one wall of the room. The Knights uncovered them, instructing me to pick the "truest" and to justify my choice.

To the left was a painting, "A Pilgrim in El Dorado." By a calm and sunny sea, airy groves showered pomegranates and dates on the mingled children of beast and man; while in the deeper shade of oaks, egg-pale hermaphrodites danced for a bearded sorceress around a magic fire, in which the salamander and phoenix thrived. The mood was nostalgic.

To the right was a blown-up pornographic photograph, full of the cold shine of flashbulb on skin.

At the center was a drawing in inks. Three elementary figures, triangle, circle, and pentagon, were linked by a meandering cord at once arbitrary and exact. Mr. Hodge coughed. He was standing in front of me. In one hand, thrust behind him, he held a white card printed with large green capitals. I declaimed the written words: "Geometry provides a plane of refraction between essential being and formal manifestation." (I said "pain" instead of "plane" but my boner went unnoticed.)

No sooner had I spoken than I was ushered out of the tailor's shop into a waiting one-horse carriage. My examiners cheerfully waved good-bye and, alone with the cabby, I rode off. I can't say how long we drove, since I fell into a delicious snooze. I dreamt of you; you caressed me; and at the moment of your suavest caress, I remembered *him*. He has become a wolf to my dreams and a remora to my will! Opening my eyes, I saw that we were turning around a colossal manhole, the principal entrance to the Dade County sewer complex.

Tradition requires that I invite a group of Knights home to meet my intimates. I'm not looking forward to it. I just waxed the floors to an umblemished sheen, and the thought of all my awful friends marking them up is more than I can bear, let alone the other reasons for not giving a party.

Montpellier is a city in the south of France—funny question. Professor Blesset of Montpellier University is to send the microfilm of a document from Montpelas. He thinks it will interest us; I hope he's right. As regards research, knighthood and the thought of your boyfriend have kept me cooking on one burner.

XXIV

July 12

Now, I work in the Arhive of the State here, so I hurry to say the last faste from Roma. On Mag 12 & 30 I 've-write, *Bona-fazio* (pope) have-take Misser *Todao's* hord and givn it to *Giovanni di Bicci de' Medici*, that he may-negoziatit. This is n't just true, it is no as simple. There is a cousin (sp?) of *Giovanni* of name *Averardo di Fran-cesco de' Medici*, he have-act for Pope ond got gold, then he re-put it to *Giovanni*. *Giovanni* a-sure *Averardo*, he will-negotiatit and have its worth. I owe to-say they're 2 Medici banks then, in Florenze of *Averardo*, of *Giovanni* in Rom. They were friend-like banchs. Then 1397 *Giovanni* make his lone bank in Fiorence, and still he 's-n't-tradad the hlippings. And this new bank rivalrie *Averardo*. And, *Giovanni* make his in-Rome bank complex-er, but all ways with no hapital, any bank have-can to-do this some time, yet there's an opinoin, they have-know of that hord in the cort of the Porpe (this is the large hustomer), so they know, he's rich, enogh to borror money from-him. *Averardo* all-so was with-out money for the treasure, but he say, it's mine. So he maded a 1st complain a round that time. The complain is in gentl words. There's fog, a bout of-who the dett the gold clippings should to pay. Be cause, Pope *Boniface* have-made detbs to both housins.

Oh your worsd of angger, a gain, they are come hards a-gains me, the sky and the city so shaek, I think the univorse must be know-ing Love—Khmer pro-verb. Yet you can to see now, your raeg is not with out cause, but with-out reason. Whewhen the bright flags of wool are put a-round the even-ing sky and make it bright, and a sweat small wind come with smells of the mountains, then my heart is to-ward you on his stock-ing knees to love you a thousand folds: *mau pheu*—"I'm you" (rs). I make sugestion, he may not be-arrest, if he do a nice gift. He chump at the chance. So, there's some good thing even in a vomit-er. Shall I say vomiter, as in Pan *uüax* means as well the man, and whawhat he make, and the to-make, thus, I'm un-sure.

XXV

July 17

Even the emphatic commas at the end of your letter left meager room for my gasps. What I ask over and over, and you will not explain, is why you must see him at all. Then to ask him to give you a present is beyond understanding. If I didn't trust you more than myself, oh, so much more!— nevertheless, it all makes me feel like *uüaxm* or *uüax* or whatever. Say, how is it that Pan is inflected—most unneighborly for an Indochinese language. That too is perplexing. Anyway, I do trust you. I know that regret for what's done is a sinful waste of time. I will measure my emotions. But please resist the flamboyance of others, don't let them tumble you into that slithery vase where so many flowers rot. "Twenty-three thousand died and the desert was strewn with their corpses." (An allegory hard to explain, but true.)

Two days ago I passed another Spindle test. It was Census Sunday, and the morning after my party, which went better than I'd expected, since Dan and Grace behaved like the civilized beings they aren't. Two men from the Knights called at brunchtime: a dignified gent (the examiner) and an impudent youth whose appearance was grotesque even by my standards—ill-barbered carrot-top sprouting above pinkish eyes, tiny lids daubed with kohl (a teenage practice here), and a harelip the color of beets. He was as respectful of the examiner as he was sassy to me.

We drove out through the northern suburbs, skirting the vast wasteland behind Slaughterhouse Crescent, with its Sunday litter of skulls. We stopped once to investigate a crowd that had gathered by the highway. A donkey—not a horse, as the press reported—had fallen into a well, from which it was being raised by the efforts of other donkeys. Afterwards we reached a pier and parked by a forty-foot, crane-colored fishing boat. The captain, who was waiting by the gangplank, complained of our lateness, saw us aboard, and started up the engines. The young rascal steered.

We rode at a desultory speed, so that I suffered more from torpor than from my usual queasiness. There was little conversation. Lunch was served by an obscure female who mostly lingered below decks. My attention was conspiratorially drawn to the designs on our plates: caducei, scale helmets, serpents biting their tails. I made no comment. I was preoccupied with keeping down the food; to this end I even refused a fine neo-Cuban cigar. Around two o'clock I noticed, near the dallying boat, an effect as of floating cloth-of-gold. I asked the captain what it was. He grinned whitely through his preposterous tan, and without answering, pointed toward the bow. The examiner was emptying onto the ash-gray foredeck a small sack of filings, which he distributed in half-inch mounds: almost touching one another, they formed a closed, irregular curve. When the sack was empty, the examiner beckoned me to watch. The vibrations of the engines were agitating the iron dust, displacing it across the slick paint. The filings gradually assembled into a fixed equilateral triangle. The examiner then asked two questions. To my surprise, I answered them without hesitation.

"Can you define what you see?"

"A triangle is defined by its center—its unmanifest essence."

"Is this to be explained?"

"No, only sensed in its intensity."

The examiner was standing behind me, and as I said these words I turned toward him, and found myself looking into four astounded faces: behind the cockpit window, the young scamp at the wheel; the captain on the cockpit roof; the examiner in the narrow gangway; the dark woman behind him. Past the stern, the cloth-of-gold was now in focus: loose-stemmed waterweeds.

A flurry of wind blew away the filings. The examiner clapped me on the shoulder, while the captain, gunning his engines, turned the boat around to speed homewards. My stamina exhausted, I lurched aft and abandoned my meal to the muddy billows of the Everglades.

The presence of a triangle in both tests seemed deliberate. According to the examiner, it was not. He explained, after I'd cleaned up, that the second triangle referred to a game played at the Knights' "mother club," somewhere in Asia. The game, which resembles squash, requires a convex triangular court. Of the reappearance of the triangle he said, "Chance is a wise master," and shifted my attention to a snakebird drying its wings on a mangrove.

On the drive home, our car stopped at the edge of town, insofar as there is an edge. The carriage that had fetched me from the tailor's was drawn up by the roadside. The examiner saw me into it and, as he left, handed me a morocco pouch with one gold coin in it—an *écu sans soleil*.

My carriage ride was long: we twice drove from the starting-point to the manhole I told of. There must be a significance to this. I have become convinced that in my dealings with the Knights everything that happens is symbolic; even if I don't know of what, that doesn't matter, what counts is that I am being guided along a spiritual itinerary. My nature has been sufficiently distracted to loosen its hold, and I am compelled into the sentiments of old mysteries—that we are, for instance, all children and heirs of one father. How they manage this with triangles *is* a mystery. Such feelings ought to be sweeter than the honeycomb; not to me. To see the

common in the uncommon, the stars in a sunny sky, birds
nesting in my mirror—delusion, delusion, I'm a doomed
machine, and can't forget it, although wishing I could.
Only in you is there neither renunciation, nor oblivion.

XXVI

July 22

My lover of camelions, it's no question and was not ever.
Other wise. I do n't like him, yet it is easy-er to manager him
with pazienze, *atr-am duvaï nob sheen-am* "I think fare well for
to-indure-him." He's so perstant, if I say *duvaï* he 'll-be wosre.
And per-haps I have a haunch a bout him... He's of name
Pindola. And, he's not long-er so crazy as the kite, he 's-
become much swettertamperd. There is a reason medicle. A
dottor cheque him and learn a "sugre defficiency" in the
blood of him. This have-make him very franetic, in other and
in de-sire. Now, he eats a milky way each 2 ours and 's angelic,
I keep him easy-ly un-der my toe. None of it is much to some
point yet I 'll chatt with you until that we met, love. I've no
pleasure in the to-ask money, but of-it have, no-more.

XXVII

July 28

They came at eight, bringing my robes, and tongue sandwiches that they urged on me, as supper was not until midnight. Three tart margaritas had put me in good spirits.
The fly was parked outside, with a limousine behind it. I
entered the carriage, the others the car. Twice our tandem
drove to the great manhole and returned to my dwelling.
The third time it stopped at the sewer entrance; I was told to
climb out, then blindfolded. One asked me a question I've
forgotten, to which I answered, "An expanding economy in
an expanding universe." (Giggles.) Another seized me from
behind and pressed his thumbs under my shoulder blades,

prodding me toward speech. Dubiously, I opened my mouth:
"Ah... um..." The laughter ended, two fingers poked
through the blindfold against my eyeballs, for a flash of
scarlet and yellow. One took my hand, murmuring, "*Dabar!*
Your land journey's over."

There was a clank of metal, I was led stumbling a few steps
forward and pushed to my knees. My feet were grasped in
turn and placed below the level of the pavement on metal
bars. Descending, I counted fifty-two rungs. The air became
damp and blessedly cool. I thumped to solid ground as my
foot sought the fifty-third rung. A short march forward, to
sounds of water faintly splashing, and three steps down onto
swaying wood. I was instructed to sit. Others clambered
around me in the boat; I felt it glide over the water. "Your
sea journey commences." My blindfold was removed.

The sewer light was dim, barely a glimmer on the glazed
vault. A voice warned, "Don't play the hinge. One look back
ruins everything."

The words frightened me: the Temple initiation imposed
the same rule. Was this to be a comparable ordeal? I kicked
myself for not bringing my flask, or some pills.

"Make light!"

I thought that the words had been addressed to me, but
another voice shouted a reply, and white and black patterns
fleetingly crossed the walls ahead.

"Where is the affection called dazzling? Where are the
tears?"

Another shout produced a flare, so intense I shut my eyes
and beheld matching darkness.

Around me the cries came more rapidly, and the walls
blazed with changing lights. The flare's brightness was over-
run with a film like blood, then mixed with creamy white,
which gave way to purple and umber. New exclamations
produced reaches of flame-color and faint yellow; dark
blue and pale blue; leek green. The smell remained constant.

We crossed the junction of four waterways. I was told,
"These are the Corridors of Proximate Session."

Irritated shouts of "Not this... Not that..." and "Never more!" rebounded to us from the lateral sewers.

"Not the voices of ignorance," my companions intoned—

"... not the voices of ignorance but the implosion..."

"... the implosion of language before..."

"Memory..."

The word moaned away down the galleries amid a salad of colors.

As the voices came alternately from either side, I found myself turning toward them. To the left there was a feeling of boundless warmth; to the right, volatile brilliance. Ahead was a dark point where the walls appeared to meet. As the illuminations ended I briefly saw one last image, a sexual tantrum, clear among the damp reflections; then my face was brushed by wet strands, we passed through some veil into a cool, empty light.

We had entered a round widening of the sewer. On one side a broad concrete platform rose from the water. Here an assembly was seated in armchairs. A quiet buzz of conversation was soothing after the shouts.

"You see, no useless ecstasy."

Our boat nudged the wall near steps. We approached the gathering. Heads turned towards us, among them Dexter Hodge's.

"Hello, hello, what a surprise! Didn't expect to see you here. Join us anyway. Sit down."

"Yes, yes," they chorused, "no matter you weren't invited. Drop in any time."

Reassured by the friendliness with which these surprising words were spoken, I settled in the proferred armchair, where I was to remain for an hour. The cushion seemed to have been stuffed with spark plugs, which helped my pious expression.

There were several dozen men, most of them well on, and well-off too. Silence spread among them, until a very old gentleman, able at last to make himself heard, bleated a wordless pitch-tone, then raised his hand and led, still seated, the opening of the Spindle Hymn:

The jester in cap and bells
Swings his bauble, lights the bladder-lamp,
Lets flow the lion's black blood
And opens the locked book
Ornate with scallops and scalene triangles,
  Hanorish tharah sharinas.

A podium stood beyond the rows of chairs. From it four Knights delivered brief speeches on "aspects of Spindledom."

The fifth speaker was the Mayor of Miami, Ayer Favell. He is the most popular political figure in the city's history: after twelve years in office, no one yet knows whether he is Democrat or Republican. His apparently extemporaneous speech was pronounced in a leathern, official voice; it dealt with Miami's national obligations as "romance capital." Mayor Favell will once again be a candidate in November, and he did some characteristically metaphysical campaigning. His rhetoric washed pleasingly over me, until at the phrase "degenerate loins" my mind cut loose, wandering among vistas of white and black until it stopped at a constellation of moss splotches on the ceiling, of a green so bright I thought they must be paintings of moss. Sudden cheers from my neighbors brought me back to Mr. Favell. He had just exonerated the Knights from beach taxes.

"Speaking of taxes, you'll be glad to learn that I've had a report from Roger Taxman. But first let me salute others, equally distinguished, who are here tonight.

"The wisest of the wise—Miles Hood." The noted philanthropist rose and bowed. He is about five inches tall. Behind him sat three squat bodyguards.

"That pillar of faith—Silex Jewcett." Mayor Favell had arranged a night's parole.

"A paragon of healing—Dr. Clomburger." He earned his notoriety during our "crazy crab" epidemic.

"Wizard of safety—Peter Jeigh." I did not understand this epithet. The Sovereign pitcher waved his one arm in acknowledgement.

"A whirlwind of prophecy—Dexter Hodge." Mr. Hodge

walked over and patted me on the back. Perhaps he had "prophesied" my admittance. His attention was flattering.

"A well of discernment—Daniel Tigerbaum." I tingled with shame. Dan, that walking snake pit! He was cited only because of our acquaintance.

"That gaggle of tongues—Robert Pindola." Imagine my surprise! This man is an interpreter.

"And now for our wandering Knight, Roger Taxman.

"Roger spent the winter visiting the Algerian province called Little Brittany. Despite its name, the region lies in the Sahara, all empty rock and sand with a few inhabited oases. Arriving in his rented helicopter at one such place, Roger learned that in the waste nearby there was something extraordinary to be seen, and that he *must not see it.* Although as polite and respectful of custom as any Knight, Roger's sense of adventure was aroused. He persuaded his native pilot to help him find the wonder, whose whereabouts he had guessed.

"They started off in that direction, flying in a wide zigzag. Beneath them the tawny sands stretched level as the waters of a bay, until they beheld a large shell-like rock emerging from the flatness. They flew near it. The rock's outer surface was scorched by the sun, but its hollow was shady; and in the shade stood the upright figure of a girl, bound and naked.

"Roger writes, 'I would have thought she were a fictitious shadow of alabaster or other significant marbles, brought to the rock through the artifice of industrious sculptors, had I not seen tears, distinct among the fresh roses and candid privet blossom, bedewing her half-ripe little apples' (that's what it says) 'and the breeze fluttering her tresses.'

"The pilot descended low enough for Roger to make out these details, and the silver chains that fastened the girl to the rock. And then, through the cloud that the chopper was beginning to raise, he saw, as he leaned from the cabin, a monstrous head rise from the sand and take the girl's leg in *his* choppers. The noise of the craft distracted the beast from his prey. It relinquished the white foot and started biting at the shadow moving across the ground. In this manner Roger, who was unarmed, and who saw the foolishness of meeting the creature empty-handed, lured it some distance away. He then sped back to the oasis.

"Confronting the inhabitants with what he had seen, he learned that the girl was a famous Berber princess, the 'angelical Farah-Sahi.' She had been captured by the local Tuaregs, who had offered her instead of one of their offspring to the Great Sand Snake. Each year the Snake exacted, as the price of sparing the oasis, the sacrifice of a virgin girl, whom he swallowed alive.

"Revolver at hip and rifle in hand, Roger returned to the helicopter. To his dismay the engine failed to start. Leaving the pilot to repair it, Roger found a camel and set out alone. For over an hour he rode, with anxiety burning his heart as fiercely as the sun his head. It was with a cry of relief that he greeted the chained maiden, still uneaten.

"Roger dismounted and approached Farah-Sahi. The Snake poked its head out of the sand. It looked more like a pig than a snake. Roger had only a glimpse of it, for the earth began shaking and the air was suddenly filled with whirling thick sand. The beast had remained, as was its wont, ninety-nine percent underground, and by powerful fillips of its buried tail had churned up a storm.

"Roger lost sight of the rock. He was groping his way through the blistering air when he felt an unpleasant pressure on one thigh. He reached down and encountered the snout of the monster sucking in his leg. The danger passed when the creature, stopped by Roger's crotch, realized its mistake and disgorged the single leg to start over again.

"Roger was determined to dispatch the brute at the next encounter. He knew that in the chaos of the sandstorm he dare not use firearms. So when he felt the Snake's maw seize his ankles, he stuck it through the eye with the hole-punching blade of his Swiss Army knife, then finished him off in the customary manner.

"The air cleared. The broken head of the Snake lolled at the girl's feet. Roger once more put his handy knife to good use, unscrewing Farah-Sahi's chains, and mitigating her thirst with an ounce of compressed water.

"Roger tells little about the girl. Evidently overcome by fear, she was reluctant to follow her rescuer. To reassure her, Roger gave her his widower's ring, which she accepted with a smile and swallowed—something that made him very angry.

"They returned to the oasis. Roger learned that after he had left, his pilot started vomiting and soon afterwards succumbed to vomiting fever.

"Scarcely had he heard this news when he and the girl were hauled before a tribal magistrate.

" ' I never blowed,' writes Roger, 'whether it was a real or a ritual trial. Its pretext was that tradition had been violated. The magistrate was obsessed with our sense of worthiness. "Which of you can swell his heart with conscious superiority? Is it you, stranger, who thinks, Better I than this animal, this garbage, this *woman*? Or you, Princess, who thinks, Better I than this Christian, this imperialist hireling, this *American*?" But we never learned the answer, because a boy ran in shouting that oil had been struck, and we all went off to see the gusher.'

"And may I suggest," Mr. Favell continued, "that our axiom was ever present in Roger's mind: *Let no man ask what this is, or why this is. He must not say it, he must not say it. For he is a Spindle Knight.*"

Facing me, he declared:

"So to you, new Knight, I turn. Welcome to our crew. I shall not describe your duties; if you were not aware of them you would not be here. Now the portal of Knighthood will open, and you must pay the required toll. To you this will be no sacrifice, since like all of us you are amazed that any man should be smitten by the luster of gold; that men, for whom money was created, could ever be thought of less value than it; or that only because he is rich, a man with no more sense than a stone, and as bad as he is foolish, should have dominion over others. Therefore draw near."

I drew near. The Mayor spoke to me confidentially:

"That's two hundred and ninety-eight dollars."

I gulped and took the pad of blank checks that he held out
(Thank heaven I'd dispatched your money.)

The Knights had resumed their hymn:

What does he hear in the bauble's swing?
What does he see in the lamp's light?
What does he feel in the welling of the blood?
The rune-rife smith at his bellows,
The herald at the gates of noon.
Hanorish tharah sharinas.

While they sang, a curtain behind the podium was slowly
raised. Beyond it lay a room eighty feet in length, lighted by
a bank of giant spotlights that bisected its ceiling. This was
the workshop of the Knights, where their precious Galahad
linen was made. A token crew now worked its cumbrous
machines.

Following Mayor Favell, I learned the stages of linen
manufacture.

At the near end of the shop, a hackler took rough stricks of
swingled flax and dashed them into the hackle-teeth of a small
ruffer, drawing them through several times, and repeating
the procedure with a series of finer-toothed hackles. The tow
waste was neatly gathered. A second worker took the clean
stricks and pressed them into slivers, a third rolled and twisted
the slivers, and a fourth wound these slubbings onto blunt
wooden rocks, or distaffs. In the center of the room, apart from
her neighbors, sat the spinster, an imperious lady in a trouser
suit of silver lastex, holding a distaff in one hand and with the
other revolving the spindle against her thigh. The spindle was
of tapered green stone, its midpoint ringed with a wharve of
gold (or brass.) Other women wound the thread on the
bobbins of a handloom, where it was woven into lengths of
several yards: bleached, dried, and stamped with a mark, these
were piled at the far end of the shop.

We returned to the spinster. I knelt in front of her. She laid
down her work, leaned forward, and tapped me on either
shoulder with the spindle, saying: "Theah... and theah... I

pronounces you a Knight of the Thimble"—the idiot! After which, casting an amorous glance at the Mayor, she resumed her spinning.

Mr. Favell helped me to my feet and, having kissed me on both cheeks, led me to a wooden construction that faced the spinster: it consisted of a stair of twenty steps on the left, a vertical ladder on the right, and at the summit a narrow platform, on which a music stand was perched, with an open book on its rack.

The Mayor directed me to the ladder with the words: "There you will ascend Happy Mountain."

I did as I was told. Two minutes' hoisting left me breathless and awash. Upright at last on the rickety platform, I withstood an onrush of vertigo by grasping the weighty book. Behind it, fastened to the lectern, a metal stem held a small rectangular mirror, tipped awry. In it I saw one of the ceiling spotlights, extinguished, its lense reflecting the bolts piled below. The markings on the cloth—six black spots like upsidedown boots—were vividly magnified by the lamp glass.

The Mayor's voice rose pompously.

"For from the communion of the inner and outer fires, and from their union in the mirror, these appearances must arise.

"For they coalesce on the bright smooth surface.

"For the fire of the eye meets the fire of the face.

"For they are thought to be prime causes, since they freeze and heat."

I straightened the mirror and obtained a sight of my hot face.

"New Knight, you have clomb the Mountain. Read us the lesson there writ."

The open pages were from Petrarch's description of Mont Ventoux; Hannibal splitting the Alps with vinegar was crossed out. I read the passage in a voice small if not still. At the words about Italy—"longing to see my beloved in that country"—I could scarcely speak.

While I read, the company of the Knights filed out on either side of me, singing pianissimo:

The jester in cap and bells
Drops his bauble, quenches the bladder-lamp,
Staunches the blood....

The weavers also left. Alone, I closed the book, descended
the stair, and followed the Knights into an adjoining chamber.
They were seated at a long table, at one end of which a
place awaited me. Aromas of broth and sauce announced
to my convulsed belly that its ordeal and mine were at an
end. The menu comprised conch-and-crab soup, filets de
flounder "Zeppelin," wild turkey stuffed with Arkansas
truffles, and honeydew melon soufflé, with wines to match.
After supper, libations were poured and there were the
other usual ceremonies. Then, with the cigars and brandy, a
three-piece band came in to play old favorites, and we all had
a good time of it, in a sedate way. Dexter Hodge introduced
me to the Knights I hadn't met; they regaled me with jokes.
(Miles Hood did not stay for supper. Dan had passed out.)
After a while there seemed to be continuous group singing.
Hours went by, and it was not until someone did a mimic
cockcrow that I knew the night was over. A samovar was
brought out. Our numbers were swelled by a gang of sew-
ermen on their way to the compost farms. They broke in
on the pretext that we had left the manhole open. They were
welcomed, and the party went on with them, although
without decorum. Don't think I say this in disapproval of
workmen. I was grateful for their presence. All my life I have
been a "have-not." At home I was a "have-not." I regard
myself as belonging to them.
Drowsiness got the better of me thereafter. I dozed a little,
then took my leave. The morning streets shone.
It's taken me hours to write this. I'm beat.

Part Three

XXVIII

August 1

Why, is Pan in-flect? You ask. Once it was n't, then home
the missions, be fore soldats and buyrs, monks mad for lingual
avance. Yet, hlever, they forse not theyr linguage up on us,
ownly show, the vantage of its struttures—of horse, we are
peedisposed to these. They show howhow one word can
to-be many, with a little twits, and we 're reasn-like and order-
most and the cort adops this eduhation. Yet in poor villages
you hear the old way, in flectsible—they have leash words
such you call hualifiers? in place end-ings. Some times the
leahs-words be come new in italian-pan. Ex. gr. *nob* was
qualify-er makin of noun, a verb, so *lucrim* "food" and *nob
lucrim* "aet", now you kno *lucri* is "eat" (as *lucrem* "I eet")
and *nob* meen "for" hense *nob lucri* has now a sense "for to et."
How ever, you must n't thingk all progross is be causa of
occodont maniacs, we do our-own. So *ticbaï* meaned firts
"run-ing from" and now "in face of, confront with"; and
like wise the antic sense is not oll losst, in my willage *ticbaï laï*
is "in flight of mud" but in the capatal "con front-ed of mud".
This is mud-heavil, under the moonsoon.

Mean while I work since middle-june at MAP, that is:
Mediceo avanti il Principato, the arhive of the Medici is

thousand of bundles, and looking in to them, I 'm go-ing nutty.

You may think, my gioy in your knit-ness is that I 'm Mrs. Knight, or you are like Roger Tax and un-screw me from the roc of my father, but it is n't, onely my brother with all truist joy my mind is fill seeping in this way and that way and two more way, and up, dwon, and to the sides, so every where it seep in every hting this mind ricc with altruest joy, mind open-ing, mature, and with graet lac of dis like and diswish.

I live in a quite pension (yet not all meels, but bred-&-brekfast.) My friend is the lone-ly chamber maiden. She 's name of Calli, the land-ing lady is Signora Videcca, who 's so please-full and many say, she is a holy, but Calli is un-sure. Nice, but only since Calli works very? Halli says me, "We shall see, howhow nice she 's in truth." One morn-ing, she stays in bed. "Why this?" Signora Videcca aks. "Oh, no thing." Sig. Videcca not replie, onely her eye broughs touch one-each-other.

I shall not, no, tell to the polize the mud-like deeds ot Pindola.

XXIX

August 6

After weeks of marooning I'm back in Mapdom. It's dull. Staring at the walls of my cupboard-size office, I approach annihilation in the perception of their near sameness—they are not the same, but almost the same; yet there can be no question of like or unlike because they are nothing; and I fuse into their nothingness. Why do Tibetans find this so hard?

Hodge has been a disappointment. Ever since my initiation he has been busy. I did manage to see him once, but to no avail, since we were not alone—after my sixth phone call, Mr. Hodge suggested I lunch with him at a diner in the area of the Ten Towns, where he was going on business; and there he showed up in the company of one E. Pater Kabod. The latter was an unattractive old man (no doubt a Temple customer): deaf, uninterruptibly verbose, and a compulsive spitter. He talked through the meal. First he discoursed on spitting, an essential hygiene according to him, whose neglect gave rise to noxious deposits of tartar on the teeth—tartar being as poisonous as arsenic, and the accumulation of venom in the mouths of snakes being due to their inability to spit. Next he warned us about the big con, showing more concern for its practitioners than for its victims. Mr. Kabod salted his talk with hypocritical pericopes such as: "It's impossible to slake one's thirst for the absolute with the possession of created things." I'm sure he would love to try.

Since this lunatic had only half an hour to spare, I hoped to corner Mr. Hodge over coffee and Havatampas. But the old man was replaced by Hodge's Tax Disclaimer, and my lunch break ended.

Grace just called to tell me, with a smarmy lack of glee, that her date at my June party has become a "romance." She "wanted my advice." Indeed. I was astonished by the grotesque echo of old times. That daughter of Saturn belongs to my cavern days, when I lived in chaos, leashed to the under wall of the globe, drinking primitive mercury and feasting on myself. To speak of my life I need two past tenses now, one for that black past which is over, one for the time that began when you stripped my scales.

Your benediction of my knighthood is undeserved. As for your accoster, do as you think best; but remember, it's a mistake to comfort our enemies at our own expense. And in future, be careful not to rumble me so: your words can excite my suspicion as violently as they do better passions. The fault lies in my character, not in your provocation—you will have to forgive me that, my sweet raggle.

XXX

August 9

I feel I am as one in Sah Leh Kot is *ticbaï laï*, but it's not mud

I come-front, but *tharaï ghanap*, end-less hours: 388. Of them I comb small friuts. I han not learn from Mediceo avanti il Principato, it 's called MAP, it near-ly drive me nut, what happen then to the tresure? Yet a bout thirtytime one say any thing of it a mong business letters and letgers from the two Medici-teams. These, from '400 to '443. The team of *Averardo di Francesco* al-ways say, the treasure owes come to us. The team of *Giovanni de Bicci* of horse respond, no thing to do. These ones, all though, do n't try to sell-it. There is a letter whewhere *Cosimo di Giovanni* ask *Francesco di Giuliano* ('41): why, do n't we soppress the busuness, you and I banks have much cash, al-so the clippings are no more to use than thousands pistol-balls with out one pistol. This mean, the clip sin is still attacc to them. *Averardo†* 1434, his son *Giuliano†* '36, grand son *Francesco* †'43, there is no grand-grand son. Then the bank and propriety are home to *Hosimo*. There fore, it should end, how ever does n't. The libri segreti go on-till 1450, the treasor is yet a problem. One can knot know, why? Other ways, all these Medici were friend-most. Re-mind your self, the taem of *Averardo* is as politicians ever be-side the other, to sostain.

Lasttime I have wrote of Calli, my friend and the chamber-ess, howhow she is test-ing the saintlity of Signora Videcca. Calli has thought: she seem saint only be cause of my to-work thus well, yet be neath, she 's tuff. And Calli a-gain a morn-ing rest inbed. Halli, Halli, calls La Videcca.—Si signora?—Why to get up your self so late?—Oh, no thing.—No, nothing? bad girl, her mistruss crys, with let-ing her angr scope in speach.—Then Calli suggest me: A ha, see, she 's not so gentle, I 'll prove her a gain one-ce. (I simpattize.)

Think much, much of you, after your 2 pages tendre & measurd. Cars like your's, give a lurch in my core. The heated weather foster keen-est rimembranzes. *Wey* for all seas be-tween! *Lemum, sheenam*—I love, I dure.

Yestoday I encunter Sig. Pindola to tak tea at Piazzale Gadda. Be fore, a slick car stops, in to it walk a man with shoes of snake, and my freind say, It is Prince Voltic— know, he 's trusted with sell of lost heritage of Medici. I re mane stil still, one-ly in my cup the water rinkles.

XXXI

Augusto 12

My feel *ticbaï laï* was not *tharaï*, so end-less, the mud have crack, out cames not moths but, the prince! And for this I write, yet with out the to-wait of your risponds, O Twang preg, this be no crime a-gaints oxidental letters-cutsom. Thus the Pindola walk with Twang a cross the green-less piazza with the tower fist-most, then "Good day prince," "Good day!", "Know you my friend...?" and emit my name, I tell to you, my courtsey so low as stretch-er cat, "What esquisite!", they talk of we shall-have cup to-gather, "Ciao," "Ciao." Think, his grand powr of Medici facts and odjects: I 'll have that.

There come too a smal-er help, from Mr. de Roover, all-ready you know, in Rome he toll of clip-ings and of *Otto di Guardia*. He is a-work in MAP, have for 20 years and still there is thirteen bundles to esamin. (Of 166.) So, I see him day and day, we put on our coffee brakes to gether, some time he have me to home to a lunch in near-from trattoria. A gain he helps—he has, a most-interest-full hump a-bout whawhat happen after 1443. Sure, *Cosimo* in-herit the proprety of of-*Averardo* great-son but bank-parts and land-parts, and there is, no patricolar things. Later (says Mr. de Roover) we shall note the regreg of *Clarice de' Medici*, as the celebrete "Resurrection Ring" by *Baroncelli* not have-became theirs, the want to give it to of-her not-yet dauhgter-by-law *Alfonsina*, and that ring made for *Giuliano di Averardo* 1430. In like-mode *Piero the Gotty* ask in 1460, where is, not to-us, the pori-tratt of *Francesco di Giuliano*, that *Alesso Baldovinetti* have paintit? A-long with referenzes to treasure after '43, these re-marks have the de Roover esteam, there is to-have-be a-nother heir. This appare so like-ly, I'm not sure how it can be true. How ever the-less it's sure, the wife of *Francesco* dies with no child.

It is to-note, a new indress on flip of this letter. I was needed to move, after Calli's last proof-ing Signora Videcca. A-gain late in her bed, and answer "Nothing" to "For what?" Then la Videcca take pin and stroke Halli. It is, the pin to roll-ing pasta. And blood leep from of-Calli head, then she run with blood into street and gry, "Look, look howhow she's a

saint!" Thus Sig. Videcca have lost a riputation, also Calli the
post as clean-maiden, and, evidently, I like her hompanion
goes, too.

I dreamed strange-ly last-night. I have walk down to the
river, and seek to ride a-way on a little boat. This, is fasten to
a tree yet not by rope, but a metal piece, and lotckd by knot-
and-bolt. The knot is gold and it is shin-ing like sunfire on
pool, I turn up on it and han-not un-scrue it. A new glow is
be-hind me, I look, it's a monk, old & strong, yet his head
is n't shave nor face. He does the glow, soon to fade, until he
speak, "It is *knot* gold!" and the glows de-part, finally at that
they're no thing. The barc is float a way evening on the water.
—I han not think, is the monk a true monk? is he a *pristwe?*
(a demon)

XXXII

Aug. 13

Your new facts suggest such a chronology as this. After
Boniface IX had commissioned him to seize Todao's treasure,
Averardo asked Giovanni di Bicci to do the job for him.
Giovanni found that while the clipped gold was great in
weight, it was unnegotiable. So he cut his losses by settling
with Messer Todao for a smaller sum in cash, released the
treasure, and canceled the Pope's debt. No one but Averardo
was the worse off. Messer Todao transported the hoard to
his abbey, where he hid it in a chest of silk, and died without
disposing of it: it lay untouched until the later abbot's
discovery. Meanwhile, in respect to Averardo, Giovanni
began the long dissimulation that his family was to maintain
after his death, not daring to admit the breach of faith to
cousins who were such staunch political allies.

All day long—it is sunset now— I've been haunted by a
dream I had early this morning. It began with my lying wounded in a street—the street where the truck knocked me down.
I stared at a wall whose surface was being slowly lettered
over, the inscription indecipherable but Gothic in aspect. The
letters started shining. I looked about. Behind me a man in

saffron robes was dismounting from a caparisoned horse. He was tall, sturdy and saturnine, with coppery skin, incandescent white hair, and black eyes.

The old man approached; his radiance faded. He set me astride the horse, then led me down an unfamiliar way. Presently he said, "A horse is a vain thing for safety. I'll take you to an inn." We stopped in front of a dark building, into which he carried me as though I were a puppy. The interior dissolved in deep browns. Light dwindled from high pointed windows; piles of manure were heaped in corners; there was a cadaverous smell. The old man settled me on a low bench and prepared a potion for my wounds. "You'll want some cascara... natural sulfur... an inch of worm spittle..." The mixture tasted like chewed paper. The old man stood over me and shouted, "Now do you know who I am? A hint: my initials are D.W. So, D.W....? D.W....?"

He removed his robe, under which he wore only jockey shorts and sneakers. His hefty body was the same color as his face. He lay down and began caressing me. Each caress discovered chinking coins along the ridges of my body, which he tucked into his shorts, mumbling "Gold in prison" or "Expenses." His beard was moist. "You don't object to paying your debts. You're no Pogy O'Brien," he said, extracting more coin. Becoming bored, he sighed "Nevermore," and left me for a brass salver heaped with macaroons, which he swallowed with gluttonous majesty. After a moment he paused:

"You call yourself a scorner of contingencies, but it's time to grasp history by its nettle-like stalk."

There was a sound of durable materials splitting, as an invisible levee cracked. Water flowed into the church.

The effect on the old man was organic. In moments the smooth consensus of his limbs gave way to pathetic marasmus. "Ah, my cancer!" he wailed. The waters rose quicker. "This my king's tomb?" he said, subsiding among them. A cascade of mascara darkened his face. "That explains those eyes of his!" I gazed on the silvery foam, expecting Venus or the Rhine Maidens to rise from his bubbles.

This afternoon brought the microfilm from Montpellier.
I'll look at it tonight. I could use help these days. The computer is now denied me, commandeered by the police. Hodge
remains as inaccessible as ever. For a whole week the heat and
humidity have been in the nineties; I feel as though I were too.

Write soon and brighten the long day's journey. I note the
improvement of your English with pride.

XXXIII

August 20

To Lorenzo de' Medici. Complaint of Guillaume
Abbot of Montpelas. How the Abbot was knowingly
defrauded by Lionetto di Benedetto Lorenzo's agent.
How the Abbot was much impoverished and the
Medici's honor sullied.

Should the Abbot Guillaume not have expected to
gain more than he gave? His hopes were not drawn
from common rumors that the chest of silk was of great
worth. He believed the tacit support that Lionetto agent
of the house of Medici, and his associates, gave such
rumors. And I cite as example one of these Benedetto di
Gianfranco, who all know to be Lionetto's intimate.
When he visited the Abbey to buy wine, he spoke to the
Abbot of certain lots of Florentine silk that were for sale.
Was the Abbot wrong to hint at the purchase of a certain chest when he was given satisfactory information
and his precise hopes were encouraged? He then endeav-
ored to transact with Lionetto himself but could not
be received, yet had a letter assuring Lionetto's com-
pliance in the affair. It is a misfortune that this letter was
returned at the insistence of Lionetto's representative
after the sale was finally carried out and the false goods
delivered. Messer Lionetto has now rebuffed Guillaume's just complaints because "the Abbot failed to
transact with Lionetto himself, who had postponed
important matters in Avignon expressly for the Abbot's
business." What? The Abbot was to blame? Guillaume

was not to blame (nor Lionetto. Yet it was he who chose that wild meeting-place.) I was traveling through the borderlands when my journey was interrupted. Just before the solitary village at Pont d'Eulh ten men apparently lepers suddenly came among us. Profiting from our revulsion they seized our horses by their bits and bridles then made us dismount. They were thieves and no lepers and quite nonchalantly plundered myself and my three monks. They took the money we carried to pay for the silk and rode off with our horses. Two hours passed before we found some slowfooted asses and thus we came late to the meeting with Lionetto. He to my dismay had just departed, having instructed his men that in his absence the sale of the silk was to be deferred, and this was a great misfortune. Needless misfortune, for Messer Lionetto himself has since told me that payment could have been made on a later day, in view of the wretched theft of my money, but no words would move his men. Such a waste! I could only submit. I watched the silk being reloaded. Great lengths of brocade were folded into the chest. The regret of the moment has not lessened, for since then my eyes have never seen such a quantity of brocade...

I've done this much of the microfilm, which is the pure quill: the draft of a letter to Lorenzo the Magnificent by the sixth Abbot. (Yours was the second and mine the seventh.) Its date is 1483 at the latest. I've pruned the text of its flourishes, which clutter every sentence: "...What I say is this, a covenant was validated, it cannot be invalidated.... My lord, do not forget the lives of poor men, do not forget the appeals of those who address themselves to you...."—on and on.

It isn't hard to guess whom the ten thieves were working for.

Thanks for your informative letters. I hope you meet the Prince again. But is it wise to see so much of this De Roover? Just who is he? I must counsel you to restrain your trust of strangers. It's not only that you may risk our secrets: you cannot guess the sexual effect a twist like you has on men of the west, especially intellectuals. I'm concerned, too, that you may not be getting enough to eat, or the right kind of food—is that why you have lunch with him?

Months have passed since I was last with you. I have only your hammock photograph to caress. I want to smell and touch you. The waning summer fills me with gloom. Two hands in their circular mimicry of pursuit cannot dissemble the face behind them that in deadly earnest hunts us down.

XXXIV

Agost 23

Now, it's sun and quite noise come from the streets, yet 20 minutes fore it were blacc thnunder and light-ing. Twang was very frighted to squat under my table for work near library windows, I feel, a *pristwe* comes after me. It is the same demon as your dracm, much water after the flash. I think many times, a flash have a no less shortlife than mustard seed on arrowtip.

Mr. de Roover is sicure, so nice, he was professor of histery at the college "Brooklyn," now retires, yet not from terribiles bundles of MAP (in fun.) And with Mrs. de Roover, she's name of Firenze! They're delihate to Twang. And she's too a enorme to-know of old ehonomix, have wrote Glossary of Mediaeval italian Buziness Terms, so beuatifull, I've not can work with out that, and when I am first gave her hand with "Good day" I was timid timid, yet soon I prey for her author-graph. In change I write her a catalog of business terms Pan and Lao. They have age, to a bout 65 years.

Your are not to think, does Twang ate what is good? Any food is a nough. And this's need-ing no virtu, all things are ease-most, they are *nob-lemum* (for that I love.)

So the Pindola accompany me to the Prince's. We slip a ice-full drink on his terraze and be-hold low houses. Pindola have said, "The Twang know much a-bout those Medici," the Prince then: "May be, that she will say any thing of their brank in Lübeck?" Twang: "O, no, it is no branch, that Gherardo Bueri and some, it is only corispondents for the bank," I tell of Gutkind's wrong-ing. The Principe Voltic look at me a dozen sehonds and then he give me a new drink.

XXXV

August 27

I'm wretched at having snapped at you about Mr. de Roover. I should have known better. I did know better—it's another case of my nature besting my intelligence. Who can approve of quarrelsomeness, contentiousness, envy, ambition, or drinking bouts? The trouble is, there's no law to uphold the imperatives of the moral will. One nails down one's bad habits on the nearest board and drags it behind, a useless brake of remorse.

I'm sending extra cush, because I don't want you eating just "any food."

Here's the Essential Remainder of Abbot Guillaume's lament. Authentic though the document may be, it's fishy. Not because it contradicts my last hypothesis and, more important, the account in Amortonelli's letter: there the chest in the abbey *did* contain the treasure. (Notice that both lots of silk were marked with "six ravens"; they have their importance. The Abbot had only to glimpse them to accept the goods. He writes of "seeing in that blazon my shield, erring in this, for it was a Medusa's head to petrify me.") The story as a whole seems crow. Why should Lionetto, high placed in the Medici bank, go off into the countryside to hopscotch like a common grifter?

Messer Lionetto then wrote he would deliver the silk to the Abbey, but he would not himself accompany it because of the distance, and he was occupied with many pressing matters, so he entrusted the goods to the said Benedetto di Gianfranco, who later claims that he only followed Lionetto's orders, and this is perhaps no

lie, but how is he to be believed when he says that he
knew nothing about the contents of the chest, which
was most certainly of the proper size (six men lifted
it scarcely), on its lid the three fish were roughly cut,
when they opened it it seemed to be filled with the
brocade that I had seen folded into it at the first meeting,
and how should it enter the mind of a man of God,
transacting with the representative of one of the
greatest princes of Christendom, that the chief weight
of the chest was a sheet of lead fitted into its base, or that
the brocade once it was unfolded was not the six
hundred *bracci* [about 380 yds] agreed on but a mere
twenty *bracci* long, although the peculiar design of sea
shells and spiny roses was the same as before, but underneath this brief sample was plain taffeta, as I later discovered, too late, and above all too late for redress
because of the manner whereby the fraud was compound-
ed, and yet I look beyond these wiles to the honor of
their master whose glory is so unjustly smirched, to
have his name affixed to a receipt for the delivery of
"620 *bracci* of brocade & taffeta" where no specification
was made of the proportion between the two kinds of
silk, and the point was passed over by me because it had
been explained that taffeta would be used to wrap or
pad the brocade to keep it clean and dry, but it was no
padding but the bulk of the consignment, which I did
not then verify, and concerning this you will ask, why?
My lord, I was stupefied by joy and fear. Joy when the
chest was opened, at the sight of the brocade with the
six ravens stamped on its first fold; fear lest this prize
be lost to me, for I could not think that Benedetto
would leave it to me if he observed what I did. And so
it was after a mere glance that I gave my approval,
ordered the chest shut, paid the price, signed the receipt.
The chest was born to an attic of one of the abbey
buildings, and fearing that any precipitation would
arouse the curiosity of my monks I waited for night,
I had had the chest carried to an attic in an outlying

building, and at last I opened it, only then I discovered the subterfuge, but Benedetto was beyond recall....

Frenzied resentment here overwhelms the text. There is one further point of interest: the Abbot mentions having earlier rendered Lionetto a service, when "Fortune enabled me to return his purse of jewels." Had Lionetto prepared his victim by having him "find the leather?"

Guillaume was on shaky ground. In buying the silk, he expected to be getting more than his money's worth, so much more that—remember the ten thieves—he paid for it twice. It was awkward for him to complain of duplicity. No doubt because of this he followed the advice of his clerk, who appended to the draft:

At the suggestion of Brother Peregrine, scribe, the Abbot has witheld this letter, believing in the end that it would bring small advantage to the Abbey, or none.

Life here continues boring, except for the headlines. The *Sun-Examiner* has trotted out the most terrifying type you ever saw: each letter is as tall as Wee Willie Keeler. Why should the Chinese want to bomb Mars? True or not, the news has happily muted our nation's "clamors of salvation in the tents of the righteous."

As for your apprehension of thunder and lightning, that is an instinctive terror; there's no squelching it. What about your Buddhist disciplines? I'm sending you money with this because I don't want you eating just "any" food.

XXXVI

August 30

To-tell Prince Voltic a bout Lübeck appear, it pleases him, he waste hours search-ing after Medici-tracces there and now not long-er, mercy mine. For thus reason he send yester-day, a thank, a censer, done of agrent, with in-it any twigs of in sense, it's of the '600, littl-est, "for home-use."

Pindola harry that gift. With pleasure: for that if the prince love Twang, to love Pindola more. Bonzo wishs to-will-work for the Prince. Now he do the manucurust, or say womanacure? It's with a for-woman barber all all day. And he will to-say *duvaï* to the work, of-it he is have enough, and who will not? aftre 15 yaers (or even, fivteen minutes.)

Yet Bonzo (Pindola) have took high way with Twang, as he will say, I Pindola gift to you Prince. No no. I never kiss that hand. He is will-hiss my foots!! It shall, to be in vert! And how? There will to-be a accidente, all most, I do it, then I salve the Pindola. He'll kiss under feets of Twang.

I will know, please, the little english speech for "there" and "to-it" as in-italian *ci*? In Pan too it's *nam*, can slid in aesy, be-tween breethes.

O froget, that rebite a bove de Roover, there was n't sorrow in the core of Twang, but warm-ing of fire soup, for it was sweet the brain-less gelosy. Abbrace thee, *lemu*, in my thoght.

XXXVII

September 3

A happy surprise has broken my dull round—days of getting out of bed not knowing whether I'm dead or alive (or feeling both dead *and* alive); the depressing station at the bathroom scale; office hours; equally tedious maps; a solitary movie after supper (yesterday *Guileless Swallows*). All is made bearable by the knowledge that you exist. I try to recognize signs of you in the trash of my life, from the morning paper to the book over which I fall asleep. I take the rest on faith.

And out of the blue, Dexter Hodge called up to invite me to a "choice" houseparty at the Beach. After weeks spent trying to see him, I was stunned; but there is no point expecting consistency from that busy man. For the outing he has taken over the Na Inn, a beautiful motel at 183rd Street.

I don't know what the program is, but with Mr. Hodge in charge it'll be the Carrie Watson. There will be celebrities, and a basketful of fashionable cupcakes. (Fashionable now means layers of Minoan overskirts beneath unveiled tops—a perplexing hot-and-cold effect.) There should be ample opportunity to discuss treasure hunting.

As for Mr. de Roover, I'm touched by your words. You have forgiven me too readily for me to forgive myself.

Unfortunately, there is no equivalent for *ci*, *nam*, or the French *y* in English.

Ever since you arrived in Italy I've wanted to ask you about an essential east-west distinction, that is, the sun—so different from your steamy heat-and-light machine, efficient but remote. It is sometimes like that in our northern cities; but in Florence, as here, isn't it intensely present, like a rampant lion, or a wielded sword flashing among us?

XXXVIII

6. sett.

The incidente was done. In this month one is making new store the Palazzo Rucellai, of-it the face is blind with bords and tube. I rent 2 work men there, one, on low baord, one at-top. Bonzo is walk-down that street, it is whewhen he 's under board I hry a cross the street and run to spin him out from harm way in to door way, then the low man spill a big brigk on whewhere Bonzo were to be. This is not a far drop and when it had have stroke Bonzo it shall have n't kill him, or hard-ly. But, now we regard a-bove, it is the high man cry and hand-shakes as although he just drip the brick, and this was the Bonzo's thought. He sit-down as a doll, I remember you before the apples truck, I was very hard not to-laugh. He call Twang many times *neng! neng!* (bellezza) and I think only on my material-subtile nose to downpush laughing. Then I say, poor tresure! he must to-eat the best lunch, and I 'll pay it, and all so a graet dottor lest he 's hurt-ing and Twang shall pay, of horse I know, he 'll not let this. And to day Bonzo think, I have save him and 'm rich, my hands are the cage and he is the inside bird. The worker men costed $3 and 2 kiss.

Florence town is more empted. It is not a worse for this. But there is a delight here now, for the dipartures. A strong spirit home to me of indolenze, I have the wish to see none one, to say no thing, to do so, and I have a desire of noth—o yes, I desire you and all though I can n't, then, to read you. *Wuc mau nam theu*, as were we here! (it mean, "would";) to-gather in the streat of warms stones.

Do not you feel some pain in that errore to ward de Roover, do fore-give your self, for my mind follow your pain and then foregive-ing, full of hompassion, this way (pain) and that-way (forgive) and again an other and another-way, a bove, and below, and every way around, pierc-ing the wrold ever full of compassion, so my mind would be a broad, spreadout, beyond the frames and esempt of harted and bad will-ing.

Bonzo tell me, to day is the first day of the Jews Year, No. 5733, he say they are so good at suffer-ing, look at how long they have practice. Is this funny?

XXXIX

September 10

I'm sitting in a Loretta-Youngish bedroom, my bare toes linked in ringlets of angora, gazing at the Atlantic over the space bar of a mighty typewriter that is equipped with fully integrated circuits and pigskin keys. The machine, so rapid that inscription precedes thought, was delivered at my request for "a" typewriter. I used it for my map notes. But I changed to the seriousness of ink to address you. Deep sentiments flow more readily from a pen than from the most responsive keyboard, the McCaltex longhand block notwithstanding.

We've been at Na Inn since Friday afternoon and are to leave Tuesday morning. It's very nice. Under the inn's bungaloid exterior lurks a small palace. The windows of my bedroom, thirteen feet high, are shaded by sun-sensitive sheet-coral blinds. The common rooms are both grand and intimate, thanks to lighting and sound systems that adjust to their use. At their center lies an enormous game-room-cum-swimming pool, whose breadth and length and heighth and depth I can hardly grasp and cannot begin to describe. At the bottom of the pool, night and day, what seems to be real fire flares into the water. One guest, Peter Jeigh, a powerful swimmer, dove to investigate. He said the flames were warm but did not hurt.

The guests I had already met are Peter, Dr. Clomburger, and Lester Greek. I knew others by name, Wolfgang Abendroth for instance. All are remarkable men, answerable to none but themselves for their eminence. The one disappointing absence is that of Miles Hood.

Early Friday evening a few of us played poker. I did so well that I considered turning out as card sharp. My biggest pot was at five card stud. I won with three kings. Mr. Hodge tried to bluff me with four cards to a straight, but I stuck it out and he threw in his hand. Toward the end, a new arrival was announced and we decided to have some fun: when Peter Jeigh's turn came to deal he would play him for a chump, using the rest of us as shills. A deck was "cooled" so that I would be dealt four tens and the stranger four nines.

The latter entered and took his seat. He was handsome, with a fixed smile paralleling his new-moon beard, whose luster perhaps betrayed a dyer's tinge. Play resumed; he was allowed to win a few hands. He enjoyed the game and tossed in his money like hay. The cold deck was introduced; I drew to my four tens and bet up the pot; but when we showed, the mark held four jacks! "Goddam it!" Peter roared, "that's not the hand I gave you." The other replied, "You have to play smart to beat Roger Taxman." He was still swarthy from Africa.

After another round of cocktails we went in to dinner. I was walking toward the foot of the table when Hodge stopped me. "Friend, you don't belong down here, come and sit

by me." It was a glorious meal. I had three helpings of the
main course, a braised stuffed-and-rolled shoulder of lamb
pie. Over the double consommé Mr. Hodge gave his reasons
for bringing us together: his respect for inner, even hidden
worth, his contempt for the vanity of the world. Afterwards
each of us tried to justify his remarks. Dr. Clomburger re-
called an early triumph, his original description of yeast
frenzy; Lester Greek spoke of new gleanings from *Finnegans
Wake*—the palindromic precedence of "Eve" over "Anna"—
soon to be published in his study, *The Confidential Walrus*; I
discoursed on the abstract beauty of maps. So it went round
the table. The evening ended with a swim.

The next days were full of sports and games. Needless
to say, when faced with anything rougher than shuffleboard
I withdrew to my room. Mr. Hodge has agreed to a treasure
talk when we drive home tomorrow.

I admire the way you made sport of Pindola; but why
bother?

Your sweetness, your immeasurable sympathy has again
left me bewildered. Don't worry about my foolish sufferings
—they are only feeble tributes to you.

XL

September 13

I can't know, why is pokre? So a mild game, I once watch
at aerport, the men are roug but in the play of mildmost
charity. They yeild their dollors corteosly, only when they
have lose, they smile. Yet with win-ing, they shake their
haeds and appare so stern with their selves, as pumished. Of
where come this beauty? Or is it but that they think, Happy
with the cards, unhappy with love (I heared so one luagh),
so stranger for in Pannam it is n't thus. A man can to-be happy, with both. Pans say, A mountain apple in one hand, a
stream eel in the left hand.

It may be, Bonzo 's good card actor, for he is be-gin to
regard Twang like my dog. And now he 's also talk talk, and
I almost ywan then he said, the Prince sholl owe to-have me

Bonzo, for the family Pindola have-be guardian of some prop-
erity from the Medici. When? (I yawn *not*.) O a bout 1466
and after. Who Medici? I serch, to think hohow I breath. O
any "ulterior discendents" (?) of: Averardo. I count down,
to twentyone. Then: I think, the of-Averardo descendens are
no one in 1466. O I do n't know, we onely keep these things
be-cause, they are history-hurious. So what things? Chairs
and chaists. Chest? 1 or two, on-them they are the *palle*, or
Medici balls, as of tradition, but them alas and no— Here I
think near by to surest-ness that he will have-say *pesci* fish and
yet make "e" last enough to be home *pesche* peaches. He
ajjoin: "I mean, people some time think they 're peachs, they
're giust balles." After, he shuts the mouth. It is, he think his
affechion mine under his discretions.

Now baby you will se why to "bother" my Bonzo, he 's
be come such an interestfull chap. As the Prince of hourse.
There-fore I press a gainst them, I 'll be a leech in side their
hears and out-suck the middle secretes of those brains. Then
I shall vomit-them-out, *uüaxm!* Thus, *naï sheenam slop*, thus,
I bear benaeth un-happiness, untill I 'm ever for yours, *me
tharaï pheu*, I say the Pan words, sweet like the milk in cans,
in to the bolster 's damp patch at each night, lonesone lonesone. Please, be a-sure of my utter-est and rimorse-less
devozion.

XLI

September 17

Your interpretation of poker is slightly wide of the mark.
It is not the players but you who are charitable. Perhaps there
is a show of self-effacement in winning—perhaps we apply
"funeral manners" to conceal the vindictive glee.

Speaking of gambling, I saw a compatriot of yours playing
faro bank at the Casino: General Kavya. He was twisting the
tiger's tail with a pluck he never showed in the field. They
were dealing them at fifty dollars a card and he punted on
every turn. Has he been thrown out of Pan-Nam for swin-
dling? Or was he sent to cruise our military establishment?

What a fate, when he could have stayed in his province, a
big tail-wagging fish in that lovely little pond! The second
alternative seemed likelier. The General was accompanied
by a U.S. Army captain, who held his parabolic sword and
was apparently abetting his play. Standing behind the dealer,
the captain fiddled with several tiny coins (antique khrots?),
clinking them in irregular, precise rhythms. I'm sure he was
tipping the cards: Kavya kept an ear cocked in his direction.
Otherwise the General did credit to his country, sheathed in
silks and caiman skins. His only weak point was a large Mal-
tese cross that flapped on his tummy, looking very Wool-
worthy among the tribal chains. I wanted to introduce myself as a Pan-by-marriage, but he was absorbed in his gaming.

Next morning Mr. Hodge and I drove into town together.
I raised the subject of treasure-hunting. Mr. Hodge responded
with a monologue on the legal problems that attend the
disposal of treasure-troves. His deluge of words kept me
speechless.

A perplexing incident interrupted the lecture. Our car had
been slowed to walking speed by the throng near the Bass
Museum. (Moreau's "Medusa of the Lilies" is on exhibit,
and for three weeks that end of Collins Avenue has looked
like London Bridge in "The Waste Land.") As we crawled
along, Mr. Hodge pointed to a group near my window:
Miles Hood, preceded by his roly-poly bodyguards and
followed by a thin, stooped figure, who as we watched gave
the famous millionaire a push, then with bewildering pre-
cision severed his attaché case from its gripped handle and slid
away with it into the crowd.

I turned towards Hodge. He looked at me expectantly,
snorted, and pushed me out of the car. I felt myself being
shoved through the slow-moving pack, and before I had had
time to resist or complain, I found myself face to face with
the thief. My own astonishment was mirrored for a second
in his eyes; then he dropped the case and fled.

"Grab it and we'll split." Hodge said. "We'll see Miles
later. No point staying and getting our names in the papers."

In fact we did not return the case. Mr. Hodge asked me to

keep it until he could make an appointment with Hood—"If he was carrying it himself it must be valuable." I've not heard from him since.

Now from the groaning board it's back to the groaning scale, and the other tediums. Only your letters delight me. I keep them scrupulously filed (this is one reason why you must be sure to date them) so that I may follow your progress in English, something that gives me pride and pleasure. The letters bring torment also. They plunge me into lust. My beloved, write me about your body. Remind me of it with new words. I rehearse the same memories over and over. Only you can renew them—you *must* renew them, repetition is a death of love. I wish I could persuade you that what I say is true.

XLII

September 20

The Prince Voltic will go in to the Mugello, at some low mounts with health. With him, Bonzo and Twang follow, as ask-ed? It is a worth-most travel, I be-leave, and also there I 'll study and think-up my hunts in MAP. If you will admit so, I must pray, Twang need a little money.

Twang can nots think, words to make love to sur-vive, when it is n't to be made, words of lust make it then any time to death. It is it that sing a poem in my district, of a tigr, whiwhich be gin

Thus of love (a) miseria (is) alas mud

like that begins all sad poem a-bout love, and can you n't catch the Pan words, *naï lemö slop wey laï*?

Thus of love a misery (is) alas mud.
A tigre hurry to the edge of the forest.
He sits behind a bread tree and chews bitter leafs—
his belly's tough of hunger.

A monkey comes. O monkey
I'll swallow your gentile meat
then make your tail as hat,
the tiger sing it, the monkey have go.

Here 's a peehock. O pee cock
I 'll chew each little-twig bone
then I spit your piumes in to the breezes,
the tiger sings this, the pecock al-ready have goe.

There is a buffala. O water buffalo
I 'll knaw aroung your schine and top leg
I'm dainty, not a house of ants,
The tiger sung, and the buffalo is gone.

The tiger rest at the edge of a forest
very dead of this much sing.
Now there are but these ants in his belly, too late,
but they, hurry out his eyes through his dentals

What is that "Waste land"? It 's perhaps a nick name of
Arizona?

Part Four

XLIII

September 24

The day after I last wrote, Hodge called to say that Mr. Hood had left town for a few days; until he returned I should keep the briefcase. I had resisted tampering with the elegant box, but this evening I tried the clasp, which was unlocked. Inside I found the June issue of *Tel Quel*, a tube of H-Preparation, checks in several figures and currencies, and a six-by-eight inch card on which a grid of letters had been typed, over the legend: "Cipher for Amortonelli Location "

You can guess my emotions.

(A withered palm tree is sketched on the back of the card. A cross marks a spot near its roots.)

We must work quicker. I enclose money for your trip, if you still want to make it. But should your friends prove un-rewarding, waste no more time on them.

If you do go to the Mugello, don't be dismayed by the wind and the chilly springs. Why in this season are they going to a mountain spa? It will be deserted, except for my hot ghost. Your refusal to write me as I asked hasn't lessened my need. I won't press the point, because I dread seeming repulsive. How often have I imagined you seated by a window, your head bent, wondering whether a certain "Zachary" is worth the affection showered on him—and you take up your bed and go home. How could I stop you? It is in you that "our" life exists. For instance, it is you and not I who make me attractive to you! This is why I long, even if only in a fiction, for bodily involvement—I want to share your redeeming view of me. I have so often relived our few nights together that they have sunk to the level of racial memory. I need new grist. Do you still not wear a bra?

This second virginity is even stupider than the first. I like it no more than you do. I like it even less than the red of my ink on this egg-hued stationery.

"The Waste Land" is a much anthologized war poem by a turn-of-the-century symbolist called Eliot—not George.

XLIV

29 sept.

Now I 'm in Rostolena. (Do you know, this was some of Averardo's proprety, when he is dead, that wents to Cosimo?) Now, speed letteres at Albergo Terme Paradiso e Fango.

I wish you, not-fear for my reliance. I belive that to not exite by un-point-ed talk, 's best. Yet, o my love-man, it shall-be un-true when I say, I did not miss you terrifly, and long-ing to-see-you. And here my poor gift to your peace, a 3° Zen story, of-such you dilect:

In the *po* test by whiwhich the 6° arch of zen was chose, there were poems. One say, "Dis-like roil dust. The probes remove the dust." The "head wing" poems are their. It said, "He 's the mind. Where, is dust?" Some lat-er Pan masters: a monk who was stak-ing bats, a young-er monk up to his id in the dust—"Are you a-staking-bats?" "No. Why?"

Then I think, to homfrot you more, of our massim: *Ticbaï slop*, in front of non-happiness, *atra-pok-atra*, think n't, *me-me*, be so, *nob lucri maï*, as-to eat the Now, *wuc Lao*, like the Laotians. "Ticbaï slop, atra-pok-atra, me-me nob lucri maï wuc Lao." Slow, you may take-on my tongue, like I your. Yet, it is here the feel-ing to be retaint, less the tongue-lessen.

The post-hard show any of the pittoresque basket work, of this the regional sheep boys are giust-ly famos.

XLV

October 5

Three days ago Miles Hood returned to Miami. Hodge drove me downtown to meet him early that afternoon. I said nothing about the briefcase, although it's painful being a crow with D.H.

The encounter took place at a new Chock Full O'Nuts. The café, almost empty at that hour, was bright with cool fake sunshine. Mr. Hood was at a corner table. As we approached, his three gnomelike attendants popped up in front of us. Smoothing their Blücher-red neckties, the crescents of their eyebrows rising as one, they welcomed us with a unison "Hi there!" Hodge greeted Mr. Hood familiarly and introduced me. I handed over the case. Mr. Hood opened it and beamed. Murmuring an excuse, he verified the contents, testing the checks with a pocketsized magnetic device. Finally Mr. Hood asked with a smile, "Where's the milk of magnesia?"

Frappes were served. While the two men chatted, I tried to catch the mutterings of the bodyguards seated behind me. "...the fat one looks like a big con type." I smiled. "Uh uh. He's a friend of Mr. Hodge." "But the boss is such an easy mark, anyone might try to take him." I turned to look at them. They were leaning forward, their heads together but twisted in different directions, so that their eyes appeared to be staring at odd corners of the room.

Meanwhile Messrs. Hodge and Hood were having a jolly reunion. The backclapping ended at last, and Mr. Hood turned to me. "What can I do for this gentleman? Have a check?" He fanned out the three papers toward me like a benign conjuror. Prudence stifled desire. "Well, let's meet next week and work something out."

There matters rested. I'm glad the decisive moment is postponed. I shall prepare myself as thoroughly as possible for it. I swear that I shall try to act the sensible man and not the simpleton.

How does this predicament look to you, in your remote and dismal village? (The young man on the postcard *is* remarkable.) The "comforts" you sent me, if not the ones I craved, did wonders. On the day you wrote them, the infernal slope I had been climbing leveled off. Your distant magic was at work, mysterious as your Zen tale. I would like to repeat unceasingly the blessing of your name. Who else ever brightened my glooms? Your words are my fixed itinerary of rescue—you are to me, dear Twang, more than a wife, more than a sister: the pilgrim's distant shrine.

XLVI

Ottobor 10

As you do with the gentlemen Hoodge and Hood, I look at it it is good. You are to remember, you know very, they may be not. And, they'll talk their little, so to have your more. Thus, aspect. It's how, I do with my friens.

You have not the true image of Rostolena village, not "deserte" no "dismal", no, they are many many here, with money, gewels, and c., very gay al-so. It is, the mud and skin festival. The springs not cold, theyr heat warm-ing all the houses and houstels, and not only, but the ways, that are cover with glass; the grottas too many and grand, in them is a ristoraunt and sauna-dance circles, very live. So, palms trees are grow a-long the walks and a deal of flowers, like the example of Buddle plants, its seed lodges in all cornices and in window embracures that even so late the cascarades of lillac flowr tumbaling down the palace facades and sprung from coigns. In them some bird sit and sing, I see two robin red chest last morning. And so they carry all clothes of summer. That is funny, with the of-health mode now followed, that of "decoctions of malt": these ladies, most rich and full of speech of great intellett, but a-round the small good clothes big blue stripes on the skins. Yet not Twang, I use but the *laï*, good mud, the ash of a volcano misched with argil, this is very sexual. Also I may be try the hure with sassoline.

This night I aet in the grott with Bonzo and the Prince Voltic. This one, is very mild and cold. He will talk, only of work (Medici). I answer of my grand knowledge, *naï sheenam*, so I bear it. After, with Bonzo I have learned the Hunch, that novel dance, it's not easy, for the Pindola likes the shout-ing as he dance of commands, so: "All-right, now, with-control abandon!" At last, I made an error catastrophic yet delight-ful, I giump 6 steps to rihgt not left. The all line of dancers fall-ing, Twang blush orange, then each laughed and kiss me (even those girls.)

Here I'm back, to write-it. You must think now, I'm not here in "glooms", it may be not the garden of Intuitive Illu-minazion, but, it is pleasant. Still I'm, dear one, a little in-drink but, at every time, your faith-full wife; and now, send you a love-ly *posti*.

XLVII

October 16

When, at cocktail time two days ago, I arrived at the Hood estate, Dexter Hodge was leaving. We had been invited to-gether, but other appointments had obliged him to come early. I did not mind; I wanted to scout the subject of the "Amortonelli location," and Dexter's absence would make this easier.

The three henchmen took me through a wing of the main house onto an immeasurable lawn. There, at the foot of the chapel tower, Mr. Hood welcomed me. It was a pleasant evening, cool, with a half moon peeping through the boughs of wisteria that embraced the round walls above us.

Mr. Hood's smiling face was emprisoned in an antique hel-met, without beaver or visor, apparently of gold. It gave him a lionish countenance. He said, "It's a seventeenth century morion, from a Spanish hoard one of my teams dug up. Look at the nifty artwork." His teams? Astonished, I tried to do as he said, and noted at the helmet's crest the figure of a long-tressed nereid emerging from ranks of fish scales. (Hodge cannot be ignorant of Mr. Hood's interest in treasure-hunting. Why has he never mentioned it to me?)

A siren sounded distantly. Mr. Hood removed his helmet while, materializing like a genie on the empty sward, a beautiful young woman proffered him a telephone on a coral tray. Mr. Hood lifted the receiver, listened, and said, "No—thirteen million." Phone and secretary vanished.

We sat down. Mr. Hood thanked me warmly for returning the stolen briefcase. The contents were worth far more than I could imagine—"The checks were nothing." He wanted to reward me.

He spoke with a gentle finality that made me awkward. But I was prepared for the offer and stuttered out my refusal, explaining that for a friend of Dexter Hodge's the notion of "service rendered" was out of place. I had behaved as he would towards me in similar circumstances.

"But such circumstances are unlikely to arise, hence my initiative," Mr. Hood replied. "I appreciate your courtesy, a quality Dex has praised in you. Allow me to say, however, that it is not only courtesy that makes you refuse. You are exhibiting the modesty of the somewhat poor. You aren't poor of course, but you aren't rich, and so you feel obliged to show that you are not interested in acquiring money, especially mine. You should be. A few extra bumblebees never hurt."

I had drawn breath to answer when something behind me crashed softly to the ground, turning me to salt with fright. Mr. Hood reassured me: it was only a little Malay dragon that had dropped from the tower vines.

Less at ease than ever, I lamely explained that I would "prefer esteem to charity." Mr. Hood interrupted:

"The fact is that I am in your debt. And debts must be paid. One day you may discover how great this debt is and simply have me thrown in jail!"

How is it that the potentates of this world always enlist

unreason as their invincible ally? This preposterous suggestion completely disarmed me. By its superb improbability, it established that it was I who was in debt to him: that Mr. Hood was an invested king, and I a fool.

I sat speechless. Mr. Hood came to my aid.

"I understand your reluctance to take what might appear to be a handout. There are other possibilities—a collaboration that would benefit both of us? I have many enterprises here that need intelligent and scrupulous supervision. Radium wells in the mangrove swamps, the dwarf-cattle ranch in the north, treasure-hunting teams—you name it."

An incredulous giggle escaped me. Speaking as calmly as I could, I said I would think the matter over. We set a "serious business appointment" for early November, then, to my inexpressible joy, the interview ended.

The meeting left me in such agitation that I can still hardly think. I have asked myself if Mr. Hood wasn't taking a vicious pleasure in "telling me the tale," but that is impossible. It's only that his offer of working on the treasure team seems too good to be true. I suffer intensely over encounters like this, which so thoroughly confirm my clumsiness. How can I face men who weave self-control, shrewdness, and (in this case) generosity into a seamless raiment of efficient character? I should prepare myself better. Next time I'll memorize responses for all eventualities. I shall clothe myself in the "trousers of stealth, the jacket of patience, and the hat of foresight." It is the cold sweat of action that ruins me. What I lack, beloved, is your excellent creed, which would have taught me that mountains are as short-lived as grass, and let me daily eat—or would a Buddhist say spit out?—the bread of immortality.

Your mistake in dancing the Hunch made me laugh, for, fancy this, much the same thing happened when I first tried it. I hopped those six steps in one spot; the consequences were identical. Such incidents can be annoying, due as they are to inattention. I'm glad it didn't make you furious. That would be far more unbecoming than a mere physical blunder, especially in a woman.

XLVIII

Octob. 21

How good that is, to be with the Hood's teams. Thus it 's
best: others pay, others work-ing, and we rich. And here also
it is a progression. The Prince is taken the Pindola to a job for
him. He 'll aid, in the sell of the Medicean remains. Now
Bonzo can better do, that Twang next be in-ployed.

Other ways they are not new events. Eccept, the graet in-
gathering of free dogs at this villagge—thousand and thousand.
They are nice, they emit large giovial noise. It is re-minding
me nights-time in Sah Leh Khot—also of an even-ing in the
spring-season, at Florence, of the "maggio musicale" (yet it
was june, still with name "may".) Have I recountt this? The
Bonzo invites me. There was a choral of dogs, very-wise dogs
train for song in Hangover (Germania), and their spezial
music by Egg, a hantata in new-Bach stile, saying "Vorkelt
nicht, berühmte Nasen." It 's splendor, in the end yet it is just
more art of the west. Only I like your opera, be cause that is
true: it is, those who make it have not the care, are they insin-
cere. One 've give the prema of one opera, "Robinson Caruso",
it is pop with the italians also with Twang.

Then how goe Mr. Dharmabody?

Here have see no opera, but yesterday a U.S. film, *nob
sheenam ghanap*, so that I pass the hours. It was near 20 years of
old, with stars Day and Jourdan. Doris and Louis are alive together in a on-beach house at the Monte Rey Beach, and he
have much free time after performing duties as famed con-
certo pianost and compostor of concerti in the Gershwind-
style, much free time to conspire to hill Doris! Thus she must
run of and she is become a air bus stewardessa. But on a day he
have manage to sneaker up on a plane whewhere she 's hostess-
ing, and—o my!

Now it 's deep night. It is a little cold but soon I 'll be sung
in bed. Warm with over-saying the one thought "we all
ways," *theu tharaï, theu tharaï*

XLIX

October 27

I'm at a barbecue given by Lester Greek in his in-town orchard. It's part of Les's campaign for congress. The guests include the invisible order of Miami authority, with lesser figures like me to fill out the boost.

Miles Hood came to the party, but I missed him. When he arrived I was away by the fire, over which seven lambs—or more likely rams—turn on a steam-powered spit. The roasting is supervised by a Gypsy-like attendant with ruby earrings, who carves with a tremendous shiv while sprinkling the sputtering meat with crystalline oil, scooped from a trundled amphora. I had decided to abandon this mouth-watering scene for Mr. Hood when Dexter Hodge intercepted me. He pestered me with attention, as though trying to ingratiate himself, and none too subtly. He may wonder what took place during my meeting with Mr. Hood: he acted slightly resentful of my interest in him. After I had unsuccessfully waved a few times to the little millionaire, he asked, "Isn't my company good enough?" He followed this lapse with praise of his friend. "Miles is truly class. Yesterday he told me that he had learned his butler was stealing his cigars. 'What did you do about it?' I asked. 'Nothing.' 'Nothing? Isn't stealing cigars stealing?' 'If I dislike sharing my cigars with my butler I can lock them up. I can't lead him into temptation and then ruin him.'"

Soon afterward he started off. "I think I'll do a little hopscotching and take some election bets," he said jokingly, or half-jokingly. Then—are there depths of sulfur beneath his crust?—wagging a finger at me: "Remember that the first-born of created things is, by identity, the first-born among the dead." In the smokeless metallic light of the salted fire these cryptic words made him quite sinister. Have I glimpsed the Invisible Jesuit?

I took a third helping and gandered around. It was hard finding company, since everyone was talking shop. I didn't mind. With that sordid crowd of busy faces around me, politicking and manipulating stocks, I thought, All my ambition, all my wealth is love! I felt like a salamander thriving in fire. Then I went indoors, found some writing paper and a drink, sat down at a table overlooking the orchard, and began this letter.

You ask about Mr. Dharmabody. The little skeezix couldn't be better. I brought him with me tonight so that he could romp. He hasn't been out much lately, and has severe belly sag, almost scraping the ground—a dangerous condition in our concrete world.

Your letter convinced me that I've been foolishly pessimistic. Mr. Hood's offer is a stroke of luck. It is unlikely that he knows much about our treasure; probably he has had it routinely investigated as a well-known lost hoard, without an inkling of its history. So I shall put his organization to work for us and draw a handsome salary doing it.

I write among dancing, singing, whooping, hollering, and drinking. I think I shall succeed. My darling, I love you to death.

L

october 31

So the progress ends, as the prince have choose, that Twang will n't work with him. He want "wite people." Yet, *ticbaï pristwi pok mem naï vin*—In front of a (bad) demone I do n't be the corpse, you say so, "lie down and die down"? It 's n't over, no *not*. Thus whewhen the Pindola toll it to me I but laughh, say-ing: Nice, jiust the to-be with you (him). And, litlte later, I unhover his eyes balls with: "O sad, I have no capitale, just the fruits of my trusty fund." "O, that is no much?" "O no, sole-ly 5 or 10 thousand lbs. every year." He will have wish to say, hohow much that he is loving me, but the money-think has detract his voice. I hold-him.

Twang yes have one regreg, the work will have give her some cush (cash?) for a more-soft hotel, and this is so small a plaint, I mind not any post to live, that is O. K.

LI

Nov. 6

You cannot imagine the rage yours put me into. It is unbearable that you receive such treatment. It's as bad as calling you gook, and not even to your face, the blockhead! Who does he think he is? Does he think the winds and seas obey him for his moldy title?

Anyway I'm sending you extra cash (*or* cush—it's the same) for a better hotel.

My business appointment with Mr. Hood took place three days ago. I had plenty of time for rehearsals, and for their spawn: new reasons to worry.

The three guards led me into the bowels of the palace, far from the lawns of our first interview. We found Mr. Hood in a windowless room whose walls were hung with old lutes. He was swinging in a deep hammock, concealed except for one tiny protruding hand, which beat time to a ditty that a young man, on a nearby stool, sang to the plunking of a mandoline:

A fine rain anoints the canal machinery...

At the final chord Mr. Hood rolled into view, handed the singer some folded bills with a word of thanks, and nodded him from our presence. He then took me by the arm, and with a silent, expansive gesture invited me to admire the splendors about us.

This began a tour of Mr. Hood's indoor domain, or at least that part of it devoted to scholarship. We visited a room where students were repairing prints of old movies, among them an early lost Laurel; another where three ham sets busily whined —one operator announced excitedly, "I've got the Dahomey *Die Schwärmer!*"; a third where a battery of computers blinked away at translations of middle Bactrian; and at last the immense library, where many young people were at work. Mr. Hood explained their tasks as we circled the room. "...clear text of Boethius... fodder for my theoretical teas... Chomskian refutations.... Here is the star of the show."

In a soundproofed cubicle a blond girl, who bore an un-
canny resemblance to Hyperion Scarparo, was reading aloud
from a propped tome. At Mr. Hood's tap she opened the glass
door to say, "Rehearsing Mommsen, sir." Mr. Hood mo-
tioned to the three ever-present attendants, who conjured
champagne and glasses from a set of Melanie Klein. Mr. Hood
pressed a glass on the young woman: "Mustn't let you get
hoarse." Then, to me: "Every day she reads to me from the
classics of history. It is an *heure sacrée.*"

From the library we entered a little drawing room, where
we sat down. The three guards left. Mr. Hood asked if as a
professional librarian I would like to take charge of his study
center. I replied that I had considered his proposals and chosen
the treasure teams as the most interesting. He assented to this
with no sign of either pleasure or displeasure, and launched
into an explanation of how the business was organized. I expected him to indicate how I might fit into it; no such luck.
At the end of his account Mr. Hood stood up and offered
politely to see me to the door. So I asked him what sort of
work I was to do.

"Oh, there's no rush about that, we'll come to that in good
time. Just think of yourself as one of us, starting now."

On the way out, Mr. Hood stopped by a small showcase
where on a bed of black swan feathers Mallarmé's left ulna
reposed. "When it arrived I had it brought up the drive in
a royal Egyptian litter, surrounded by musicians performing
the death scene from *Socrate.* A banner day."

Farther on, in a capacious niche, stood the primitive, half-
size statue of a horse. Its outstretched forelegs and cringing
head were full of unhorselike obeisance. One eye was painted,
the other was a rosy globe of crystal. An alarm clock was set
in its brow; long cracks spread out from it.

"It's adobe," Mr. Hood explained. "It was made by a noted
wizard of the West, Bernheim Wood. He once visited my
childhood home on the Rappahannock. For some reason he
was very taken with me and gave me the horse. That day I
stopped growing. The sculpture has no beauty, but in that
glass eye is stored tremendous scrying power. I often use it.

There's always something going on, it's like a twenty-four hour movie." He peered into the glass eye. "There's a lady in a sari digging old papers with a spade. I met her once in Rome. A handsome fellow is helping her. I know him too. As a matter of fact, he works for me. Take a gander." I saw nothing but faint pink tracery. In a tone of regret Mr. Hood said, "It's because you don't believe. You don't understand."

It is said that at Lester Greek's party Mr. Hood pulled off the deal of his career.

I left feeling saddened by Mr. Hood's establishment, or by his role in it. He is too much the master; his kindness is always tainted by condescension. For instance, he handed out money not only to the singer but to the workers in the other rooms. It's hard to imagine Hodge so pretentious—although I find Mr. Hood much nicer than Hodge. Perhaps the richest people feel obliged to behave this way.

I've been wondering whether my angry words about the Prince weren't a mistake—whether a temperate view might not be best. I say this not only because I naturally tend to peacefulness, but because his rejection may have been simply meant to increase your desire for the job, at filling you with "admiring fear" so as to get you cheap. He may also think that you have not shown the respect due his station. I understand you in this; but I also feel that we are bound to honor those who deserve it, which sometimes means those who expect it. So don't give him up; cultivate him a little.

Perhaps my own fear has produced this watery advice—the unfamiliar fear of being left stranded. As I see more of my new friends, I understand them less. I ask what is to stop them from some day tossing me to passing fishes?

But what other reasons could the Prince have for treating you so shoddily?

I'm sitting in my library cell, swaddled in silence. Election Day has emptied the building. After this letter I must start work on a lecture: next week, I am to address the Knights on "My Visit to the Far East." I shall enjoy telling them about you and other matters crucial to Miami life.

So long for now.

LII

Nov. 10

You mild concil is to late. Went to Prince Voltic table and spake in a big public sound. I 've say godbye *duvaï tharaï* for ever to that one! I say, first, Italy is a moundain of *laï* mud. Then Florenze is *dhum pristwei vini*, so, as a stingk of demon's horpse. The cultura is no thing, only for balance of pagments. I say those opere of Verdi and Pucci are *uüax*. I say, Duccio was a pornograph and Fra Angelico is a jew. Then, his grand mother is a cooked egg, his mother is a post-nose drip. At last I call him a hommunist and one hommosessuale. The Voltic is be come red then white then gone. Follow an other storm. Bonzo is much angry, say, Twang has not to risch his job, for the soddifaction of try-ing on names that fits.

Thus, I have n't power to "cultivate the prince" or, "deal with him" in some way. And, he has all wear-out my wanting to pleace or dis-please him.

I leaft Rostolena village, a round, there was ballons of smoke from the bomb fires, oh I like to eat it. Here I 'm with-in a comfy pension, in Florence. I have sistemate, all my notings from MAP bags at the library here. I bring my learning up to day.

Do you remembem, the de Roover think, there will have to-be a heir to *Francesco di Guiliano*, be cause the personal possessions are not gone to *Cosimo*. Then, this heir shall still wish to have the treasore. For this I look all the mentions of tresure after 1443 (that year *Francesco* dieds.) That all most get me ready for the nut bin. Mr. de Roover know where they are the libri segreti (counting books), but other dohuments in MAP are mangled with one the other, it is like, a mattman do it with porpose. Yet, these days are n't guasted. If many names are named near the treasure, one onely came back, in year and out year. This is: *Salvestro Sguardofisso*. He have have stories with i Medici, I do not recount these now, it is just the matter, he persersist toward the gold and I thought, it is him the her. How ever that name wring no bell. I leave MAP and consolt the State Arhives. The 2nd name (Sguardofisso) had no ante cedents it shall be a knack kname may be. I find him —on elettoral list, San Giovanni quarter, 1443-1466. It 's a good sign,

S. Giovanni is of dominanting class, and of *Francesco di Guiliano's*
family. I cearch more on, at the end I find this list of the "arroti" in the
Balia of '58, on this *Salvestro* is wrote not Salvestro Sguardofisso no
not even Salvestro di Francesco Sguardofisso yet *Salvestro di Francesco
di Giuliano Sguardofisso!* So it is secure he is of those cousin Medici, I
was right. Mr. de Roover is right.

But then, why is he not said, as of Medici? Why not, as *Francesco's*
hereditor? Who was his mamma? If were a fine lady, it shall be hid,
that *Francesco* were the father. If she were low, he can have adapt the
child, even marry this woman, even more get her annulld if she is
esposed al-ready, with his great power. Yet not this nor that. So it is one
soluzion, that the mother is *Francesco's* slave.

I can not tell of it now, Twang has such hunger, now down
to the dinning room. It shall be in a new letter.

Now I'm turned. O my *lemu* & *neng* I am to night much in
thooght of you. I ete a lone. Of ten I am drinking you healthy,
so I can say, I'm "deadrunk" for you're sake, this is better as,
"I die for you," I think.

LIII

November 14

The Knights held their scheduled meeting, but without my
lecture. I was very disappointed. There's no doubt they're ex-
ceptionally busy: it's the season when they must organize the
parades for the Miami pre-Lenten carnival. The forthcoming
one has its special problems. Last February a festival barge,
burdened with two hundred frolickers, sank in the lagoon,
thus reopening the problem of safety hazards. In addition there
have been complaints about the theoretical structuring of the
pageants.

Hours of discussion resulted in no specific plans. During the
intense and sometimes dazzling crossfire, I contributed no
more than a requested yes or no. But when it was decided that
the difficulty of our problem demanded "superior enlighten-
ment," I found myself picked for the inquiry. The methods
used were better suited to the Egyptian Temple than to the

Knights: we held a Shakespearian lottery. I was chosen by
the childish rhyme "Eenie meenie minie moe, Catch a bugger
by his toe," and told to open a volume of the poet's works
at random, reading out the first words to catch my eye:
  "Exeunt omnes."
The Knights were bemused. They decided that we must
next consult the municipal mascots: a family of porpoises that
lived in a vast glass cube within the floating museum of maritime replicas. We drove to the harbor and found the sprightly
creatures sporting about the oars of a trireme. My companions
studied their gyrations with great seriousness.

Perhaps I would have been sympathetic to these eccentrici-
ties had it not been for an incident that occurred before the
meeting came to order. I had looked forward to seeing Mr.
Hood, but he was absent. Instead, Hodge delivered a note
from him. Mr. Hood said he was still unable to see me, but I
could work things out with his "confidant Dex Hodge."
Hodge was watching me with an unpleasant smile.

I had wanted to bypass Hodge: his knowing air showed
that he had guessed as much and was pleased to have outma-
neuvered me. As if to aggravate my disappointment, he began
lecturing me about my appearance, looking at me as if I were
some kind of dogheaded-abortion as he addressed cruel words
to points of my dress and physique.

So when the Knights finally disbanded, I drove home to my
bathroom mirror. The view depressed me. My five-month
stye peered back at me from a garnishing of permanent spots
—as for the rest of my outward being, I'll skip the details,
even though you might view them with charity. I used to
think that I should remind you of myself, that I should *make*
you see me. I did not then understand that love is better than
sight and will do without it.

Reflection helped me from the depths. I thought, it is better
to have the nettles sprouting in one's face than in one's mind.
Slowly I cheered up. I decided to relegate Hodge's meanness
to the category of past accidents, to face whatever the future
would bring—which at that moment was a party at Dan's. I
spruced up, set my sails resolutely, and cast off into the evening.

I've told you what Dan's parties are like. This was the exception. I felt it the minute I walked in. The air abounded in that unstrident gaiety which we call natural but which is no more natural than waltzing. Dan had installed his Koolflare, a low calorie fireplace that has brought inhabitants of hot climates the pleasures of the hearth. Made of coal-colored stone, with fire spouts in the shapes of mushrooms, it bathed the room in friendly light. There were few guests at the start, but among them were long-lost acquaintances, and I was amazed how much I liked seeing them. I was a great success, too. My old friends were full of admiration for my recent socializing. Dexter Hodge had brought a troop of pretty raggles, and I hit it off with them like Dean Martin, conversationally, of course. This was balsam to my wounds. Dex was his old affable self, treating me royally.

Late in the evening Dan gave us stork steaks cooked, I think, with speed, because the party turned wild. People kept swarming in. In the confusion Dan bit Dex and some other guy got punched up. But I escaped intact.

Lester Greek was elected to congress by a large majority, winning the "content" as well as the "form" vote.

On my way home, I plucked the enclosed from a wayside bush, forced into unseasonal gaudiness for the greater glory of Greater Miami.

LIV

novem-bre 18

Ah! my pointsetter blossom! Dou you know, I hatch my self with to-pity for that you gathered it, with this premise of summer on-it. There is too room for the toes of some bird. Still I 'll keep it longer than it shall not have stay on the bush, that is very sure.

Your speech of the fests, *nam me slop*, in this is non-happiness, *wey!* for I will have been to the great cerebration in my capital, of the Namma Ghaï (it is "royal shrine"—*namma* mostwise is the hut shrines of peasants make from bamboughs, but this one is all from mud breaks and piastre, then guilt.) It has been this week. It shall be no matter.

Then my belove I shall bring to the honsider-ing of your aspect no ciarity but admoration, all is good even the spots which I look-on for gewels. But one thing (perhaps), you are a little very fat. Yet I know, you have try to slender down, and that will happen. I, shall not force you to that, it is so clear. I remember my unkle munk as he talks to some Lao's (some Laotians) of to-not-eat-much, he needed not to forze them, his exsample of haleth and sense was so cleer, he had the knead only to draugh their attention to this point. That was like a wagging well-joked with the hwip handy that wait on a flat ground. It's at a crisscrossroads, a intelligent driver mounts and he know to driver the horses. He take the reins in the left and the whap in the right and he diriges the hart here, there, whewhere he wish. So you *ticbaï pristwe*, turning against the demons, those of cunger, drive your senses clever-like, separe your self from that what is bad and lead toward the just conditions of the brain, for in this road you'll make grow in you and strong the Doctrine and the Diet.

In my life there is again change. For the Pindola beg me, think not the Prince so evil, and he first beg the Prince, think Twang is not so evil. The Prince cedes, Twang may then work beneath him, but he will have "series referenzes of haracter and onesty." These, I can ask of the Mrs de Roover. Yet I do not decide. I shall go one again to that bath station Rostolena and think, and write to you more about whewhence come *Salvestro*.

LV

November 22

Good news at last: good as gold. Mr. Hood is making me a *partner* in his treasure corporation. I can't wait to turn out as dallier in the prairies of abundance.

The news was doubly sweet since it followed new nastiness from Hodge. Yesterday afternoon the Knights visited a master weaver's shop; we were to choose fabrics for the carnival parades. Hodge picked me up, and on the way grilled me in a fashion more suited to a heavy gee than to a man of the world. He questioned my motives in going to work for Mr. Hood (as if it had been my idea), and cast doubt on my qualifications in a very rude way. And then he asked me about the "so-called Amortadella treasure." I instinctively corrected him, thus revealing my knowledge of it. And what were the chances of finding it? I thought them impossible, since there were no maps. This apparently satisfied him.

It didn't satisfy me; during the visit, to recover from my panic, I stayed clear of the other Knights. Loitering in the shop near one old-fashioned contraption, I was addressed by its attendant. He explained that it was a device for "throwing" silk—for twisting strands of raw silk into usable threads. The machine consisted of two concentric drum-shaped frames, a fixed outer one and an inner one that turned on its axis like a revolving door: just like an old Florentine *torcitoio*. (*Torcere* also means to throw.)

The Knights returned from their tour. When he saw me, Mr. Hood took me aside. He announced my partnership with evident pleasure. I mumbled a protest or two, which Mr. Hood waved away. I emphasized my lack of experience and, particularly my ignorance of the Amortonelli treasure. Mr. Hood exclaimed, "That's of *no* importance."

Then why, I wondered, had Dexter Hodge brought it up? I believe Mr. Hood. It's Hodge's role that I question and, I admit, resent. Yet at that moment Hodge acted in a way that disarmed me. To celebrate my promotion he offered me a night on the town, with the full treatment—dinner at the Fontainebleau, the Monkey Jungle Baths, parties, the works. Elated as I was, I accepted, and that evening we had a merry time. Dex organized an *ad hoc* gathering for cocktails; then, after a wine-drenched meal, we went semi-invited to a fancy bash on the ocean front, whence I had to be half-carried elsewhere, though I'm not sure where elsewhere was. "Ah, but a man's reach must exceed his grasp..." I ended here in Dex's private sauna, where consciousness is vertiginously reasserting its claim, and where I'm trying to write you with this dripping ball-point. I do remember refusing the Baths, which are really a glorified panel store. Of course I didn't want "a" woman.

It's hard to keep my thoughts from the success that awaits us. I can't see how we can fail. I shall have access to what my partners know, and this in conjunction with our own information may be all we need. Besides, I shall learn of *other* treasures and be able to claim a share. Does this materialistic optimism seem foolish to you? I swear that I desire wealth only for peace; not to swagger among men, but to secure my own apple tree in which to swing unseen.

As for my "very fatness": until last night I had kept strict tabs on myself. I wear up to seven layers of clothing, including a winter coat (ludicrous here), and jog every day in this attire until I can breathe no more. I take hot baths. I sweat for hours, reeking of baked salt, under that hottest sunlamp the sun. I eat only a quarter pound of red meat every twenty-four hours. No breakfast, no supper, just one meal and some apple snacks. No liquor except for a rare glass of Bass. Sometimes I take a strong laxative. By these means you can almost make out my bottom rib, and my clothes have been taken in *half a yard*. Do you approve of me now? Of course, there's lots left.

Your turnabout with Prince Voltic saddened me; I mean on your account. The task I imposed has brought you this humiliation. Your perseverance would set an example for the disciples of Achaia and Thessalonica, and I appreciate your selflessness with wonder and pride. I know that our work has been dull and its results, so far, insignificant. But like the black-mustard seed, once it takes root it will grow so high as to dominate the garden, and all the birds of heaven will find room to nest in it.

LVI

Novembrr 26

Why do you not expressed no interest, in that I tell you of *Salvestro*? and his mother, that I find to have be a sclave? I wait during two letters, yet now I tell you anyway, you are able to take it or live it.

I learn, all in Florence keep some slave then, who had two bits of money. Thus too the plain preasts and the monkess, the church admit the trafic, when it is unfaithfuls who be boaght and sold. These are spedited in ships many many from Black Sea and Alexandria, in Italy they are soon a pane in the head, the Petrarc names them the "household enemies." Yet not the mamma of *Salvestro*, was of-none the enemy (maybe, not-wanting, of *Cosimo*?) Beautiful—"bellissimma di viso con un busto assai adatto," this isn't hommon because most of those slaves have little pocks and then the hwites of the West slashing their face or pric a tatoo so you can tell them if they scape.

They give to the mother a name *Mantissa*. I have found the bill of her sell to *Francesco*, 15 febb. 1431, with this name and her years 25, and those words of her beuty, also: "Since she is perchased by the breaker *(sensale)* one week agone, she's had no harm," and speek of "care of previous owner well hognized to all us" but without some name, or hint of who 's; and the price 60 florins that is much.

Otherway (I shall say below) I find *Salvestro* born in the november of that year, has the *Francesco* jump upon her like a hot dog? However he is not a beast if he have done that, he had to-want a son so long, then he's assolute kind to her, to the son. And, his spose dies: he waits, the decent wait-time, then he freeze quickly *Mantissa*, I have this act: "Mister and slave presenting in the chambers of notary, her liberty was conscended because she has served him with sollecitude and as the laws. Kneeling front of her master *more priscum et antiquorum servando* she places her hands withinside his hands and implore him with the most great veneration and humiliation to befree her as in the roman use; after this her master let fly her hands, said, Be fre, be the Roman citizen, freed from some and all servitude to-me. I notary present draw up the deed. And she 's that free as she is born from a family free."

Then, truble. *Francesco* want to make the birth of *Salvestro* leginti-mate and so he will adopt him. In the church some said, no, *Mantissa* was not your amateur wife whewhen this boy is born, still your old wife was there, only with a regular honcubine in your house *non ut famula sed ut uxor* can it be adoption. All right, so this mater needs the Arcibisp's dispense; *Francesco* will go to him, I think it is *Antonino*. But this one must "consulk with who has intelligence of the sobject, and in church and in lay, he must talk of course to the Priorate of the state." And, divine whowho dominoes the priorate? It is *Cosimo, duvaï tharaï* to that hope!

But *Francesco* will interpose an appeal; then too soon he's dead. He shall have give to the mother and the son his cash, his light belongings, yet could not his great lands and houses and they go to the cousims. Any months before that he dies there was the election (of '43), there was new rule and he can push *Salvestro* into the first grup of handidates. You know, this is that time when the incluse not just those seduti & veduti but their relatives and it means sons and grandsons there, so *Salvestro* after this is in some political bodies. He has not true strength yet a distinction, with this he's going on to argue with *Cosimo* about the treasure, his tesoro dei tre sciarrani.

That is something, that is enough.

You are content with the going to work for the Hood, and the joy is good, however you have much hope, I fear that this shall fall. But it is not too bad, execpt for the sadnes, for here, it is all arranged, the Prince and Twang breathe in the same breathe-rhythm that is friendshift. "Give-for and get-for," as your saying. And he wants to "pick ripe frutts of the mind" of Twang, so I drinking and eating with him much, and this after-noon even golving together. Bonzo is as glad, he sleep all the day. The golf is hard, in my *phrap*, after a hole I only do the potting, I'm O. K. in this. The Voltic is today well-formed, he say, and his balls are straight. Then he shows something for the one who play wicked, and become furios with theirselves: near the very hard holes one see that I think are old-manner from-rain shelters, no, there are in them a lady with some whips, she's dress in sharp heals on botts under lather dress. So the man-player has hit balls in berries, he smile at the play-enemy, very gentle manly, and he come here and is bitup, then back to game all relax. The Prince know these nice ones, I'm meeting three, and pretty, Tisiphone, it is the most pretty, and Alecto, and Megaera. Others have also most harmonious ancient names. But then, I ask, where does the tense play-ladies go? For this the prince has a frown, it's the cold moment of our new intamity.

Bonzo after tells me, the girls are very fine prostatue—that is his word, no "whore", I suppong it is a pretty-er as we say *battazhum*? I have forgot your lessons, now for you a Pan new dictum—*Battazhum ticbaï, nob-me lemö üin*, with to-mean "Cofronting with a *battazhum*, love be-come an idea." Some say *vin* not *üin*, "become a horpse," it is unrighteous. The sense, is to justificate the wores.

That also is well your vast diminution of fat. It is, like of a giungle of salad trees which near one village or group of cabitations is invade by creeperers and in this comes a man whowho desire that the trees wax and blosom, for he bear them good-willing and friendlike sentiment. He huts and off-bear all the torted branchs or the evil-doing creepers to the end that the wood he clean and tended even with-in. He foster at that time the wood growing straihgt that is well come, in the manner that later the tree incresce and svelop. In that way you detach yourself from that is evil and fat and are clinginging to the just estates of mind, thus you push up in you and strong-then in you the Doctrine, and the Diet.

It has been nice, to re-see the Etuscan landescape. The life in Rostolena's alway grand, and *wey*! it must be asked, some dollars, I therefore need a new war-robe. This is a small *slop* but I cannot else. It is for the coldness too. Fogs have start.

LVII

Dec. 1

I write from the lower depths of hangover: a hangover procured at my own expense from four sidecars, a bottle of New York State champagne, and six snifters of Drambuie— hardly enough to justify the wreck of this day. Indulgence has only deepened the trough of my depression; more about that later. Since I can think of nothing else, first let me explain the hangover.

Yesterday I was asked to tour the library with an out-of-state colleague. For once the chore was fun, thanks to the personality of the visitor, Mr. Alfred Korn of Phoenix. After an afternoon in the tape stacks, we went out for drinks, and he came home for pot luck. Unfortunately, between the third and last sidecars, we had broached the marshy topic of "simultaneity versus linearity." Quoting third-hand examples from modern art and physics, we praised the former as a principle of thought and action, while condemning linear logic as archaic, inefficient, and dull. Our ideas were vague, but enthusiastic; and in our alcoholic simplicity we decided to put them into practice with an experiment in synchronous cooking.

On the way home we agreed on a two-course menu. Alfred would make spaghetti with fish sauce, I a giant vanilla flan. On arrival I had a first, fleeting qualm when Alfred complained about the absence in my larder of fresh sucking-fish. But he resigned himself cheerfully to canned tuna and set himself to chopping onions, accompanying his task with a *sotto voce* "Hallelujah Chorus," to which he fitted his own text, "Non-sequential awareness!"

I had meanwhile turned on the oven. A burgeoning appetite sustained my expectation of a satisfactory dinner, and I set to work with gusto. But after I had assembled my ingredients and utensils, and was separating the white and yolk of my first egg, Alfred startled me with a gasp of indignation. (The egg flopped into the bowl entire.)

"You mustn't do that," he said. "It's against the basic principle. If you break things down into their components you submit to linear tyranny at its worst."

"Alfred, you can't make a flan if you leave in all the whites. You peeled your onions, didn't you?"

He considered these facts.

"Oke. We shall allow Zachary to divide the egg. But it's heresy."

It was a few moments later when, declaring "Now a few nuts to complete the spectrum," he spooned a jar of *marrons glaçés* into his sauce that I realized how high he was. I was no less so: I was simply less inspired by our "idea" and more interested in eating. I had got my elementary flan into the oven without disastrous omissions or commissions. Since

Alfred plainly needed more time than I, I left the oven door slightly open. Alfred had finished his preparatives and had begun, normally enough, frying garlic in oil. But as he poked the sizzling cloves he became restless, and this restlessness culminated at last in a wave of impatience that visibly overwhelmed him. Before I could intervene, uttering a petulant shout of "No, no—at-onceness!" he emptied the contents of the saucepan into the water set to boil for the spaghetti, and dumped after them all the remaining ingredients: tomatoes, carrots, onions, herbs, tuna, chestnuts, and the *pasta* itself. He turned to me with a chuckle. "It's the whole concept of time —not chronology, but the moment as critical nexus of reality."

That moment arrived all too soon. There was a preparatory growl from the pot, then an irrepressible gush of orangish foam rose up like a thunderhead at sunset—rose up, swelled, and collapsed on the stove in a languorous hiss, sputtering over the incandescent burner as it coursed down the front of the stove, and into the oven, with its cargo of muddled grease. I was helpless before that roar and surge. Alfred was shining with anger and surprise. The vision was brief: the fuses blew.

Since there was no top on the baking dish, our meal was lost. We consoled ourselves with the champagne and a basket of fruit. Alfred wanted to start cooking again, but I had had enough. We drank away our disagreement.

Several hours later, and fewer ago, my head and innards woke me and drove me outside. No hart ever panted after the water brooks as I did for Bufferin and air. Shuddering I watched Venus and Mercury dancing above the low new moon.

Nothing is more adventitious than a hangover, but this one seems the outward and visible sign of inward and invisible gunk. My nerves are shot. First, my rapport with Mr. Hood broke down again. The responsible agent is without possible doubt Dexter Hodge. Unfortunately, he has become Mr. Hood's right hand in the treasure enterprise, and I must have all my dealings with him. I dread that he may try to eliminate me from their plans.

On top of this your letter came. Perhaps I'm unduly sensitive, but it left me with the feeling that you were becoming someone else. I can't believe you do this on purpose. But without wanting to you have filled me with doubt. You speak of your life with the Prince and Pindola, who is after all only a failed rapist, as though that was what mattered to you. You reproach me for indifference to your account of Salvestro and his mother. Why *should* I be interested? I am down with worry and find this research, no matter how ingenious, irrelevant—especially when you tantalize me with the continuation of the dispute over the treasure. How much have you learned from that? Are you sure Salvestro kept his official positions? Was his presence in governing bodies a reason why the election of 1443 was annulled? The Medici clique called it *lo squittino del fiore d'aliso*, because of the lily's stink.

And there is this request for money to buy clothes! It's so unlike you. Besides, I cannot possibly afford expenses of this kind. You know I do not begrudge you a real pleasure, but I dislike spending money on a fancy dress which will only be worn once. I don't want you to look strange, but I certainly can't spend very much for this. Now it seems to me that there are things, in the way of clothing, that you need more, for instance warm undergarments, since you say it is turning cold and damp, and someone like you from a hot climate must take very special care not to catch cold or worse. In my opinion there is nothing on any occasion prettier than a Pannamese *phrap*, and wearing one would allow you to dress warmly underneath without looking bulky.

This may sound petty, but it is not for any lack of affection or concern. Quite the contrary. You must understand that I feel particularly frustrated by my disappointments here and that I am dismayed at the same time by the distance between us. Perhaps it's my liverish imagination. I don't mistrust you but for heaven's sake let me know what you're doing. It isn't that I want to dominate you, I'm happy if I can influence you even a little. But I still have to know who you are, and now I feel as though in a moment of distraction I had turned away from you, and when I turned back, you were gone.

LVIII

Decemb. 5

It is that only some silk I want, for to make *phraps* perhaps one two or three, that is it all. I've not wish to expend that money to a dressmaker or yet to shops with the dresses off the pig. No it is nonjust, Zachary! Already I've buy the underware with old money. Yet now, there is nothing for silk, and I shall have needing more for life expenses and cannot ask, for some or new. It is not grave and Twang'll do-make however. *Sheenam sheenam* I bear it, I do not mean reproval. I say *duvaï* to the more money and I shall not miss that. My mind to be *theu, theu* "we" and it is all.

But then: the presence of *Salvestro* is "reason why the election of 1443 was a null." *Pok atram pok naï!* I do think thus *not!* It was nothing to do. *Salvestro's* there yet in '45. Also he have support *Cosimo*, of course, in the politics, if the Medici are outthrow perhaps he loses the treasure ever. *Cosimo* had not a worry lest the *Salvestro* compete in a bank, for *Salvestro* had not the bank formation, his father wrote of that in regret; and so the father may be for it have enter him in the election because this is for "uffici intrincesi ed estrincesi" and they, are offices with payments. Last, it was *Cosimo* & Co. whowho wide the lists for seduti e veduti (wish, to make stabilished families stronger there), if he's a-worry of *Salvestro* he will not make his walk up to a public office so facile. And *Salvestro* is grateful and always vote-for Medici.

These mistakes, of dress and of the Florence politic, I think it's you're mind is overthrow with mudnanities. It's that it is like a jungle of Salas trees near a good town or some dwellings that is overtaken with savage vines, full of twisty boughs, and other discoragement. Please, you are to practice a small mastery of the breasth, simple and cuts the heavy weed. So, thinking of just that real air in-coming and out-going, say: Thinking of cessation of confusion I breathe-in, thinking of the cessation of confucion I breathe out," so a few thousand time, with relax. Then, all-calm, perhaps: *pok lucrem pok lucrem pok lucrem* I eat not I don't eat I will not eat, and so fourth (not).

You see so, I'm again at Florence. This is to recerch about

a little statue of gold, this the Prince have given Twang to sale. It's of late 15 century. Thus, once more into that Laurenziana. Also because it is coming back from the S. U., I must have to stay about two hundred hours in the Hustoms House, almost I go to insanity, it is so big and in it, no person knows more than one part of one law.

Yet I use my visits into the Library, that I look more for us. And thus, I'm very busy. So much preoccupation, do not admit me to think about myself. It is some felicitude.

I am depart from Rostolena in just time, on that day I see the snow prows have come out near the road way side, they wait for the first falling. Is that true, there are *pristwi* of the snow (daemons)? It here is cold too. I thank your expression of a fear, that I don't care myself about hatching a cold, and the like. Yet I am enough careful when I am a-wake, it is at the night the clothes are kick upon the floor and I'm espoused to the damp until coolness awake me, and the cold billowcase.

Part Five

LIX

December 9

This is the black time of year, even here in the sunniness—
blacker here. Dry canes croon in the wind: my heart slept—
wake up, heart! Sleep buried thought and feeling in stupidities,
and "I" spoke them to you. Twang, your husband is sometimes insane. My last letter! Black blood scolloped from
the soul's cellars. How can it have happened? Solitude? Gazing
on past miseries with the fondness of self-hate? If only at such
times I could board a train, and in a few hours find you,
to get back on the way to happiness (the way next to which
I am my own ditch), the way that you opened to me, sweet
lyon of the morning, piloting the tramp out of his compost
years, with his joker's baton and rig, dumb as blended Ajax—
the ultimate T. B.

Contrition holds sway in the essential realm; elsewhere,
mild thanksgiving. At lunchtime yesterday I stopped at the
treasure office for a routine visit. The receptionist surprised
me with the news that Mr. Hood was expecting me. I went
in fearing the worst. The little gentleman received me courte-
ously. "Waited to be sure you got this," he said, sliding
printed sheets across his desk with a pearl-pale finger. A glance

showed them to be a financial report, with the heading "Key Biscayne Dredging Operation." I said that there must be a mistake. "I don't think so. Cop a peek at the last paragraph." This announced a distribution of dividends, concluding: "We inform you of your share," with my name written in against the figure $2,170.

Confused, yet not wishing to appear inept, I found nothing to say. Mr. Hood broke through my discomfort: "Dex did tell you that you'd been cut into the pie?"

"Dex" hadn't. Nor had he lacked the opportunity: I had seen him at Rilkie's over breakfast. The meeting had already lowered my opinion of him. He had remarked that he was "just hopscotching"— in other words, making book for the counter clientele. It was hard to believe: Dexter Hodge, tycoon, prominent citizen, Spindle Knight, doing the work of a petty criminal! Perhaps he thinks of it as slumming. He said nothing to me about my dividend, although he spoke to me for several minutes, glowing rosily in the morning light, rambling on about this and that, the luminous windbag! Should I warn Mr. Hood about him?

In the office, wariness compelled me to point out that I had never heard of the Key Biscayne operation. "That's all right. You're part of the outfit. You're entitled to your share. You can't imagine what a difference it makes having a bright man around. And you're a lot sharper in business than you let on. Don't think I don't know it!" I thought I must be dreaming, but the two grand prove I wasn't. La vie she is a little crazy. It's nice to be taken for a slick pro once in a while.

I'm sending extra money for your expenses, comfort, and all the *phrap* material you may desire. I'm glad you're dressing warmly. Be careful next week, during the "Wotan freeze." It's a short, bitter pre-Christmas cold snap, when Wotan, or Odin, supposedly abandons the north to fetch back the sun.

Trying your recommended exercises has been only partially successful. I concentrate satisfactorily during the breathing out part, so much so that I often forget to breathe back in. This leads to dizziness, once I even fainted, though very briefly.

LX

december 13

From here and from there I glue-up a tale of *Salvestro*, from '43 to '65, how he quarrels with *Cosimo* and then, with *Piero de' Medici*. It is un-yet-finished. It will be not-ever: for, the libri segreti afer 1451 are been lost, after this the peekings are slimmer. In the general, the song of *Salvestro* is the old same, in his letters, in his spoke pleas to the cousins (I think too, if I'm right how I read the *Cosimo's* reports): that the treasure "dei 3 sciarrani" was truely-bluely of-*Averardo, naï*, so, of his afterbears. Yet the manner of *Salvestro* change from the earlier pleasant slow by slow, return violenter, more scourteous. But not the answers. *Cosimo* write ever gentler after *Salvestro* be the last *Averardo* leaf. That I do not understand. *Cosimo* had not such much need for the *Salvestro* vote. And still he will never write the forgivable words of resentment, that acridmony of *Salvestro* has replies of consideringness and offers of hompromies.

That little statue is sold, but not by Twang, by some other working in the Prince's organism. It is hard news, for there was long work, and some hopes.

Then, second trouble, that my noce is stuff. Never before. Twang apply some resulution disciplines, say, "Now thus face with the demon in nose," *Naï ticbaï pristwe maï neng-dek—duvaï duvaï* farewell, yet he don't want to leave! He walk in my mouth when I asleep and wipe off the smooth damph.

LXI

December 17

More news from the office. Mr. Hood called me in to inform me that he and several "colleagues and competitors" were organizing an expedition for early April. Its object will be the treasure at Key Betabara. The expedition will be financed by individual members of the different groups, with profits to be divided accordingly. Mr. Hood was giving me a chance to join. He said the price of admission will be steep.

He also made the venture sound *very* important. I did not

ask too many questions, because he was in a foul humor. His accountant had tried to play him for a savage by salting the books. With me Mr. Hood was gentleness itself, but a platinum light in his eyes betrayed an inmost fury.

What shall I do? There are reasons against participating: the money, the time taken from the pursuit of our treasure— but what if *this* were our treasure? I worry about being left out of future projects. There seems to be no straight answer, and I burrow under the problem like a daffy gopher. It's surely not that complicated. Which way do you counsel? (The way that will bring you here quickest—rapture of that parousia!)

Sorry about the statuette. Your golfing friendship hasn't made the Prince exactly frank in his dealings with you. Console yourself with the thought that he isn't fit to unfasten your shoes. (Not that you need bother to show it.)

I guess your cold was inevitable. For sleeping, better than drops is to smear a little mentholated jelly under your nose. You should see a doctor.

Your progress with the treasure is admirable. We've narrowed the gap in our knowledge to the few years between 1465 and 1483. What a marvel you are, dear Twang—

Twang Twang bo bang
Banana fanna fo fang
Fee fie mo mang
—Twang!

How happy I'd be lolling with you in a banana orchard, how I'd love you when I saw that you were looking at me, and that you loved me.

LXII

December 21th

It traspires, *Cosimo* in 1467 wants to export the horde of clippings. He try to does this in a trade company, where's a partner with *Francesco di Nerone Neroni*. They conseal the gold in any silk, but *Cosimo* doesn't tell *Francesco* this and then he learns about the surrebterfuge from *Salvestro*, who has found in about this and attached it and ruin it. Yet not before that *Francesco* tries to get more money from *Cosimo*. Here, 2 letters of *Francesco* about it, condensated.

1. *To Cosimo de' Medici*: You made mistake to draw from our contract so fast, without listening my view. If it is fact that I arrange the trasport of the chest of the silk to the foreign, you were not so onest to hide the true content. Yes, I understand that you almost must be secret, but you shall have give me an alert to the dangers, that I shall have may been expose. For this spezial treatment of it shall have be necessary of course a little more of expense, to caretake of such a wonderful spedition. Do you do this, no, you unsolve the partnership, I guess you will punish me thinking, I'm not loyal, but who is punish? You too, because the company has have a lot success and why will it not still.

2. *To Salvestro Sguardofisso*: (about at same time): Look, whewhere my fidelity to you has bringing me—*Cosimo* has disciolved our company. Now, I say, I'll get my revench, you will get your property. Yet in the meant-time your indisecretions afflect me, they do the get-back more hard. First, I don't know, that you be right in that congetture. O. K., Cosimo has write as he has confess, "ho facto torcere il oro in un pezzo di seta di 500 bracci," I agree as good you are much suptle to think it mean, the little piecings of gold are "throw" in the silk, but he did maybe not signify it. I do not denegate, that man is diabalical enough to do so a thing. Yet, your are not-wise, to verify it, so you say as you do, with the question to this one here and that one there, and there. All weaver in Tuscany be now has, heared of the treasure. Where you demand of the marks upon it, I reply: Cosimo said only then quhen he first instrugt to ship the chest offf, that it (chest) and as well the silk within that have "i segni familiari". Now be careful of going in Bologna, the plague has intered the city, &c.

The nose isn't weller, yet this shall be not *tharaï* alway always, *ticbaï Twang neng sheenö* in the face of nose I shall bear.

Yes, yes, you are to go in the venture with the Hood. He want you to do that, he'll distain you shall you not, and all so months to be with Hodge & Hood, and you will lett the offortunity go past? To this you are to bag, burrow, or steel the money. How, are you making so much complihations? It is complete useless. And yet I know, such matters are not less or

more real in this materio-subtle world, for: *Nob-ma, stheu
ticbaï nam pok-ma*—O Being, all in front of it is not-being, a
love-most sayso of the Pans. But, whewhere you are writing,
"There seem to be no straict answer," POK *atram* POK *naï*, I do
not think thus, or this way, or this.

It's becoming very frank in concern with the figurine, and
I pull-off myself my shoes. The Prince send me yesterday the
commission (12%) from the selling. With this come apology
for the retard, and to do vivid the apologies a pottery of green
plants dark green, that will not die in my chamber. I believe,
this is the Bonzo have made that to happen, so I am full to him,
of grateful, and affection.

For you in this paper Twang folds a twig of smelly rosemary.

LXIII

December 26

I have accepted Mr. Hood's offer. You were wrong to ac-
cuse me of making complications. The decision would only
have been easy if Mr. Hood were a simple person. I wish he
were simple, even a simple tyrant. But it's a subtle not a heavy
hand that maintains his hold on his employees and friends—I
almost said subjects.

He was pleased with my decision: I could now expect to
make a considerable sum. "Otherwise, as some kind of ex-
ecutive, you'd have had to settle for a salary, or a measly two
per." How much could I put up? I asked what was the mini-
mum amount? "That depends." I would raise as much as I
could. I suggested contributing "certain maps" as part of my
stake. (I did this to provoke some indication of what Mr. Hood
knows.)

Mr. Hood seemed largely, although not entirely, uninter-
ested. He concluded with a slightly brisk suggestion that I
start raising my share without delay. Perhaps he took the offer
of maps as an attempt to buy in cheaply, but I doubt this—he

is always praising my integrity.

What a gloomy time this is! To celebrate Christmas the palm tree outside my building dried up and died. An adolescent goon has already lopped off most of the fronds. I stare at the stripped trunk and wonder how to get a piece of that business, which Mr. Hood described as in the millions. My means are so pitiful. If only he had refused the maps outright, or named a sum. His ambiguities have left me in a desultory fever.

These worries have aggravated a case of holiday insomnia that will probably kill me. At four every morning I turn on the lights and stare at the objects in the room. There's your sprig of Tuscan rosemary among them: the Virgin's rose, so timely come, laden with fragrance and thoughts of weddings (funerals too). I wish you had spelled out a few words of affection to set next to it. Somehow your last note was not so treasurable as your former ones. But your light shines on.

And the discovery of what happened in 1457 is a triumph. Such patience and intelligence bring hope for everything—I even imagine the dead palm putting out new green. (It won't. Here, spring means only turning on the blower connected to our God-given radiator.) It is at last clear why the chest of gold is a chest of silk. This is as valuable as having the map: we now know what to look for. Of the work we had set ourselves, you have already done more than your share.

Of *course* the bits of clipped gold were wound into the silk when it was "thrown." Since only one or two workmen were involved, the secret could be easily kept. Later the threads were woven into cloth, weighty but otherwise unexceptionable. No wonder the Abbot suffered over those lengths of brocade!

That Cosimo describes the markings as "familiar" indicates that there were fish on the chest and crows on the silk. Both sets are so *familiari* they appear in every account; and the treasure even took its name from the fish. Were the crows a weaver's mark—can you check this? To the Abbot they were sure signs of the gold. What I cannot fathom is how the real chest reached the abbey in time to be sent to Barcelona. But doubtless you will solve that enigma too.

As for your persistent cold, I think—well, perhaps I should stop "thinking" and send you a hug.

LXIV

Wey Twang me ticbaï pristwe o god I'm face to a demon, new, it rise in me like boil water, it is making me very conflicted, for that the gentle Bonzo, whowho has be so kind to Twang, so affective I think, he is hookered by an other, a dark native, and that woman, do not smile and laugh much such as our ladies, O no but of clever tragical, it is not good, I hate that her dark of-chick-fatt soul, and she is nothing good for Pindola, more, and more he has suffer from that one draem he dream, that he is a dagger! I will *uüaxm pop vin* uomit over on the corpse, of-her, when I shall can. Yet this is not the way, I must know, *slop pok duvaï pok*, a misery is not for ever evr. Still the water foam-hots.

Then I think too, of your words on these letters of *Franceso Nerone*, yes I think of you remarkings on *Cosimo*, how there is no difficulty to believe when he says that those marks are familiari that they can to be crows and fishes—*pok atram pok naï*!! Is it that you desire still, that I expedit to you the italian dictionary?

Exceptively there has been some business pleasure. The Prince gives me a hameo to sell. I was hearing of one american collector on the visit in Florence, I go to the cotel, it's a snatch. The pleasure is, to gain money by Twang's self. The Prince please too, sending me a new plant-pot. Before it, and those other, I have sit, to write these lines, and they semble to be waving, so I do now, acrossed the Atlantic.

LXV*

December 31

I must write without an answer because I'm becoming a psychosomatic derelict. I can't sleep. Fatigue keeps me awake —body in a spasm, head full of rivers thundering toward a nameless sea.

The trouble is carnival. For us Knights it has already begun. Most of us are busy decorating the streets for the parades (the first takes place in four days.)

Decorating is a poor word for what's being done. After pavements and sidewalks have been scrubbed, housefronts repainted, commercial signs removed, and ill-aligned buildings straightened, a continuous decor is installed, with paintings, statues, three-dimensional gardens, street-to-roof tapestries, arcades of flowers, canopied intersections...

The cost of this is shared by the city and a few wealthy citizens, who are given certain streets as their responsibility. Although they generally turn a profit from carnival through a multitude of concessions, these individuals must be able to put up hundreds of thousands of dollars. Many Knights meet this requirement. Others less rich are at least refurbishing their own properties. But I, in whom any such pretensions would be comic, have been given another privilege. I have been made watchman of a glorified parking lot. It is called the "carriage patch," it lies near the Bayfront Park Bandshell, and in it the processional carriages are abandoned between parades.

I must devote two hours before and after office work to my new job. It is not only a tedious but a useless one: the lot is enclosed in vibrant wire. I was forced to take it; Dexter Hodge did most of the forcing. This morning he drove me to the patch, as if I couldn't be trusted to get there alone. "Don't be fractious!" he kept saying, even when I had stopped complaining. He took pains to convince me that being watchman was a mark of great esteem. Miles Hood had held the office last

* Special delivery

year. "Right, Phan?" He turned to Phanuel Asher, another Knight he'd brought along. Mr. Asher agreed. After this double testimony Hodge went on lecturing me until we reached the patch, where he left me with a genial wink.

My two hours then, and most of my afternoon stint, passed in undistracted solitude. As watchman one may not read, write, or even sit. I sniffed the mortuary smells of the carriages; gazed hungrily at "The Dragon Spit," a Chinese restaurant across the road (as bar-b-cue it was simply "The Spit"); or listened to irksome strains from the bandshell, where the All-Miami Youth Brass Ensemble rehearsed *The King's Dump*.

At six, thoroughly bedraggled, I had a visit. A car skidded up to the gate, and out of it bounded Mr. Hood's three guards, their red neckties fluttering as they leaped towards me. Backed against a barouche, I withstood their harangue, loud but not unfriendly:

"Hi there!"
"Hi there!"
"Hi there!"
"Look at *you* ..."
"... in your cold gold prison!"
"All alone!"
"No twist, baby?"
"No twist, *sir*?"
"Don't be grumpy!"
"*We'll* find you ..."
"... a slattern to your Saturn ..."
"... a Venus to your ..."
"Don't mind us."
"We've been sniffing sulfur.'
"Shouldn't we tell him?"
"No."
"No."
"He'll never blow."
"He's no crow..."
"...but he won't blow."
"He's not snider..."
"And you can't knock him."

"Bobble him a little?"

"Let him wait for the moon."

"But hopefully."

"It's hopefully you must wait for the moon."

"Bye now."

"...bye now..."

"Bye."

They hopped into their Dodge and drove off. Were they drugged (from "sniffing sulfur")? Character-judgments aside, their nostrils did foam slightly.

I had brazened out their litany, but my inner structures were shattered. I stared at the orange elephant floating over the gate, symbolizing the people of Miami, and felt myself going crazy. I'm not much better now, waking from a doze, everything wrapped in deep silence and the night half spent. Your words... to preserve me from terrible forces, all these men—

I'm helpless without a sign from you. I feel as if I were being swathed in endless black fabrics and stowed away.

Everything is in confusion, the Knights, me, us. Can't you make a short trip here and bring some light?

I incessantly repeat your name against the Lesser Sanhedrin that confronts me. Your name is my non-ancestral totem.

I write because I can't bear waiting for your letter and to ask, can you make that trip?

LXVI*

Janu. 3

It has been time now, that I wish to speak secrets to you and thus, as soon as your specially delivered letter has awakened me from delicious slumber, I think it shall be now. For I know, since the middle november, the letters to you are be open. So I control in the letter of 21 dec. There was in it, no rosamary! But the opener think, it falls out, and he put in one. Your

---

*Because of insufficient postage ("Unauthorized Enclosure") this letter was returned to the sender, c/o General Delivery, Florence.

thank you ensure my knowledge. However, here is a twig truly from la Twang.

For I am in some minutes to snuggle this away, past any spy, to a post office and speed this with my proper hand. Yet it will be right, with after letters, to do old way, then they will not suspect. To mail secretly, is terrific it must be rare—not again.

Now I quick shall say of markings on chest. Read this sentence, that I cannot send because of those opening, from *Averardo* to *Giov. di Bicci*, 1403: he is speak of *Messer Todao's* gold: say, "e quei 25 sacchi furono portati dalla vostra gente, nella vostra casa." I inscript it but in the mind, it is maybe non-exact, no bother. For you must perceive, how signifying this is? And not for only what the marks then are being, but it is a flash on the late "travels" of that treasure.

The cretin Pindola knows nothing of it, nor the Voltic. Bonzo ignore even, the life of *Salvestro*. His family custody the things of "ulterior descendents *Averardo's*" he don't know there be one! You shall say, So, what? I say, Nice to be 1 up over them!

Also, I have Pindola in soul mess. Twang entirely brain-flush him. That other, dark woman? Twang rent her, from one-horse bordello. Thus: Pindola wishes, to penitrate in Twang. "No. But let me introduce, Signorina Dark. Can penetrate in her, please." He does does. O after, crazy with the more wanting for Twang. Two day before, he visit; I "forget" his mars bars, he enter psycho-psexual glycemia frenzy, he spends memorable New Year day mostly shouts and yells things like, "Where all the vulvas (*fiche*)?" even I was worry concerning the neighbor effect. I have write to you my jealousy sentiment, to hover my truth. This is truth, a chinese say: "In the men a desire is mother to love, In the woman love is the father to desire." And how grand his desire for Twang (yet not so much, as her love, for thee.)

Ah poor one that you suffur, only now it shall be, *wuc naï stheu slop lucre theu*, as this all inhappiness eat up us, yet it is but now, and after, you shall chuse for yourself an house; which Twang will like, because you like it. Now, or soon, I am coming to Miami, however it must not be seen, you must not say it, seem to know none. But use some way the two words, they will tell Twang, you wish her to come, she will come. The words, I choose: "dictionary" "Pogo O'Brine"

After, I answer crazy anythings, you will ignore. Then tomorrow I am to write a "real" (false!) answer to your letter, it is for Bonzo and the Prince and their spies, not for Zachary.

I must need, about dollars 50 plus to pay the quick plane billet.

And always now I must fill the letters with lyings of many color, be as twisty as that *bukhaï* tree. Yet it's no matter, not the lies, not any things, are I. Remember, what is "me"? One is to inspect, so reflect: The eye, the observed form, are not "me". The hear and sound, are no "me". The tongue and the tasted are not, the "me". The knows and the stink aren't "me". The body and touch are not "the me". To consider that those 6 personalizzed senses and their objects do not make a "me", this is the perception of inpersonality, O relief and purify, to Twang, to you I trust, although like all even that is a cool dewdrop lasted no more than trace of stick in water. Yet does this afflict, if then one am satisfied in meditation and distachment.

(You must lie also, for they shall have open your letters, as much.)

It cannot be said, more. Such little is this "airletter" paper stamp blue-light all in one. And never, the enough place, for speech of my loving.

LXVII

jan. 4

To behold your trouble is as, to behold water troubling and mudded. That not-desire to know and think, with doubt, hesitating, small commitment, and mindwander, it is call "skeptic doubts". That is an obstackle to advance, you shall liberate the self from them. For a sample, can be said such, naming now the doubts "the Demon"—

ticbaï pristwi	*nob me*	Face to the deman,	for to-be,
pristwi	*pok me*	"the demon	not be
pristwi me	*pok-ma*	the demon is:	not-be"

or like that, to show what are two paths

| *pristwi lucre nob-ma* | demon eating the not-being |
| *pok-ma lucre pristwi* | non-being eats demon |

There may come clearing in some water; or think:
it seem, the conditions of life are a terror. Thus, they're disgusting. Then, throw them away, and comes through inspection the imperturdability, the reflection on the unconditional, dismisting the conditions.

Well, for that trip, you do it better and you will voyage to Firenze, just as I say in my lastest letter. Perhaps I shall lean you the money for trip? (Exattly so I have said in my late letter.) From these objects sold of the Prince, the hommissions are adding together.

O what to do with that Bonzo, once so dear? I tell him, he must let go that brown woman, it is bad to him, sad on Twang. He says, O left her any days past, but the men's speech are incredible. Just as he in english then say, he will "eat on locusts and wild money," *per fare penitenza!* (And that does, what mean to mean?)

LXVIII

Is it you or I who is losing their marbles? I needed help, not a sermon. I try to be Greek with the Greeks and Pan with the Pannamese, but your advice is very obscure. So is everything else you wrote, and especially the references to your last letter. Do you really want me to make the trip? If you do, say so unambiguously, that's the main thing. (Why in the world do you offer to pay for it?) Wouldn't it be easier for you to take time off from whatever you're doing? Or are certain problems too pressing—what indeed am I supposed to think of

this incredible jealousy of yours? "Dear Bonzo!" Jesus! Finally, I never asked for an Italian dictionary.

These misunderstandings make me the more eager for us to
get together. I hope you are fit as a fiddle, and ready for love
again. I am hunky-dory which means only normally depressed. I am so tired that I can no longer feel strong emotions of
any sort. I swallow neat rye like spring water, and hamburg-
ers like pills.

Standing around the carriage patch is still what is most
exhausting, because it's so frustrating. Of course it prevented
me from watching the opening parade. It's the first time I've
missed it since the war.

Carnival began, as it always does, with the entrance into
town of our Mystery Guest. Somewhere in Opa-Locka,
temporary but grandiose gates have been built. Outside them
the Guest's escort first assembled: heralds and ambassadors
from all fifty-one states and several neighboring countries,
with bands and retinues. There were even interplanetary rep-
resentatives: this year our kohl-eyed clowns play the role of
"Venusians." All were ceremoniously refused entrance until
the Guest's arrival and made to don orange cloaks and caps,
thus becoming honorary Miamians. The local citizenry already wore orange.

Invited to "preside over Miami's destiny as romance metro-
polis," the Guest appeared before the gates. He was greeted
by the black and white Mayors of the city, and by the Black
Virgin of Dade County, who is chosen by lot from the poor
of her community. They ask the Guest who he is. "Are you
Hermes Trismegistus? Are you the American Hercules?" He
replies, "Call me the Pilot," promising only to reveal his
name at the end of the festival. The welcomers crown him
with orange leaves and give him the tokens of the city: a wand
wrapped in crossed spirals of turtlehead, and a gold coin.
Advancing to the gate, the Guest drops the coin in a slot above
its lock, and with the wand strikes a bucranium adorning the
lintel. Thereupon the massive plywood doors swing open.
Before entering the city the Guest asks the Mayors to grant
pardons and paroles. His flag precedes him. It shows a white

ship on a black ground, symbolizing "Miami under the Pilot's Guidance," and until Ash Wednesday it will replace our banner as city emblem. As the flag passes through the gates, a baby hare is released and scampers down the empty expressway: a reminder of the "fun" aspect of carnival. A moving grove of oranges trees followed the Guest, turning this way and that according to the rules of a time-honored dance. Then came the Black Virgin, the Mayors, the ambassadors (the Venusians rolling among the rest like hoops), and the cortege of floats.

Their destination was the city center, where the Guest was to initiate a new dance. He stopped on the way to pay homage to a new statue of the President; since the work hadn't been completed in time, he had to lay his wreath in front of just the horse. This lapse may cost us the Dixie Carnival Cup.

I saw nothing of this, except for the hare, who found his way to my backwater and stared at me for a few seconds (exit, pursued by a scamp.) Much later, a float appeared. It exhibited a pastoral scene. Under spangled netting (dawn sky of stars and sun), among pale grasses bordering a mirror (icy pond), a donkey nosed about the roots of a tree; a gray lantern was nailed to its trunk, an empty bird's nest perched in its boughs. Title: "The Phoenix."

The slovenly old man driving the float wanted to park it in the carriage patch, which was unthinkable. He pretended to be an old friend who had "done me plenty of favors in his time." He called me fink and Pogy O'Brien, and his raggle stuck out her tongue at me as they lurched off.

The expression "eating locusts and wild *honey*" is from the Bible—perhaps a barbaric Jewish custom. It means "roughing it."

LXIX

J. 11

It is shame, the honey not money. For in Pannam, some eat "wild *money*"—flowers of a bursh of the grots who are few, so, precious, also delicious. The eaters are men wild too (but these, not clowns: hangry thiefs.)

And this sobject money: may you remember, that that Twang ultimately has requested.

What sadness that you will not learn that teaching for consolotion. Is it simpler, these mottoes? *uüaxē slop*, retch woes! *lemō maï*, love the now's *pok atrō* not speak (think)! *mō!* be! The aim of the arrows is, contemplating transmorphations dissipate the idea "stability". Thus (he said) brother, a monk with the mind full of impurturbability, pierces one way first, then in a second, a third, a ford; similarly over, below, around: and in everyplace being one with all he'll penetrate the world with his mind full with impeturbabality, the wide, grown, unlimited, hate-free and malevolence free Mind.

Also I wish, you once will say, you would like some thing, because I like it. This recalls, soon I perhaps have a thing, that it is we both like (and look!) much, much.

Now that trip, it is not a matter to Twang, that you enterprise it, that she. Or, not all. Yet I shall believe the first plan is that we follow. I shall think, Giannuary 19? Thus I'm glad when you mention a dictionary. It is also interesting, that Mr. O. Brien is come to the town.

LXX*

January 15

Your letter was a big help. O.K. for the wisdom of the east, but what about the trip? That little phrase "or not at all" left me feeling coshed. Or were you just drawing the long bow? It would be cruel to exercise your English when your husband's sanity is at stake. What do you mean, the first plan? Say what you expect and want! Why is this meeting such a problem? It's like organizing a party in Gander in the pre-jet days. Why reproach me for not sending the money you asked for, when I promptly furnished it? I hate this talk of money

*Special delivery

and wish you would stop it and not transform yourself from a woman of wit and beauty into a dun. Especially now, when I need every penny for Key Betabara.

I suppose that "I should like what you like" means Bonzo. My God, I thought you'd taken him for a chump, not a playmate! What was the story you once told me, when I smiled at one of your pretty compatriots, about the rival pigeons that fight over a mate, and both die? The moral was: "Two dead pigeons will not warm the broads you sleep on."

How I have come to hate this time, how I long for our life to begin! I don't much care where, as long as it's not here. Not only because of the present. Miami has an original, other taint. When I was twelve, my parents brought us up here for Easter, and they lost me when they started home. Since we had been traveling with another family, they assumed I was with them. I had in fact gone to see *Random Harvest*. Afterwards I was alone in the city for three eternal hours. I was then punished for hiding myself deliberately, which I had not done. Miami became a place of doom. But anywhere else. I won't be difficult, I only ask to be with you, and with Mr. Dharmabody if he lasts—he's getting awfully gray about the paws. Not much outside activity, perhaps a movie from time to time, but mostly at home, a life of patience and compassion. I promise not to start a shell collection or design a coat of arms. Roses perhaps. I would be content to sit with you and watch the rain fall in the pool.

The fiesta continues on its boisterous way. The Guest has engaged in the first contests to prove his supremacy: golf with the Black mayor, jacks with Ayer Favell. The games will grow in violence. Once all were violent, since the festival originated in Ghetto Riot Week and it was necessary to rechannel its ferocity.

I have felt less out of things lately. One of the dance floats has been moored opposite the carriage patch. These floats, now scattered through the city, are manned by professional dancers who demonstrate the new carnival step, the Muffle. The dancers wear costumes illustrating the Muffle's theme, "The Melancholy of Anatomy": body tights dazzlingly embroidered with diagrams of the skeleton, the circulatory system, the musculature.

The Venusians have already introduced a parody of the Muffle that is supposed to be as popular as the original. At the second largest float, near Interama, only the parody is danced.

LXXI

17th Jan.

It will be best to say, there is no trip. This will make expressions of regret, by you, by me, which will be accompanied by thought of aversion, to blow up the conception of the Lust. Yet can you, my beloved, so calm your soul, to think quiet? You make it, by the *laï* in the mind, that mud, almost not able to be satisfied of destachment. I shall reminder, and do you, that the life in time is is a wheel, and one point sole of the rim touching the earth, a creature is alive but at the point, the rim's points gone by are death, the points coming are not alive, when they come the now will be dead. It shall be new creatures.

Thank you also for your espresso letter that raised me nicely early, so I could enjoy the day to the full. And I think, when you tell that life together, there lack perhaps some sufficient excitements.

Or it is so, when the rain fall on the mountains tops, in aboundance, the water follows the sloping fills the splits, these latter fills the marshs, they the lakes, overflooding who make small rivers, the rivers feed grand rivers, they, fill up an ocean. By parallels, are created the activities by ignorance, consiousness by activities, name and form by consciousness, the 6 actions by name & form, contact by six actions, feeling by contact, desire by feeling, becoming by desire, birth by becoming, suffering by birth, repulsion by knowledge and comprension of things, and the knowledge of extinction of ignorance. And so, on. You, a vespral lake streaky with wild colors, wild longings for holding of the sun that setting.

Therefore and again as first expressed, Jan. 19 will have the sun rise.

(That second, librarian object of our desire has a sure record here. I think it's mine—but, "ours", it shall be always *theu* we not Twang.)

In Pannam it's said, *Pok Lao nam sheenam* not even the Lao (tions) can bear (in) it, when a joy of hope is strong strong, so that breath be past mastery. It is improbable that this Twang not be dead, bended to the near point of coming, on that wheel. And that it turn there, to new "now", but stop!

LXXII*

...person-to-person.
"Would you spell that, sir?"
Em see capital see ay el tee ee eks.
"And your name, sir?"
Mr. McCaltex.
"I'll call you back in a moment, sir."
What's that?
"I'll call you back, sir."
Oh. This noise... damn car race....

"Your call to Florence, sir... Miami calling Florence, two six nine three seven seven, to speak to a Mrs. McCaltax, m as in mother, c as in Charlie, c as in Charlie, a as in able, l as in love, t as in Tommy, a as in able—"
E. As in eel.
"... e as in easy, x as in X-ray."
—What the last letter please? Ics?
"X-ray."
—O.K. One instant............ It ring now. *Albergo Camerlenghi? Si domanda dagli Stati Uniti la Signora Maccalteches, Milano Como Como Ancona Livorno Torino Empoli ics—come xenofobia.*
—*Non ci stà quella signora.*

*Long-distance telephone call, Miami-Florence, January 18

Operator, wait a minute, operator—

"Yes, sir?"

Try her maiden name, Panattapam, I guess I'd better spell it.
P as in pilfer, a as in angle, n as in... nuts?

"Nan?"

Yes, Nan, then angle, terrible, terrible, angle, pilfer, angle,
... man.

"Nan?"

No, *man*—m, as in mud.

"The first name, sir?"

Well, actually it's double—Tro-tsi, t-r-o... like Trotsky
without the k ...

"Groffsky?"

No, Trostky, Trotsky I mean. Never mind. Just say Twang.
Tang. Wing. Angry. *Neng*—no, Nan. Gong.

"Florence, please ask ..."

—I hear last name, but first?

"Tommy, whisky, oboe ..."

Not oboe—

"Yes, sir?"

Nothing...

"Tommy, whisky, oboe, Nan, George."

—*Si domanda un altra persona, la Signora Tvong Panattapam,
Torino, William-Holden, Otranto, Napoli, Genova, poi Palermo
Ancona...*

—*Ma questa signora non ci stà. E fuori.*

Operator, let me speak to her.

"Do you wish to make the call station-to-station, sir? '

Yes, I do.

"Rome, the caller will speak with the answering party.
Go ahead, sir."

Albergo Camerlenghi?

—*Si, signore.*

Dove la Signora McCaltex?

—*Non saprei, signore.*

Uscire?

—*Credo che sia partita.*

Come? Come?

—*Credo che la signorina sia partita.*
Dove?
—*Forse in campagna.*
Oh. *Lasciare messaggio?* "Arrive tomorrow," *scrivere: a come addio...*
—I understand perfect: "Arrive tomorrow."

LXXIII

Jan. 21

My trip to Florence was the eighth gothic tale. It has left me a shambles. My body doesn't know what time it is. My mind hankers for the night zones.

Now, safely home, I can admit a fact I spared you: I am hopelessly frightened of air travel. It's foolish, but what does that change? Before departure I consumed half a bottle of pills, but they did not blunt my flight-long terror. Only when I landed in Fiumicino, wondering where you were, then remembering that you couldn't know my flight, did wooziness come. I hardly dared drive. But I crawled to Florence in the little rented monster, its steering wheel digging into my paunch, and found the albergo; where to my stupefaction I learned that you were still away. I pestered that poor lady about you, but she couldn't help, although she did make one call. (To whom?) For the rest of the day I walked through the dank city, yearning to find you, expecting you around every corner, eating meals of various sizes, sipping numberless coffees and drinks, not daring to telephone your friends for fear of compromising you, in fear of them, sinking through sluggish currents of exhaustion and disappointment like a pebble in a tank of crude oil. Night came, no news of you, I was taken to your room—your room!—touched your clothes, sniffed your scents, laid between your sheets. It was awful to sleep without you but fatigue and Valium won. I never heard the alarm: I was awakened by a stuck horn. There was no sign of you. I didn't dare stay away longer. So after leaving the note and money—don't take me for a Pogy O'Brien (how did you learn that expression?), it was almost all I had—I drove back to Rome for my return trip. Before boarding I absorbed so much *stravecchio* that I felt someone else was taking the plane.

What a flight! With the money I had left, I had hoped to prolong my non-existence with a few splits of champagne. A wedding party had reserved the entirely supply, so it was back to bourbon, which sobered me immediately. I was sitting next to three bronzy orientals, one mother, one father, and one pretty girl. They may have been sweet souls, but I was never to find out, for at the moment of take-off they buried their heads in shawls and scarves, a dismaying sight. Soon they started vomiting, missing my Flagg Bros. boots by fractions, and they did not desist. I tried to "be something" about this and concentrate on reading the *Sunday Times*, but my general love of the human brotherhood wasn't up to the occasion. I changed seats.

Festive Miami seemed no haven to the returning traveler. From the air, Funland Amusement Park was visibly swarming. A doze on the bus ride into town left me stunned with accumulated weariness. Outside the terminal, waiting for a cab, I began chatting with a personable young man. It was at least a minute before I realized that he was a carnival mannequin. I couldn't believe it until I touched him. Indeed touching him was irresistible: he was more real than the living.

Reaching my apartment I at last found out where you had been. It ended one painful uncertainty. Christ what a mess. Why didn't you wait? My anxiety now fills sky and earth and day and night. Even before leaving I had been completely distraught. You may have noticed in my room a coffin-like carton and a suitcase which despite its appearance was not made of human flesh. They had been confided to me by an elderly neighbor, Mrs. Roak, to be deposited at the Rome airport— she is soon flying to Italy to visit an idiot cousin and was afraid of being overweight. Mrs. Roak stopped by half an hour before my departure, yet I forgot my promise. I was that bewildered from worry (from the pills too, perhaps.) How do you think I feel now? I have no energy, no confidence. I feel that I've been tried as silver is tried, and found to be tin. How can I stand firm in trouble when I can't even stand up! Outside of you there has been nothing to give me hope. My work at the library is disreputable and I am frequently told as much. I haven't found a trace of the map. I wrote to Avignon and Harvard for help: no replies. Mr. Hood might just as well live in Peshawar for all the attention he pays me. And yet these things would matter little if I had seen you—if I had not lost touch with you. It's unpleasant to blame you, but who else is there to blame for the wasted days and nights, the money spent, and the terrible expense of passionate affection? I begged you to explain your desires and you refused. What a miserable time for us, or for me. Perhaps someday I shall see why it was necessary to drink this vinegar first.

LXXIV

January 24

Yes, it was the cause of regret, and of so much amazing. Yet I have told the plan, it is more than I seize. My two days in country also bring less than the homfort desired. But that sad fear in the airplanes, it has not conflicted me. The plane move at a enormouse speed, that is true, but there is less fearing when was in them than when explained it from far away. I am frighten for you therefore. For my very small trip, it was in the train, I borrowed money, so I am thanful for your thought, to leave any, my very dear.

However with the tumult of your arriving, my most dear friends the Prince and Bonzo learn my absence. When I am returning, in evening, they called upon me. From your cause my reputation has suffered injustly. So why did you not tell me, you shall come? These friends will have believe there is secrets from them. They cannot think I shall be gone to country, however I show my cut ticket, that in some way I have thought to keep it. Then is it friendly, and they will stay to converse. But Twang is weary, so into a great cycloon of yawnings that in five minutes I think I blown them out from the room and was asleeping at eight p.M.

Can it be consolation, that one other thing we search, here, there, is here? And of course it will be in Mediceo Avanti il Principato!

This town is as you saw her, gray with coldness. One expect the river will freezes. The moving images are dull. I read some first mistery stories, and play fooling games of card, that I enjoy, with the little girls of the hotel lady, she you met, who is ever more helpful (is this the good word?) about mail.

Than I think, you are in need of being more accurate when you are writing to me.

I have remembered, the contemplating of the estate that is being without desire shall dissipate the idea of pleasure, and I repeat this, Contemplation of a state without desire dissipate the idea of pleasure. Zachary it is hard. It is too strong to master, the buddist way, sometime. I tell you: *Wey, Twang dek laï, Twang nam me vin.* But: *theu mau neng* and *theu nob-me neng.*

Part Six

LXXV

Jan. 28

The tail of the cat
Fell into the vat
The tail of the man
Fell into the can

Do these lines perplex? So did your letter. What kind of explanation is this—your "trip to the country"! Doubt may be a good spur to the imagination, but you have abused it and me.

You are perhaps weary of my groans; there has, however, been a special disappointment. Yesterday at noon Mr. Hood invited me into his office. He seated me in front of his vast desk to address me in fatherly, adamantine style. I copped bad news. Sure enough: "...reports from the field...speed-up...expedition advanced to early March...." After these words had burned into my marrow, he added, "You're the first to be warned, so you can muster your resources. Others who shall be nameless might want to force you out. By the way, I gather you and Dex are friendly again. Ten days ago I saw him outside your place. He was talking to a cute little lady in a sari, or whatever it's called in Siam."

The office was aglitter with white suits and shoes, and papers flashing among his glamorous male staff. The tumult seemed to enhance the light and perfectness of his eyes.

Now what?

It shocks me that your letter doesn't contain one word of apology. (Or mention meeting Hodge.)

When I left, I made the mistake of walking a few blocks to let my blood subside, and so wandered into the cross-city dog race. This event is probably unique in the history of carnivals, and for good reason. It is open not only to greyhounds and other speedy breeds but to all dogs—the prizes allow for size, age, and weight. The result is twelve hours of pandemonium, aggravated by the many owners who, lest their entries weaken in the way, follow them from Coral Gables to the far side of Venetian Causeway.

I was so preoccupied that not until I was upended by a low-flying basset did I realize where I was. Getting up, I was consoled by an unwelcome Samaritan—an affectionate wet-snouted boxer bitch. When I tried to shoo her away, I was accosted by her wroth owner, who yelled at me, turning redder with each stubborn word, "Wh-why are you b-b-bothering B-b-b-beya?" (Bayer? Bear? Baby Bear?) At this moment enthusiasts on either side began shouting—"Come on, Apollo 20!" "Get with it, Gabritius!"—thoroughly deafening me. During six volatile seconds I expected Beya's master to strike me; but he kicked her instead.

The rest of the day was better. There was nobody at the office, and I wrote off a few more maps. The evening stint at the patch passed quickly. I had Chinese 'tweeners across the way, then drove to Haulover Beach Park for the evening show. I arrived well ahead of time. The stage was bare, nearly all the seats empty. A noisy speck appeared in the sky, flickering in the sunset light: a helicopter carrying the set for the performance.

Tobacco, the ballet of the day, was part of a festival series about local products. It was worth the price of admission (actually I had a free ticket.) The scene was the island of Tobago, from which the plant was once thought to derive its name. We saw two Indians perform a *pas de deux* extolling the magic virtues of the leaf; four priests scatter tobacco shreds to calm wild storms; and seven witches conduct rituals of worship with fumes from wetted clay pipes. Then the corps de ballet, as a crowd of snuff addicts, did an energetic sneezing number, and finally a patriarch gathered young men from all the nations of the earth into a brotherly Smoking Academy. This was unexpectedly moving. A timely Havana-colored moon rose over the beclouded dancers.

Diana, my sister, is here on business. She had asked me to an after-dinner party in her hotel suite, to which I went out of politeness, and had a marvelous time. I was the only man there. Although tough as a tank, Diana was almost motherly. She steered me clear of the virginal twists for whom I naturally yearn to a riper triad of sisters named Asham—Marcia, Molly, and Aline, of whom I decided that the first two were sufficient unto the hour. (Aline seemed lion-toothed as well as haired.) Diana somehow depicted me to those girls in irresistible lineaments, and I enjoyed a moment's adoration. This even helped cure an intolerable boil—but I shall not irritate you with details.

Which reminds me—I haven't deciphered your Pan phrases. When I first saw them, without translation, I admit I clenched my fits in annoyance. I shall look through your letters for the explanations. Did you really think I would remember all these words?

LXXVI

Jan 31

No more again Pan words ever. (Yet they are the language that dreams. And secrets.)

And was Twang to think? the gentleman asked for the time of the morning, still your door will not responds, is the Mr. Hodge.

It is more for Twang to reprove: your trivial joys with women, what a bath, fish in mud, they can smile, it has make

you stuprid. You must contemplate the word "decline", to
dissipate the idea "closeness". What is, perception of impu-
rety? One is to inspect, so to reflect: the parties of his body
from the sores of his feet to the ends of his hairs is in every
sense subjects to the corruption. See that, this is the observa-
tion of corruption. Then the consciousness too is horrupt:
appears, is dissolute. It must be to renounce the joying of life.
It is Twang that has love for you.

These are the later years of *Salvestro*. Never does he obtain that treasure. After 1457 he's abandoned hope, he knagged the cousins cowever
on till 1465. The next year he joins *Francesco Neroni* in the conspiracy
to throw the *Medici* over. Salvestro is reveal in *Neroni's* wide screen
confession. So the new *Balía* of *Medici* men votes him into exile Sett.
11 1466 because he has "take up wheapons against the fatherland."
(So, of each conspirator.)

Then for 15 years *Salvestro* wanders through the proximate countries of Italy. He looks perhaps for friends to his rights. In the end he
calls his old old mother *Mantissa* from Florence. From Venice they sail
together away on the long trip back to her homeland, he will become
there a spices merchant. Goodbye, *Salvestro Sguardofisso*.

That *Mantissa* I trace too back to before her arriving, to her insurance
policy, this is taken for her during the awfle journey from Tana to
Venice, it is for 75 gold florins, except if she die from leaping willful
in the sea. That sea death was often, so kind the white Christians to the
colorful infidels.

It has been as in my expressed fear, that the Prince is un-
pleased with me, after that sudden arrival of you. So he tell
Bonzo. I know nevertheless that the Pindola will sustain me,
and my worth. It is a strong leaning to have him thus. Although in this day he is something sulky, after drinking
much white whine.

Can you remember, the same *Francesco Neroni's* fear, when he write
to *Salvestro* in '57, of indiscretion? He was just. I find a letter of the
Florentine merchant *Pazzino Cicciaporci* date 1460, here he speak of
"certain tresor weaved into bolts of silk." Before he die *Beccadelli*
mentions that too, in a little satiric poem. This means, the news goes
even to Naples.

Once you tell me, that of the first Italian missionaries in

Pannam, those very first that come by land, in the ending of the 15eenth century, there are some baptismals, marriages, deaths records still, they survive my climate, and if this be true you have photograph these for your mission? Then, may Twang request those microphilm, together with the next check.

LXXVII

Sunday, Feb. 3

It's unfair to condemn me for a few instants of distraction. Neither Marsha nor Molly Asham counts for peanuts. You imply that my resolves to avoid insignificant people are not sincere. This is wounding.

And there you go dunning again! Didn't I send you money last week? Forgive the expression. But each time my feelings reach out toward you for esteem and friendship and all that is soft, you clutter them with trash and dirt.

Furthermore, I'm down to my last bumblebee and bean. The day before yesterday I went to the office to make the contribution to Key Betabara: $2,200. This included every penny I could find. I even closed the hometown savings account, that I'd kept out of nostalgia, sixty-two dollars and thirty-four cents. The trouble is, I don't *own* anything.

Mr. Hood was busy but received me. Among the comings-and-goings he sat in basiliscal dignity, with quicksilver eyes. He heard me out with evident disappointment. The sum was too small. He showed a touching sympathy with my plight—I almost felt obliged to comfort *him*. He explained that I needn't put up a dime for his sake, but there were the other backers. He had already defended my interests against outside bids.

As if to confirm these words a relay of men swarmed around us with messages from banks and financiers: offers of ten, thirty, fifty, and once a hundred and fifty thousand dollars. My depression sprang a new icicle at each figure.

Mr. Hood promised to support my candidacy a little longer, and urged me to get busy. I assigned the twenty-two C's to him as proof of my good faith. Then I went around the corner to The Glass Slipper where, although I had planned a leaf-and-fruit day, I had three slugs of philosopher's wine.

Well, the multitude of the isles had better ready themselves. I shall go with those others if I have to hang onto their boat with my teeth. Is it unreasonable that I should feel so violetly about this, that it should have become my sole obsession? I know—don't ask me why—this treasure and ours are the same.

I am day after day in a state of exceptional nervousness. My insomnia is entering the hallucinatory stage, with purple crows nesting in my pillow. Not only the dismaying turn of events is responsible for this. I'm still groggy from my trip, and each day our carnival makes repose a little more problematic. At night spotlights of great power play over the city and cause the most swaddled window to glow. Nor have our ears been neglected. Noise flows relentlessly from peculiar electronic devices that amplify distant sounds and diminish those nearby. Thus one lives among vast echoes of ducks and Indian choirs; at dawn cockcrows issue from a phantasmal barnyard.

Another network of speakers broadcasts carnival tunes. The music has been planned like a grand operetta: a few songs are reprised with ever-increasing frequency.

The worst moments, the ones that wake me up for good, are the silences. A capricious glider hovers over Miami, projecting a beam that switches off all sound equipment beneath it. When it passes over my block, the effect is of doom.

At least there are no "surging crowds" in the streets, so that I can stretch my legs in peace.

They're playing one of those songs—

> I may be black, I may be red,
> I may be yellow, I may be white,
> I may be red, yellow, black, or white
> But I'm blue

Meanwhile the Guest pursues his irresistible dance, and the daughters of Judah dance for joy in his steps.

It's time to wing this on its way. The library will send the microfilms you requested. Why do you want them? Their condition is bad, but they are legible—they were preserved by your "breathing vases" during their long burial.

LXXVIII

2.6

What, then, is the "bumblebean"?

My dear Zachary, I have now assemble from the measureless Medici paperdom a dossier almost complete of the treasure. That is now folded beneath my unwriting hand. Yet the most important, most desired, lie within my head—in the archive, mess where only Twang can find; so in my head.

O I'm so sick of this seedy old dwelling. There is a dog of household, friendly, and so great that I can ride him, last night this ridable mut open my room and pipi in my slippers, not of glass. But shall Twang maybe move to a worst place if there is no money?

However my brain is clear, and yours is most not. It become very necessary that you think: contemplate "considered contemplation", this shall dissipates the idea of non-contemplation.

LXXIX

Feb. 10

Enclosed is a check. It's smaller than usual. If you ever peruse my letters you may be aware of the local shortage.

Last Wednesday, after several attempts to see Mr. Hood, I managed to speak to him by phone. In desperation I told him about my access to the maps in the library and suggested contributing some of them as part of my stake. I even proposed *our* map. (If the Key Betabara treasure is the same as ours, my map won't tell them much they don't already know. And if it isn't the same, it's certainly worth as much going after. How can I lose?) Mr. Hood was surprised that I had a copy. Then I was obliged to explain that I expected to be in possession of one very soon. This is true. There are only 138 maps left. He promised to think it over.

Yesterday Hodge came to the patch. He brought the tidings of Mr. Hood's acceptance, but maliciously concealed them for a good half-hour. According to Hodge, Mr. Hood disliked the arrangement. It was bad business, and he was only agreeing to it out of friendship.

Dex was disgusting. One minute he was sneering at my poverty; the next, he insisting that we "bunk together" on the trip. (He may have another insist coming.) Admittedly I was ill-disposed towards him since a few nights ago he had an intimate dinner with Grace to which I was definitely not invited, and Grace confided a lot of things that Dex refuses to divulge. I tried to show what I think of him but he refused to notice. If this sounds like ingratitude I can only say that I have no strength left for gratitude.

To speed up my map research, I've been replaced as watchman. What a relief! This afternoon I took an hour off to stroll through the decorated streets. At least the weather has been pleasant. Each day comes in like one of an endless succession of ambassadors from the kingdom of Prester John. However, the night moons are fuzzy.

Of course I saw only a tiny part of the displays. At street level there is living sculpture; higher up, Cinerama screens on which immobile personages appear. (Their purpose is to encourage meditation.) The live shows present great scenes from comics, television, books, or history. At a sports intersection one might see "Casey at the Bat" (books) and "Mickey Owen's Mistake" (history). Emphasis is placed on the subject's ethical or philosophical significance, in both these cases close to the Buddhist notion, "Only impermanence is permanent."

(I should mention that no decorations survive the end of

carnival. Nevertheless, first-class designers compete for the privilege of contributing their work. This is one reason for the high quality of our celebrations. Another is that while most cities import their festival staff, Miami maintains its own year-round. But most important is the community spirit that fills us all during carnival time. We become members of one colossial family.)

There were few people in the streets at the time of my walk. Everyone was at Interama watching the archery-plus-rhetoric contest. For his turn the Guest appeared in the skull-and-bones suit that he wears ever more frequently.

Harvard has sent the letters written to Lorenzo de' Medici by his representative in Lyons. They are of little interest. One or two mention the treasure. In August 1481 Lionetto complains that a chest of silk marked "as you describe" with black birds arrived "incomplete—much darnel but no wheat." It was essential for the prosperity of the Lyons branch that the rest be sent. Later Lionetto repeats the complaint, adding that several buyers are interested in that "particular silk," which he has widely advertised. However, after the signature there is a note: "...I am glad that at last this devious gold has escaped its ultramontane destiny..." The letter, incidentally, is a copy in Lionetto's hand, and was kept by him.

Now we know how the treasure reached Lionetto. I couldn't care less.

I have had more sleep at night, but spoiled by dreams. Friday I was on a beach that I had never seen. My father was walking along it, gray, unshaven, in tatters. There was a giant fly closely following him. There was a man who was also my father sitting in the cockpit eye of the fly. There was my first father withering as he trudged through the slow sand, finally stumbling, then crawling on his knees, then prostrate. Meanwhile there was a wet salty squall blowing a smudge of fish scales over the large eye where my other father was sitting; he stopped the fly and got out, walking towards the ocean and giving the prone body a kick that broke it to piece. There was my surviving father clean-shaven and rosy. There was a girl splashing in the waves—you. Your wet tresses were even

straighter than usual. There was my father who started playing with you, but I saw little of that because the sight of you
was too much and I woke up in a tumult of semi-pleasure,
bathed in my own slime. It was the first and only time in my
life this has happened.

LXXX

February 13

That you decide to deliver map to Miles Hood is all right.
I approve. But, you will not find it, I think.

I'm much anxious, lest you be condamned to having always these nightmares at night and broodmares at day. It is,
again, the *pristwe* "demon" that visit you. He will seem to be
of the third class (out of illusions sustaining egoistic arrogance)
but no, poor Zachary, it is of the first class—bad outside influences, of such we say,

"They bring fear, they pass through changes, innocent
things have terrifying appearances, unoffending women will
appear as bewitches.

"Very early, between three and four of clock, you will feel
that you see tigers; from five to seven, unoffending rabbits,
yet who, nevertheless, scare. From seven to nine you will feel
that you perceive very bad dragons, or turtles. From nine to
eleven you will have the impression that you see snakes. From
eleven to 1 you will have the illusion that you see horses.
From 1 to 3 the apparitions will be of sheep; from 3 to 5 of
monkeys. At dsk the illusions will be of vultures and crows.
In the shades of night they will resemble dogs and wolfs.
From 9 to 11 they will have the appearance of pigs, or repig-
nant things; from 11 to one, of rats racing off and mice. From
1 to 3 you will see the apparition of cows, that threaten and
bring fear.

"So assailed, remember what time, and remove these appearances. Call them by names. They will vanish."

Practice the halt of thought, the mind will quiet, and the
armies of Mara will vanish. Perhaps too should you have a

micetrap if that is the hardest hour? And sometime change the color of the upbolstery?

My friend Bonzo is a dearest friend. He has smoothed the Prince, and presents to him my knowledge of the treasure dossier, for negotioating. I'm closer to him, than ever.

This most: contemplation of "vacancy" will dispel ideas of adherence.

LXXXI

I stay in the library day and night. My guardian angel still seems to be out to lunch.

Day and night, but there is no longer any night. A horde of permanent flares has been loosed over Miami. Each generates a downward thrust just strong enough to keep afloat. They emit an aqueous sparkle. One is now bobbing outside my window, these lines ripple in green light.

With little more than a fortnight to run, the carnival knows no pause. Outside, on the campus, a Ferris wheel revolves through the dark hours. Thousands of smudge pots are fixed to its rims. The riders are murky blobs behind the turning flames.

Tonight I had been invited to an elite gathering at the Brissy St. Jouin. The evening is devoted to the "Inner Muffle."

There was no question of attending. I have chained myself to one cycle of gestures. I peer into a map for several hours, usually emptying even my 69 fountain pen ("Writes with both ends") as I retrace its topography and place-names. Another map drops into the winnowing basket. Eighty-five to go.

There have been no more than three words exchanged between me and another human in the last week. I exclude Hodge, who checks me out daily, no doubt on orders from above. When he finds me still working he gives me a glassy-eyed, six-pointed stare into which I read a savory mixture of repressed disappointment, boredom, impatience, condescension overlaid with a very slightly exaggerated air of

courage in the face of insurmountable obstacles, Sydney Carton, Joan of Arc, this hurts me more than it does you especially in the pocketbook yet I go on unflinching but with the
satisfaction of letting you know all this. He is justified—that
is the horrible thing. *A* horrible thing.

Your letter was at least short. Your words of encourage-
ment concerning the map made things so much easier for me.
Does taunting me give you that great a satisfaction? Or do
you not realize how harsh your words rings? Such as giving
up the idea of "adherence." You are cruel to a generous nature, which has a tenders for you that makes your least ill-
humor afflicting. My rock drying up? I only hope your vitriol
will turn to Victory Oil—it sets the wheels turning all right,
like an unquenchable hotfoot.

The library by now will have sent the Pannam microfilms.
What do you want them for?

Here's the sun. I greet it with a camel yawn.

Now back to maps, eyes sharp, box those shadows, running
in place breathless, stupid pursuit of that unfading wreath!
When I think of those others, who heard of the treasure two
weeks ago, and who will get more of it than I who have
thought of nothing else and labored for over a year! Many
will have been called and all chosen, except me.

Yesterday the Guest played macro-tennis with the Mayor.
Next comes the bowling contest: jet-propelled steel balls and
twelve-foot exploding pins. Boom boom!

Often I feel that if I could follow the workings of old Wittgenstein's mind, these puzzles would become clear.

LXXXII

February 20

The microfilms have arrived and I thank you. They fill
personal needs.

"Prince Voltic has established a legal claim on the treasure."
I say the words and will yet not believe.

It is true: Prince has a legal claim, and international, on the treasure. Bonzo show me the paper, that was deposited a year ago almost. Can it be possible? Is there some thing to do? For you also this shall mean an end?

My mind, my heart are shaking. For: it is necessity, that I am honest with the good Prince. Oh well, I make myself contemplate "renunciation" to dissipate the idea "greed". Have I not told you as such? so:

One following the Teaching does not harbor thoughts of desire (every sensual whatever it be) that may arise in her. But she avoids them, she tames them, she annihilate them. She does not harbor thoughts of rage or resentment, no, but she averts them, she tames them, she annihilates them!

It constitutes the perception of renunciation.

So as perhaps to help you, I have been at once reading the *Tractatus.* I fear my intellectual standard must be under below, I can't understand some thing when I read the plain words, over and over.

And that is that my understanding might follow some feeling of life which I can feel from the proses or verses, familiar to me. I have read late writers of your country, frequently I sense this feeling is a of loneliness and isolation of the modern man situation in a world of civilisation and technique, a feeling of depression but the trial to conquer it too. Such as Robinson Jefferson, as example.

I do not, though, read only the mods. Thus, in recent days I learn from Origen that on the Lost Judgment the blessed souls will roll into heaven, for they will be resuscitate in perfection, as spheres. Do the *Medici* think of this when they make their marks?

O water ruffled by strong wind! You, have omitted to set on your last letter its date.

So, remember: *Evvivano le palle!*

LXXXIII*

Feb. 24

It is 3 A.M. I just returned home through streets full of maskers. It is our one masked night. The powers that be decided one is all we deserve.

I've found the map. It was forty-first from the end. I feel like both seed and fertile ground. That's speaking like a fool but if there is to be bravado I too can indulge in it, after this drudging. Fuck the Prince. No stumbles now!

I have here glued half a stick of Juicy Fruit gum (at three cents a stick) which is the greatest proof I can give you at present of being, with my whole heart, yours.

What the hell's Tractatus?

LXXXIV

February 27

Because you need to comprehend Wittgenstein I read the Tractatus, his early broad book, but not so bad, as you say.

Now every day Bonzo is pursuing the Prince, to negotiate with him, the map for a share of the treasure. I have told him, go very slow; so I don't know if yet they are talking gravy.

It makes me think, if I must eat many meals more in this *pensione* I shall go on a hunger stroke. However I have the luck that Bonzo buy me a meal nearly each evening.

And your map—it seems so far so fantasmal. Is it real? Is it really unreal? As I once said to you, things must disappear, and even so consciousness of them. Therefore, contemplating the consciousness as well as any thing (e.g. map), you are to think of it impermanent not permanent, miserable not happiness, impersonal not a personality—you are to feel aversion to it; take no pleasure from it; detach yourself of it; give it up.

Thus, you do not pile up *kamma*. For, we know this:

*Postcard.

The act has no actor
And no one gather its fruit;
There is only the succession of empty phenomena.
Other than this no view is right.
And while acts and their honsequences succeed
In obedience to the law of causality
(As the tree follows the seed and the seed the tree)
No first beginning is perceptible.

Twang shall ask, send the mask you have wore.

LXXXV

March 3

Forgive my delay, caused by dicease in the family.

Mardi Gras is only two days off, thank God—no sooner had I found the map than I was ordered back to being watchman. The resulting exhaustion was a match for even my insomnia. Today's parade ended my duties.

It was a continuation of the one with which the festival began, and followed the Guest from the City Center, which he had then reached, to the waterfront.

I missed the start—it is supposed to have taken place in an atmosphere of high dedication, so high that Mayor Favell was unable to speak—because I was busy defending my vantage point. The only person in front of me was a petite lady cop in a magenta "spectator sportswear" uniform.

The street was a lively spectacle. The pavements were strewn with fresh laurel and honeysuckle. A pot of incense fumed on every traffic light. Above me a trio of Flügelhorns stood at a picture window and from time to time blew a peppy fanfare. From cornices and roofs smoke-machines uncoiled ropes of color, as did the hovering flares that so brighten our nights. The crowd flowed about the food-and-drink stands, which sent smells of fritters to my appreciative nose.

The live shows scattered through the city had been moved to the tops of buildings along the parade route. I could see one of them: playing the legendary Willie Mays, a batter stroked baseballs in elegant parabolas over the rooftops.

From time to time the glider passed over head, stunning us with silence.

The parade began with seven groups of animals representing the continents. I noticed that Dex had leased some spares from the Temple: two razor-clawed avocado bears from Peru.

Then came various guilds, appropriately costumed. Among them were the designers of the festival, who got a big hand; lawyers (they carried a coffin-like mock-up of Blackstone); professional transvestites of both sexes who held up the parade with a squabble as to how the "Ladies first" principle should be applied.

They were followed by the succession of floats that is the pride of our festival.

First were the enigma floats: scenes depicting undisclosed proverbs. On the first, for instance, one saw a man with corked ears contemplating a sheet of music, while behind him a blindfolded girl, gesticulating skyward, vainly implored him to look where she was pointing. On the second, an old fellow in striped garb sat on a green platform surrounded by water, gazing toward the horizon past a sign that read, "Property of Lucifer." It wasn't hard to guess that the first float stood for "The blind cannot hear, nor the deaf see"; the second for "A colonial escape must be singly bred"; and the third, "The button leaves a mark of fear."

Next were the allegorical floats, giant figures and settings. It would take pages to describe them (they lasted two hours) but some titles were: The Big Number, The Assassinated President, Armed Peace.

Musical floats followed—brass bands, pop groups (one of whom sang the Mayor's verses to the newest Mrs. Favell) and a chorus performing in counterpoint the three hits of the carnival. In the soprano one heard "A Big Basket for Fruits," a presto tongue twister sung with miraculous ease; in the tenor, the languid melismas of "Trouble my Depths"; in the bass, "I may be Black, but I'm blue."

The dancers were next. The "Anatomy" floats are now peopled with mannequins: when they passed, only the Mirror Man flashed among the dummies. The other floats were live and various. On one, dancers spelled out the words of a significant text. It is hard to say how this was done, but it was done.

At the end came an animal dance, with llamas, elephants, kangaroos, and other charmers. They were followed by people dressed up as the same animals, performing the same dance.

Throughout the parade the Venusians carried out their antic role.

The cortege at last disappeared towards Miamarina. It was there, last night, that the guest won his final victory over the Black and white Mayors. He manned a jib crane set on a gantry running along two hundred yards of waterfront. In the cockpit of another crane, at the opposite end of the gantry, sat replicas of the Mayors. Charging towards each other, the cranes collided near the middle of the gantry with a bang that shook the suburbs. Six times the derricks clashed indecisively. At the seventh the Mayors' tipped sideways, fell into the harbor waters, and vanished. The Guest had justified his title of Chief Pilot.

It is at Miamarina that the festival will end. It has entered its final, aquatic stage, symbolizing instability and metamorphosis, preparing us for Lenten changes. The parade, when it reached the harbor, continued straight into the water. Floats, Venusians, and swimming animals joined the host of carnival participants already immersed: pilotless boats, "float-in" movies, trained squads of dolphins and fish, and swimmers finned-out as fish. Ordinary swimmers then began dipping into the chilly water. Later there will be boat races and battles, with prizes.

I visited the harbor in late afternoon. The thousands of swimmers made the scene worthy of D. W. Griffin. However, all filming is forbidden. No one in fact can keep any record of the carnival, written, painted, photographed, or taped. The festive structures chosen for permanence are our only memorials.

The Guest's winning crane is to become the scaffold for the great bonfire of Tuesday night. It has been christened *thalamus* or marriage bed—Aphrodite's, because the water festival celebrates her birth from the waves. The crane has already been draped with an immense net, on which the population of our sinful town will abandon its "instruments of pleasure," everything from swizzle sticks to Kahlil Gibran.

Meanwhile the Guest, now Chief Pilot, his duties done, is to spend two days carousing with Miamians great and small. On Tuesday he will conspicuously join in the last wild dancing, kissing all the pretty girls he meets. At midnight he will unzip his mask and, casting it into the fire, reveal his identity.

The time will also be given over to public confession, in these circumstances a joyful and salutary experience. The Festival Directors have been accused of organizing these confessions, but the reproach is unfair. They are absolutely spontaneous, and are organized only to make sure someone is listening.

The last confession is the Guest's avowal of his name.

I myself must "confess," dear one, that my map is as real as an Easter egg. I find it to say the least puzzling that you question its existence—methinks my Twang no longer trusts her Zachary. Or is this more Buddhist theory? What about "your" map? How can you negotiate with it—do you expect me to send you a copy?

Of course, theoretically, you are right: knowledge will undoubtedly vanish away. Meanwhile I have the map and I want its "fruits," the whole and palpable knowledge of it, before it and I return to the burning fountain. I have no desire to sit out my life like a blind beggar on the roadside.

For the first time in months I feel sanguine about my future. I've seen that Mr. Dharmabody is properly boarded. My *kas* are in good shape. So, out of the desert and into the sea. Wednesday morning will see me and the others headed for Key Betabara.

Ah, the *Tractatus*—by Wittgenstein I meant Charlie Witt-genstein, who used to rope for the Locus Solus kid. His specialty was "finding the leather."
Check enclosed.

LXXXVI

March 6

Yes, it's indeed my own map offered to the Prince. Bonzo has done this so well, and the Prince says Of course, since I must use it to find that treasure which is mine, part of that can be yours. So it is done! Not your untrust yet unbelief confuse me, me-think your mind is of water-veiled-with-mosss, for I six weeks ago have told you of the desired docku-ment that is in *Mediceo Avanti il Principato*.

Now Bonzo and I have made a certain agreedment and to honor it he has at last take me to his fatherly house, and there through many obsolutely fine rooms, like the autobus sta-tion! And he asks, Shall we visit my dear the Averardo Room, I thought he say avocado with in mind your charmer bears; but, Averardo.

It is very nice too, for histerical reason! I have meant, that is only a storoom attic, not eleghant as others, not used much, with such dust one was needing a lot of broom for manoever. But very interesting. There were fine very plain chests, for the chairs are mostly sold with the Prince, a cross was on one, plain too but plainly renaissance (15th c.), a Roman coin was there. We opened one very large chest, there were the Medici *palle* (Balls) on the lid, and on the inside stuff also, when Bonzo opens the lid, Oh so heavy and slow—the floor of that room was wide board—there were seventeen small windows, I shall say 120 cm × 80 cm—the beamis of the ceiling were painted with the same color as the plaster between, pinkish cream—some black cracking went along them—on the walls were a so-so so-so "Woman at the Marketplace." A 19th cen-tury tapestry of a railroad train, very holy. *La Tolleranza Tra-dita*, by Unknown.

Often I say, concentrate on detachment to crack up the hardnut thought "covet."

Well, did you know our marriage is not legal in Italy?

Thinking of your letter from *Lionetto de' Rossi*, I renote this from *Lorenzo the Mag.* to him, writing of the treasure. He *Lorenzo* say that he has not yet tried before to sell it because it is so notorious but now he's short of cush and want the gold negotiated quickly and discreetly. So, he will send it abroad. It will come in a box of old brocade where it is still since *Cosimo* tried to send it away through Pisa. It is so old brocade that "the silver marks at the end of its bolts truly now look alike black crows." He says it is 500 *bracci* long. He promises to let *Lionetto* know, when it will arrive. "I promise to tell you, when it will arrive."

Part Seven

LXXXVII

Early Thurs.

Back yesterday evening, up all night. The events have left me feeling like a fragment by H. D. It was absolutely an awful time. I'm going to have a banana and a swallow of Epsom salts then get into bed and weep sore. The sun, about to emerge, can pursue it's magnetic way without me.

LXXXVIII

March 8

This business seems to completely have fallen through. I can't tell how. The breach is beyond repair. I expect no redeeming event, but would like an explanation. Eschatological tensions rend my bones, unsoothable subintestinal knots! and you will soon be berating me I know it, and not wrongly, don't go easy, bray what a fool I've been. But tell me first if your map (I do believe it) looks like this:

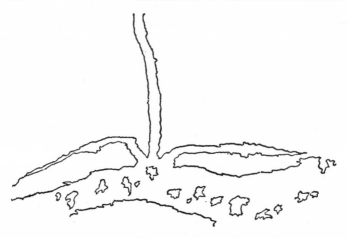

(Somewhat like my voice-print when my voice say "eye.")

We left Wednesday. The morning was clear, the town quiet. The unmasked Guest had "rescued Aphrodite" at midnight, and before dawn the two of them had boarded a rocket to be shot into space. Through empty streets a girl's cool voice broadcast the Lenten proclamation that forbids "blasphemy, games, sodomy, concubinage, renting houses to panders..." Hodge, in charge of the expedition, directed my driving. To make sure we were free of tags, we meandered through back streets before taking the highway to the gulf. At Naples I turned south on a secondary road, stopping after two miles by a weedy graveyard, our rendezvous. We settled down to wait for our partners. After twenty minutes a car slowly approached. From it stepped two uncommunicative men, nondescript for their reputed standing; perhaps they were, like Hodge, mere delegates.

Our boat was at a marina five miles to the south. It was ready; we set off at once. We plunged into the labyrinth of inshore channels bordering that coast. Hodge and the captain used an enlargement of my map, discussing locations in the Ten Thousand Islands to which it might correspond. It was then I learned that we were not in fact going to Key Betabara. We were looking for our treasure after all, but it was in some other, unknown place. Hodge acknowledged this. I felt

THE SINKING OF THE ODRADEK STADIUM

reality slipping a little farther from my grasp.

Hours passed in slow search. The configurations of the map approximated many sites but coincided with none. The coast and shores turned from sand to mud to other-colored sand. Flat clusters of mangrove and palmetto accumulated monotonously. Hodge became sour and a little frantic. I found myself cheering him up, busying him with questions, like the idiot in Grimm distracting the witch from her pills. Our companions somnolently fished from the stern.

Occasionally we saw other boats, or glimpsed tourists along the shore roads, but for the most part the landscape was deserted. It was with some astonishment that, exploring a channel that resembled a detail of the map, and issuing into a cove or, more properly, a well-protected estuary tallying with the map in every particular, we found that the island at its center—our very goal—was a nudist camp.

As we approached and cut our engines, an old man started shouting at us from the water's edge.

Hodge grunted irritably. "That's the resort director—harmless. This is Key Mingori. If I'd known, we could have saved half the day." Sunset was near.

The old man had a mane of white hair. Erect in spite of his years, he looked, with his short staff, very Stan Musialesque. He wore an open jerkin embroidered with shells and thorny roses. Something in his manner suggested that he was expecting us. I wondered if one of our agents had alerted him, but decided that my suspicions were due to his lack of beard.

As we came ashore he concluded his diatribe, of which I only grasped the final sentence:

"The black men shine redder than your moth-eaten gold!"

At our approach he raised his fingers to his eyes, which were obscured by gray cataracts. Adroitly he flicked them away, and put on orange sunglasses.

This old man was Mitchell Mauss. He has been famous among the local Indians ever since the tribe with which he was living was stricken with epidemic diptheria. Mauss taught them a technique of deep yawning to tear the suffocating diphtherial growths, saving many children. The tribe rewarded him with the gift of the Key.

Mauss developed the island as a small resort. His clients are shy nudists—people who believe in nudism but find difficulty practicing it, and who are fearful of ordinary colonies with their requirements of strict nakedness. On Key Mingori nudity is only encouraged, never enforced, in accordance with inner needs.

Mauss welcomed us and, despite the late hour, insisted we tour his establishment. He presented it as a very moral community. There were beggars stationed in inconspicuous spots, hidden by richly ornate screens "so that donors would not feel unjustified superiority"; in a recess of the shore he showed us a vast submarine corral filled with sea beasts—"A gam of milk whales," he explained. "But we don't milk them now, because they're fasting—yes, fasting. It's for our benefit. The knowledge of their privation fills us with remorse whenever we eat. Whereas if we ourselves fasted we might fall prey to smugness." At our approach many a square snout had risen from the agitated water.

Opposite our boat stood an old, sickly palm tree, A rusty pie dish was wedged in its upper branches. Underneath, traced in faint disjointed pencil strokes, drawings of Alpine scenes were clipped to the fronds; and close to the ground an iron cross, perhaps the shank and stock of an anchor, protruded from a gray scar in the trunk (almost fell down, said nothing of course.) To a ring in the cross, two thick ropes, one long, one short, leashed dissimilar creatures: a young woman who slithered in the powdery sand, combing her hair with a sea urchin, naked except for an anal star; and a huge, unmoving boa, whose body coiled around a driftwood log.

A young man stepped up and declared in a shaky voice, "This is a private club." The director reassured him. To us, touching the snake's eyes, he said, "He's afraid. Don't you be."

The young man had risen from a group that was seated in rows on the ground. It was watching television programs on five sets arranged in quincunx—

The doorbell's dinging, maybe that's news!!

LXXXIX

March 8

Now, just, I have had a police visit. The three men came to my room, all say *Ciao!* loud at once, and look every place —under the bed they do not need to bend they are so stumpy! They say (good English), What's this? What's that? Watch out! "Scandalous prodigality of rush wealth" and so funny threats. I acted bewhildered—I *was* so; and proclaimed my innonence. They go.

No more to write now, for I shall telephone the Pindola to ask him what this intruding meant.

But I forgot to tell, that your beautiful description of carnival's final was appreciated to no end, etc.

I must also calm myself, so: "thinking of wretchedness against ideas of affection and clinging."

Now, I'm calmer. Perhaps I saw those policemen some time else? Yet I take it for granite they are real.

XC

Continued March 9

The doorbell was a mistake.

There was this X-shaped arrangement of television sets. Three commercials, Ben Gazzara's twentieth dying year, and a quiz program emceed by Mr. Hood.

Hodge shouted out to the boat, "Bring the tools." Tools meant picks, shovels, guns.

He was leaning against the dessicated palm. Mauss said, "That cross *looks* so old," rubbing his hand over one rusted knob. "What salt air does in a few years!" Hodge glanced at him. Mauss continued: "If the old Spaniards had put it there, how high would it be now? As high as the pie dish?"

Hodge's disappointment was so plain he almost looked human. I groaned in sympathy.

Mauss said, "I remember one big palm, about ten miles south, with a cross sticking out twenty-five feet up. Somewhere around Key Isabella, hard to say exactly with all those mangroves. A cove like ours..."

Without a word Hodge turned toward the boat. I stopped to mumble our thanks. On the television screen Mr. Hood was presenting two hundred thousand dollars to the quiz winner, the Miami chief of police. Mauss went over and switched that set to another channel.

I heard engines start. Our boat had weighed anchor. I ran towards the water, shouting hopelessly in the growling dusk.

An Indian nudist appeared, brandishing a feeble torch: the boat turned back. He led me through the shallows and supported my swim with a strong scissors kick.

Safely aboard, I watched my benefactor return to shore. It was nearly dark. Above the Gulf unseasonable lightning glimmered like a defective bulb. Supersonic bats, popping like corks, issued for their nocturnal hunt.

Over the engine noise Hodge was shouting his contempt for Mauss's colony: "...Back to square one.... Substandard realty for the dissolute...." He was his repulsive self again. However, he dried me off kindly. I would have preferred plain signs of his evil heart; but you can't expect a suffragette to grow whiskers.

We anchored off Key Isabella for the night. I hardly slept. Around midnight one of the partners emerged from his apathy to start cleaning the firearms, which he said were in an appalling state. The night passed in clicks and shocks.

At sunrise we resumed our search. The day began fair, but by eight o'clock a fog thicker than Mogen David wine had clapped down on us. We persevered until noon, staring into the beclouded branches of every passing grove. The captain finally announced that search was futile in such conditions— we would return to port. We inched our way into the gulf, headed north, and docked at five.

Our partners went their way. When Hodge and I reached Miami, he reminded me that Mr. Hood was waiting for news. I suggested telephoning. Hodge was adamant: "Can't cross the old man."

In his office Mr. Hood was having drinks with three gentlemen of opulent mien. He introduced them as our principal associates. One of them was known to me from Spindle gatherings.

Hodge reported the failure of our search and recommended that we start out again as soon as the weather cleared. Mr. Hood seemed disappointed and, even more, perplexed. He politely asked Hodge for a full account. Hodge said that he would draw up a report in the morning. An ice-pick note entered Mr. Hood's voice as he insisted, still courteous, that he and his partners learn what had happened. Until then I had scarcely listened. Abruptly, through fatigue and depression, terrible suspicion surged. Were things not as they seemed?

Mr. Hood was watching Hodge with an appalling, predatory stare.

Hodge began recounting our trip in wearying detail. Often he turned to me for corroboration, which I cautiously supplied. As he described our visit to the island I saw him stop in amazement. Mr. Hood had risen from his chair and stood shaking his smooth hands at Hodge. He was white. One reads of people going white but I had never seen it happen. Mr. Hood was the color of wet plaster.

"So that's it!" he said, his voice thrillingly quiet. "Do you expect me to buy that, you cheap hood?"

Grasping the arms of his chair, Hodge blustered, "Who do you think you're talking to?"

" '*Whom* do you think you're talking to'! Now, don't tell me you spent thirty years with the papes and never learned how God made a tree." Mr. Hood turned to us. "Don't you see his game? When you drive a nail into a tree trunk, it stays put, and an iron cross is no different. It wouldn't climb as the tree grows. He's in cahoots with Mauss. By now the treasure's in the Bahamas, the whole eight million. You fink! You despicable fink!"

Mr. Hood crossed the room and slapped Hodge's face (since the latter was seated, it was on a level with his own.) Hodge rose and began strangling his tiny adversary. This is the last thing I saw clearly. Purplish smoke seemed to fill the room. I yelled, "He's ruined me, he's ruined me" and I threw myself at Hodge. I was ready to kill him. The others pulled me back. Hodge, himself in a fury, again lunged at Mr. Hood, who had scrambled behind his desk. I wanted to stop him but there was no need for that. I barely glimpsed the silvery pistol in Mr. Hood's hand as he shot Hodge point blank. Hodge gave an ugly groan, turned toward me, and a jet of hot slick blood spurted from his mouth over my shirt. Then he collapsed face downwards.

Mr. Hood acted with dispatch. He searched Hodge's pockets and found the enlargement of the map. "Where's the original?" he asked. I gave him the ancient document, which tore where the blood had soaked it. "Burn them, they're evidence," he ordered. One of the men wrapped the maps in newspaper, set a match to the bundle, and dropped it into a metal wastebasket.

"Now we'd better lam it." He said to me, "I'll take you home, you can clean up there." To the others: "Gentlemen, stay here until I can dispose of the body. No one must enter. I'm sorry you're involved, but we must work together now to make sure our names are not associated with this hoodlum or his death—even if it's an obvious case of self-defense."

The men agreed. They were stunned by the violence. Mr. Hood took me down a back elevator to the parking lot, where his car and chauffeur were waiting. It was late; we drove through empty streets. Mr. Hood saw me to and through my door.

"Don't budge till you hear from me. I'll take care of everything." Then, with a smile sad but warm, squeezing my hands in his:

> "...If thou art rich, thou'rt poor;
> For like an ass whose back with ingots bows,
> Thou bear'st thy heavy riches but a journey
> And death unloads thee."

He has been my only consolation in these grim hours.

I feel sick, sick, and never so alone. Alone, and vulnerable, in spite of Mr. Hood. The police will come straight here for me. I feel conspicuous as a flying elephant. I have no energy, no confidence, and no glimmer of comprehension.

But why tell you how I feel? There was nothing but you to give hope, and now I guess there is not even you. Without your strength and thought I would never have undertaken this and now you have deprived me of them. It's unpleasant to blame you, but who else is there to blame for the wasted days and nights, the wasted money and the expense of emotion? I beg for help and you answer nothings. Here's a check for what's worth.

XCI

March 12

It is very sad, Twang sends you much thoughtful strength for your trouble, but then I have such: the policemen are sent after me by an American the Mr. P. Asher, who bought last December that cameo. It was false! I telephoned the Prince and he said, "Ssh! Nothing to say on the telephone, come." He already knows. It is so bad for everyone of us, so that he, and Bonzo, and I, and all are about to fall into disgrace or jail. It seems, there is no way out as if they had surrounded us with rollers of bobbed wire!—but the Prince "will do all he cans."

I shall answer one question here, saying that the two maps are the very same. But do you see, it does not matter? (Because the treasure is a belonging of the Prince Voltic, wherever it is found, or lost.) Not a matter anynow.

And I think for Twang, for Zachary too, to remember: perceive evil and suffering, think of them collapsing the stupid idea happiness. And:
Stillness within, knowing:

> Suffering exists, but no sufferer
> Action exists, although no actor
> Extinction, but not one in the least who dies
> Although there is a Way there is no wayfarer

(And to face them I have not even any pretty clothes, just just these old hateful ones.)

XCII

March 14

This has been a day of varied emotions, bringing as it did my ma's will and accounts of her death.

There has been no published news of Hodge's murder.

My mother died last Wednesday, while I was mucking through the fogs. She had recently fallen ill, as I wrote you. (You did not find this worthy of comment.) Her death was therefore not unexpected, but no less terrible, especially as I could not attend her last hours. She was a perfect woman, "glory and beauty went before her." She must have been disappointed in me, her only son. She never however showed anything but affection. Thank God she didn't live to see me in court. The mother ate sweet grapes, and the son's teeth fell out.

She was buried today and I drove down for the funeral. Mr. Hood would not let me go sooner. In his tactful way he even tried to dissuade me from making the trip at all. He finally agreed to it and ended by coming with me! It was a godsend having him there. There were moments, such as when I beheld my coffined mother in her beloved pearls and shawl, in which collapse was near, and at those times Mr. Hood straightened me up with a word or look. He was a comfort to everyone and made a strong impression. Diana thought he was a doctor.

The funeral was ghastly. It's true that my other (and I admit greater) anguish may have deformed what I saw. Everybody behaved as if they were menstruating. It might have been a snake that was being buried. It is degrading that a woman so generous and cheerful should be a pretext for such meanness.

On the drive back tonight I asked Mr. Hood what he meant when, just before the blood flowed, he referred to Hodge's "years with the papes." Mr. Hood replied that for most of his life Hodge had been a Jesuit priest. I couldn't believe it. I said that Hodge was as unlike a Jesuit as possible, witness his latest hairdo. Mr. Hood said, "That's why he was called the Invisible Jesuit. You were looking at a Jesuit but you couldn't see him."

Miami in Lent is deader than an empty gin bottle; I am the fly inside it. Mr. Hood tells me to be patient. He visits at least twice a day—his concern is amazing. He is chary of news, probably out of discretion. He says we're getting the breaks: no doubt he's making them.

I have taken out protractor and compass to try and collate my sketchy copy with the real life maps of the Geodesic Survey. They never quite match.

It is uncertain what the police are doing. Mr. Hood may have arranged matters or perhaps they are being clever. They can issue John and Jane Doe warrants and fill in the names at the moment of arrest.

Thank you for your frequent and sympathetic letters.

XCIII

March 14

Yesterday again I saw the Prince. (It was near bath-time, and he appeared in a down-to-the-floor lamé bathing robe, and with eighteen curl springs in his hair. He is, I guess, so queer as the three dollar coot.) Oh, he is good, and great. Perhaps those curlers were mastery by suspension, pushing away the five hindrances by metal concentration, as a jar tossed upon moss-covered water split the slime. He had decided, to take every responsability for himself: and we shall go free from peril. It is not a foolish way; for "justice will stick to the biggest stick." I gush my thanks. He almost cried, saying no more can we ever meet. Generous man! Of course I give him Medici papers, map and explanations, anything that may help him in his battle.

It is so lovely, that in this situation everbody from the

Prince down has been one hundred per cent. Thus can Twang practice the contemplation of high intelligence to shake away the idea of material attachment, that dump of ice.

So you too should find such a discipline, notably after this disgusting slaying of which you write. Also I find it a degradation, that you copy insults out of your old letters to me!

XCIV

March 15

Bonzo and I have escaped Florence, we shall go to Lerici for a long hide-out. I think much of the idea of extinction to erase the consciousness of ever having been born. For

if mental actions are the result of ignorance
and consciousness is the result of mental actions
and name and shape are the result of consciousness
and six-sensual action is the result of name and shape
and contact is the result of six-sensual action
and feeling is the result of contact
and desire is the result of feeling
and affection is the result of desire
and becoming is the result of affection
and birth is the result of becoming:
suffering is the result of birth

We are spending the night in Lucca, charming renaissance city waiting for the next flood.

XCV

March 18

Saddened by news of the mother's death, Twang has climbed to the cemetery of this town Lerici, to think with you. Now, after tears, my dear Zachary, I must remind you life is nothing. Were you so attached to your mother? You,

also are subject to death, already. With or without this attachment to her, you are dying. It would be better, my friend,
to disengage yourself. It was better, to think of your dead
mother as you would think while looking at a cadaver, if you
worked in a crematorium.—Some objects of contemplation
for repulsion:

A corpse two or three days old, blackish-blue, it is decom-
posing; a corpse picked by cows; a carcass of bones hanging
with blood-sputtered flash, which worn muscles hold. together; bones—dessevered, whitened like shells, piled in piles,
crumpling from exposure, falling to dust. Then: "My body
is of this type, has this fate."

It is called also the perception of instability. Impermanence
even in the moss on these grave stones among which i sit to
write, the sad sunny wind, the hungry cats among the dooms.

I am in some despair also. The little town, the little life, is
empty, except for fear. This morning as I awoke I see old
curtains, old glasses, and the empty dish. I am ah thankful for
Bonzo, here, it is nothing other.

I remember another say, say

> Thinking of the cessation of desire I breathe in,
> Thinking of the cessation of desire I breathe out,

again; again.
Of course it is only an example, this word "desire".

XCVI

March 19

Just saw Hodge, alive and kickable. Was close to breakdown,
staying in day after day, so went to eat at the former Nova
Luna, a dyke bar on Scheherazade Blvd., now an Armenian
restaurant called Leander's Hideaway. Enjoying a succulent
grunt-kebab when in walked the visible Hodge. He had a
drink at the bar and left; after which the barman confirmed
his identity. I wish someone would confirm mine.

Unable to reach Mr. Hood by phone, now awaiting his visit to pass on the dire news.

Could you send copy of your map? I hope you made a copy?

I am rather dead. Also suffer (paradoxically?) from epithelial oversensitivity. Couldn't shave for days, water is fiery as rum, etc. Underneath, soft anesthesia of desperation: the shock seeing Hodge a distant one, a sonic bang from overseas. You notice I didn't move. (Should have shot him properly!) Less distraught by him than by fear of being caught by somebody from the library—have been on sick leave. Yet must quit that job. The derangement is certainly worsened by so much solitude. When I asked Mr. Dharmabody to please pass the salt I realized things were bad. Later I hitted him. I hope he's too old for me to infect him with my neuroses. His looks embody my my feelings, with black-ringed eyes and straggly hairs. I find no pleasure in his sight.

XCVII

March 23

It has become impossible to tell whether it is worse hearing or not hearing from you.

Mitchell Mauss has been arrested for theft of a treasure trove, by law the property of the state of Florida.

Mr. Hood did not come the day of Hodge's re-emergence, nor the day after. On the morning of the 21st his three bodyguards appeared at the door. They were subdued, barely whispering their unison "Hello there!" They handled me a large envelope. The map was in it—the map I had seen burn. Also a note from Mr. Hood. The partnership was being dissolved, because of danger. Contributions to the expedition were being refunded, less profits already paid: $2,200 - $2,170 = $30. Hodge was best forgotten, "victim of the cackle bladder." The whole affair should be forgotten. We had been misled. The map was of no value. The treasure had never reached these shores.... At the end: "Zachary, you're a nice man. Take my advice and pretend it was a dream."

Before there was time to show my feelings, which if my present existence were not posthumous might have been lion-like rage, the three of them rattled off an antiphonal midrash or mishmash warning me that I was liable to prosecution for stealing state property (the map), and reminding me that Mr. Hood was on the best terms with the chief of police.

That night the hair fell out all over my body. I am denuded from crown to sole. I might have foreseen this. I have felt as though some unknown law were being written into my vitals with a drill; this is its public form. I shall next grow scales.

Mr. Hood is not to be found. His house is boarded up. His office has not closed, it has disappeared. The space is occupied by a simulated-pearl distributor who claims to have been there for years. I cannot think of anyone who could testify to the contrary.

There is little left in my shrunked world. Your neglect (contempt?) has turned books into blank papers, friends into [*illegible*]. It appears I shall have neither savory meat nor blessing. Perhaps I am to be the fatted calf. Unfatted: these worries have revealed many a bone. The thyroid may be affected.

My depression is thck as a chocolate brownie. A cackle bladder is a little rubber bag filled with chicken blood and held in the mouth. Bitten into, it shoots the blood forth.

XCVIII

March 28

Indeed, there is no hope in that world of yours. It would be best to believe Mr. Hood, Forget. This, and that. For you are attached to deviation, and this has made you a pariah. Remember, it is not by birth that one becomes a pariah, but by acts.

So you have acted: when most gently crossed, you fall into

anger, screaming, etc. Look at Bonzo—humbled for years by
the women whose hands he must shine, often by the Prince,
and life, yet is ready always for more. It rouses atrocious
feeling in me when I think of your way. And now even water
annoys you so your hair is falling!

Also you have acted: the sorriest occasion is an excuse for
you to put forward your lust. Our nights together, always
you slide to my side of the bed; later you ask me to write
dirty letters; and so forth. And Bonzo—true, he did that first
attack but since, look at him: nights and days with Twang,
and he still waits. I start to find him rather sexy!

You act as if your heart were a tiger's, you kick away my
questions, my thoughts and all my sentiments, and you claw
at friends with hate. As for Bonzo if he sees one eye of mine
opening he strains to guess its desire. You wish to shoot
Hodge. Know that they who would shoot will be shot!!

Is it then a surprise that I shall want to forsake a pariah of
such irritability, sensuality, and cruelty, and marry the mild
man Bonzo?

We must remain here until the danger pass. I would prefer
you do not write. Later, I shall tell you what is to happen.
Three nights ago there was a fire in one section of the Laurenziana, I suppose you have read this in the newspaper? Many
private citizens bravely rushed in to help evacuate the rare
archives.

XCIX

Why not the whole truth? Surely you no longer care about
its effect on me. You need only admit it. This is no attempt to
convince you of anything, or to judge. You are beyond the
pale of judgment—at least of civilized humanity—among
Tartars you might get a hearing.

Nearly a year ago a first suspicion slithered through my
brain, and was sent scurrying. In your letter of July 3, "Who
is Montpellier?" you naïvely asked. Yet on May 12 you had
written of Messer Todao's house in Montpellier. You will

remember those words, these very words, you who forget nothing?

This was the scheme. That gang knew that we librarians had access to the Donation maps. What better prospect among them than a middle-aged bachelor slob? So Mr. Tittel, agent of the highly respected International Red Arrow and my "accidental" traveling companion, collared me on my flight east to plant the first information in my unsuspecting head; and in Bangkok he delivered me into your irresistible care. I was solidly hooked, "marrage" wiped away all doubt, and you bravely agreed to work alone in strange cities on our behalf. I passed into the hands of Hodge, whom I met as I had met you, at the initiative of a stranger. You urged me to frequent him, to take up his proposition, after which I was propelled into dreamy Spindledom. Whenever I was calm enough to be capable of reason, you inflamed me with harrying news— Bonzo Pindola's assault, your frequentation of him, your ill-treatment by the Prince, all communicated in the certainty that knowing you alone in a foreign land was torture to me. Meanwhile your refusal to punish Pindola started the long fuse of jealousy smoldering through the burrows of my mind. I was tantalized with reports about the no doubt fictitious Salvestro to convince me of your zeal; and with your arsenical Buddhist moralizations which, when you ran out of affectionate phrases, were to prove your devotion. Finally you engineered the catastrophe of our transatlantic non-meeting, probably without leaving Tuscany; thus exhausted, I was lured into the unlikely partnership with Hood. They got the map from me. They certainly have the treasure. And they means you.

Isn't this the truth rather more than less? Isn't it the work of your desire?

As for the things you mention, we will forget them, if you please. I have no wish to remember them. If there is evil in me it will not be learned from your crusted tongue.

More last words, not many. I don't expect an answer, it doesn't matter, you will at least hear me. I expect you want to complete your revenge on me. I do not need to learn that

an incensed woman is dangerous. You have already made
chaos of my dull globe. My ego is like a torn kleenex. But do
whatever seems most delightful. Our marriage isn't binding
here either, thank you, so go right ahead with Banjo. Only it
must be said that I have loved you as old men love the sun—I
repeat this, since resentments leave only half-recollections, I
have loved you beyond any wish for life or death—it is
something I would not want you to forget, the merest jewel
for your left claw.

C

7 Pok Laï

*Piu Lemu! lemö vin maï uüax pristwi. Theu mau neng, wey
tharaï duvaï. Wuc Lao stheu atran, ticbaï maï slop, naï: theu sheenö
laï nob lucri nam aïndap.* (eels)

CI

This chump never blowed you were turned out to hopscotch. You let him find the leather, and he copped you for
the pure quill, when you're nothing but a crow. It took a long
time to bobble him but now you've knocked him good and
he feels like a heavy gee had slipped him a shiv. Well, no
twist will ever beat this savage again, not if she hands over
her bottom bumblebee—it's cheaper loaning cush to Pogy
O'Brien. Don't you play the hinge but stick to the big con.
You're a class raggle with a grand future, even if this mark
knows you're snider.

CII

April 10

Dear Doctor de Roover,
    it has been very long, since I had the pleasures of lunching
with you or Mrs. de Roover. I have not, however, forgot

how much your help. I have thought, you shall like to know if I found anything out about that treasure *dei trè sciarrani?* Yes.

You will remember your intelligence of Otto di Guardia's hoard and the clipping; later, your great guess, Averardo had that bastard son whom then I could discover (Salvestro Sguardofisso.)

I suspected that treasure, its going to America; yet only suspect; then learned (two sources), on the chest were three perch "crudely carved", by Nicola Pisano. By Nicola Pisano, never! Crudeness and his name cannot mix. It was plain, that chest was false. Yet was it thought, was it meant to be thought, true? I have wondered, who saw the very gold, but in Florence? Nobody. Only the silk wrapping, I will tell you about it soon. Next I learned that Averardo accuses Giovanni di Bicci of taking Mr. Todao's riches in *bags*. Later Cosimo wrote Francesco di Neroni, about its markings: on the chest, on the wrappings, were *i segni familiari*, the family emblem, thus balls not fish. The name *trè sciarrani* stuck only as a memory of the first, fish chest.

Cosimo has the treasure in his Florentine palace, but too notorious to use, and Salvestro watching. Cosimo hides the clippings in a chest of silks. He asks Francesco di Nerone to export it; no mention of gold. Then Salvestro tells, and the plot fail through.

Again the treasure sits in the palace. Useless, but they will not yield it to Salvestro. Did they fear he'd claim pictures, land, jewels, banks, anything? They feared he was Piero's son! (The slave mother had just been in Piero's employ.)

In 1465 Salvestro is entirely their enemy, joins in the great conspiracy. In exile, after, he frightens them; then leaves Italy.

It is 1480. Lorenzo de' M. is short of money: he will sell the clippings, in Lyons. And he makes the plans for this with Lionetto de' Rossi. But in the next year new luck comes to him. The family shuts the costly bank in Venice. The Medici are welcome back in Rome, some pope's debts are paid. Those political "reforms" start to work, the state of Florence is lapsing between his hands with the public monies. His plan changes.

I learned this from one unscrambled bag of MAP—have you yet reached it? There was the correspondance between Lionetto and Lorenzo of those years. The letters before were known only from Lyons (Harvard). One of Lionetto complains that a chest of silk is not

full, hurry with the rest. In this copy, after the place he would signs,
there is an addition. It reads, how happy that the gold has "escaped its
ultramontane destiny." Look! this is not what it seems, it is no part of
the letter but of Lorenzo's answer, that I have found. Has Lionetto
copied it there for the fact, as a signal of disappointment, of irony? I
shall not know; but the meaning of "ultramontane" is France not Italy.
The treasure did not move. Yet that word became evidence of its
coming to France.

Many already believed this. Lionetto started the lie. You remember
he was then badly straitened. He wanted so much to sell the treasure,
restoring his assets. Now I hope I shall make you happy, and you can
fit a new paragraph in your book (p. 301). Lionetto sent two balance
sheets to Florence, one confused to the manager Sassetti, one clear to
Lorenzo. You have wondered why, and I tell you: Sassetti did not
know the plan of selling, and must be beguiled. Lionetto hoped the
true account would make Lorenzo help. It did not. But Lionetto decided to act as if his wish had been granted.

By this time he had excited some buyers. He told the immensity of
the treasure, also its distinctive signs: three fish carved on the chest,
ravens stamped on the wrappings. (False! never ravens, only the Medici
balls agains. Those birds were hatched from Lionetto's misreading
Lorenzo's words, they were that the markings on the silk are so tar-
nished they "truly resemble black crows.")

Lionetto sold some chest to the sixth Abbot of Montpelas. He was
foolish and paid a gold price for taffeta. After a repose in the abbey, this
chest was carried to the new world, with its reputation still glowing. •
I can tell you its American history, when you so ask.

The gold lay in Florence. Lorenzo had decided to melt it down
later, "with strenuous precautions of secrecy" (Memorandum to
Sassetti, MAP Filza 34, No. 344; no mention in the *libro segreto*.) It was
never done.

When the Medici were expelled in 1494, the new government let
the mob plunder their palace, it was "sacked from roof to cellar." But
in that mob, calm, came the Pindolas, rich oilmongrels, attached to the
Averardo clan. Salvestro's father had bound them to be loyal to his
bastard, and they helped him. During his exile they sheltered his mother, and departing from Italy he charged them with this final task. They
should recover certain possessions "close to my heart, albeit modest

in their worth." These had been part of his inheritance, seized by Cosimo, so he said, kept by his successors. Salvestro breathed no word of the gold. During the sack the Pindolas retrieved these things and took them to their house until Salvestro's return. They remained there, undisturbed until last year, when a few were sold. The chest, full of rotted silk, did not move. Now it is journeying forth from the scholarly realm, and my account must end.

I hope you had no trouble from that fire at the Laurenziana. Other friends were I think both burned and arrested.

May these pages have pleased you, dear Doctor de Roover! If you so desire, I shall send the exact sources. Convey my expressions of unforgetful friendship to your wife.

Sincerely Yours,

Tro-tsi Twang Panattapam McCaltex

CIII*

April 13

Zachary! I understand! One letter lost! Not the *i* in "marriage"! But this blue secret one, quick read it, only now it came back to me, for I sent it from the "General Delivery, Florence", and last week I wrote them for mail coming when I am in Lerici and here (Genova)—look on it, they have marked redly "not authorized enclosure"—it is my own, Twang's sprig of rosemary that had brought it back for more stamps, but why should I return to that post office, it is the sprig I sent from my very window pot that has poisoned the time. I have thought in late weeks, he is acting his part very well for the spies, even: is it truth? a little only, my Zachary, for that is more than I can think long without dying. Today this letter comes, not until today because of the strike patterns, and before when I wake up—I came into a hotel in the first mountains, for their sweet air—I have seen a daisy, a tardy orange, a cow: I ask, what joy will come upon me? It is you. I can

*Special delivery. Letter of January 3 attached.

understand, and you shall not be lost! Oh I admist that the
tears stream down my cheeks. It is as that which was tumbled
is raised or what was hidden is unclosed, some yellow rose,
like the right road pointed to she who was lost or a light
brought into the dark for those who have eyes to see. Yes
my cheeks are wet. Come to wipe them with that torn kleenex. Not as that other trip then I believed you must have the
softest brain! Because you write "dictionary" and "Pogy
O'Brien", that is some accident, and you think the lies I com-
posed for them are true, I have such miseries inflicted on you
it is not to be thought about. Now it shall be new, and today
the New Year starts in my country, I say Happy New Year
and this and all other that ever I shall speak to you is true.
True as it can be born, wrapped in kindness of love, for in
these lying letters I have said some real things, I thought, I
shall not waste all the time I shall tell him of our believes and
thus my short course in Buddhism but not meant so cruel,
indeed there is truth in my words over your mother, whom
I bewept so, I must flee into the graveyard, yet it was from
my shame to have never kissed the hands of her who gave
you into the world and this, is selfishness; however I would
not have spoken with that cruel written tone. Never! my
Zachary.

There's too much, to tell now, together I shall tell everything, we can smile and weep about all that. But some explanation—for instance the treasure was always here! That
story about the abbot, and Amortonelli, that was crazy to me,
then I think, you are fascinated by the intellectual problem
viz. map, but Twang think rightly: cash. And other mistakes
—*familiari* only meaning "family", and sacks bearing the
treasure, and *torcere* not to "throw" the gold only wrap it, as
many did in that historical period when the exchange rates
were bad, and the crows on the brocade, a stupidity of Lionetto and making for me early suspicion because when I hunted
through all the timely papers there were crowns, crosses,
croziers but never crows! There were only ever the Medici
palle, their balls as in the shout *Evvivano le palle!* so I write this
cry but it misses you. No the treasure was always in Casa Pin-

dola and that day Bonzo showed me the remainder of the Averardo heritage when I saw the old silk I have a pulse of about eight hundred, and he saw nothing. He believes those stories.

Ah the Prince, the Pindola, they are giggles—are such the tough men of the west it is to be the famous yellow takeover. They thought I shall seem to come by accident into their company? they shall make me so dependant on them, then trap me, then scare me absolutely off? I know when I meet little Bonzo he cannot rape a sponge, most clearly they are longing for that map. Now they have it. The police scared me to give it to them!?—do they think I have no memories, these "policemen" that invade my room were with that Hood in Rome as he argued modern thought. Quickly I decided, I must win Bonzo from the Prince, and never leave the Prince to suspect me, and it was for this our letters were the clinch. Sometimes it has been hard. For the American trip I had to sneak out in the mask of an old dame, that I made from the padding of my quilt, some pasted across my brows. But only now can they know.

Thus it was: Bonzo and I escape out of Florence. In a day the Prince notifies Bonzo he has shifted all blame onto him. So, Bonzo can say to me, watch out, I Twang am an accomplice, I shall better stick to him. This is so he can stick to *me*, to watch me, not let me warn you, should I know their plans to use the map. I was content for I needed some time to harass the Pindola about the chest. Already I grasp Bonzo tight—we shall marry! That is the "certain agreement" that at first I did not explain. So foolish the man was, it was I Twang who must beg him to marry with property in common—he thinks still that I am rich, he thought I asked money from you because I'm so tough I shall not lose one cent. I teach him, it is wrong for a wife to own more than a husband.

In Lerici we wait, nothing to do. I'm hard to him. One day I say I want that chest as an engagement present, he said, a stupid idea, it weighs some quintals. I twrist his arm harder. Still he thinks it cannot be, also it is his father's. I said the old fellow's gaga, I want the antique silk, some will be found

from the rot to sew into my wedding gown; and promise to
be nicer to him, oh much nicer.... O.K.! He orders that the
chest be sent in a truck. That evening on the beach, I must
(dear one you shall please forgive) I must, so that he keep his
mind away from that decision, I consent to "grant him my
favors" as he has always begged. So I "screw my courage to
the sticking point," and vice versa, but he becomes so surprised that he was not able to fuck me. He just falls prostate
to my feet. No matter, I have warned the police to be near
and I tear some buttons in the dusk and scream and Bonzo
is in the jail as rapist at last.

I kept the man there as long is needed. He cannot call the
Prince to help, not without revealing the joke about the
Prince turning against him. Then I let him out, annulling
charges. To Bonzo I said that on the beach he hit me in one
of his madnesses and I thought he wished to kill me. He con-
not remember through the shocks, I insist and scold him and
he believes, such a kreep! and even's lowly ashamed. I say
then, Off to Florence, prepare our wedding, it is Pan custom
for the bride to be far from the coming husband, away! He
did not want to go, it was a terrible struggle, but since it all
took place inside him, I did not mind.

Meanwhile the Hood had come to Florence on March 22.
This had made me think there is trouble on foot; this is why I
force Bonzo hard. Hood must first have thought that Mauss
had stolen the treasure, and made him arrested. But he learned
soon there was no gold there, they had dug up a chest of bad
silk. (And are they the first to know this—for Amortonelli
and the captain I think never could look themselves into the
chest, they believed the weight, or did not want the shoveling
sailors to see.) I deduce that after this, they all look again at
my letters and know the secret is in the Medici archives. They
must have those bags, while I am kept away. They start the
fire in the old library, so they can run in and "help". This was
a guess, I only heard information on the radio pogrom; but
next I read two burned in the fire, their names were of the
little bodyguards. They must steal the bags of papers with the
numbers they found in my notes. Well, I telephoned the

police to look for those papers at the Prince's. They are several arrested. Not Hood, he's a wily man, you were my dear one in the hands of a very bad hat! Yet Bonzo arrives in time to climb aboard the padded wagon.

So now the Prince and Pindola shall drop their marbles where they may. Poor Bonzo, again in jail! He's wrong for such work, being a sure psychopath—those rages, those callapses. It is said, also, that only old age can cure the psychopathic personality, and if there is a thing Bonzo does not wish it is the growing old.

Hastily I must tell you one last discovery, then I shall run with a taxi to the central post office and send you this. I confess, I have indulged one extra research. It was because the name of Salvestro's mother, not the Christian one given, but her own from the east, is Twang—or, *Tuan*, but even now the Italians call me thus. I have laughed and believed nothing but chance there, yet anyway I inquired. She was twenty-five years old in 1431, therefore she was likely born in Tana, or better on the way from Tana and this is why she had no marks. Was her mother able to be Pan, and so far from our country? That was not probable, it was possible. I wondered: where did Salvestro go with her, when he left Italy? And asked for your microfilms. One more thing to love you for. The missionaries are established in time. So I could learn that Salvestro the Spice Trader came there, to Pannam Tuan's home, he has married in 1489 and his children were baptized later. I laugh some more and write my father, and he has told me that in a little chapel at the village Namma Bamma there is a western portrait of a male that has been cleaned last year, and scholars call him Francesco de' Medici! Salvestro's father! That village is next to ours, to that village where you came to me, my Zachary, and consider it is perhaps from Salvestro that I am born, with his mother's name that is saved through our family, a rare name, and also my first name, in Pannam this is a reference to my hero protector, usually of legend, but think that Tro-tsi, Salve*stro* Medi*ci*, do you recall how we called you Kri until I could master your beloved name, cutting off the last sound to mean the foreign word? And therefore I shall be the treasure's heir? *Evvivano le palle!*

For I have it. That chest came to Lerici, I climbed into the truck, opened it. Under the shreds my arm stuck into the gold bits from the fingertips to my elbow. I filled one palm for expenses, and your ticket. At once I had brought a big chain and bound it and without leaving it off the truck forward it to Genoa. And after I released Bonzo and he left to Florence, I followed.

The affair is done. Early I went today to the shipping offices and made almost every arrangement, it was only not possible to get much insurance, tomorrow I'll argue more about that —it is for this why I did not write until this afternoon, it must all be done! Oh that letter made me bad in business. A gentleman asked, "What must be the date of arrival?" and I answered, "He is the most exquisite of men." Another desired to know, "Is there a Burmese address?" I replied, "Perhaps he will be here Sunday." One needed to be told, "How are we to declare these goods?" "Not leave him for an hour!" were my words. Yet the matter was concluded, and at noon the chest was already sunk in to the hold of the *Odradek Stadion*, a vessel that is property of the Malta Cross Shipping Company of Panama, chartered by Metternich Services Anstalt, a Swiss-registered company with offices in Liechtenstein, fitted out in Greenore, Eire, carrying U.S. equipment, and a Dutch captain and crew! At least, it keeps the Panama flag. It will carry the box to Rangoon, best market of gold in this material-subtle world.

The weather is of heaven, *langoureux vertige*, spring fever. Through gentle air, my mind fills up with such a goodness of love for you, my beloved and ever-desired, towards the west expanding first, over the seas, promontories and islands that make you distant from me, thinking: you are to tell me today as you see these words, that I shall very soon have the honor of kneeling again at your feet when you consent to come here, oh most soon. For until that hour I can live only in expectation of this, meditating on your perfection. I shall tell you, the vainest man never found in his mirror half the beauty I see in you, your way, your voice, every glance motion and gesture has such radiance my whole being is possessed and there is no life for me except in the hope of your affection. I cannot say it, only I love you with the most wild passion that ever came into woman. I wish my life's action to be discovering of means to convince you that you are preferable to everything pleasant on earth. My mind is so full, so full of you, Zachary! It swells in this goodness all of love over the world, then to the north, now I see some lightning of first summer warmths, and it's as I shall feel of you when first I see you distant, still faceless; and south, there are I believe shells on the beach and I remember that never will you collect them, I'll be a shell you can just walk on my uncollected skull if that be your pleasure; and east, the sun, the golden sword of new life! Come soon! And up to the sky, a big blue cranium—no that is not the flower name I want, but you can understand I desire to symbolize my desire, while below the earth would have me of course reminded of Mister Dharmabody, you must bring him no matter how old and worn he has become, and I think I must make him to bite me for that blow, it was not you it was Twang inflicted that. So much love within me, spreading about, what is there it will not enfold—perhaps my typhoid germs? which were yesterday innoculated into me, and it's plain the immunizing produces a tough form of that disease! It pierces the whole world. You are to be emperor of the world in my explosion adoration, I'll drag you *nel giallo della rosa sempiterna*, do you know, into the yellowness of the eternal rose, that opens, clambers, casts perfumes of praise to the sun that lasting springmaker, and I shall hope, it does not make your hair grow again, that smoothness is pleasanter—the bodily hair is what most disconcerts in occidentals, and without it also your fat shall be a gentle smooth quality only with hair is it terrifying. I shall pluck my pubis smooth as yours. Yet Zachary, do not although I say these eat every food, not for fat and thin, but I shall recall, "Whatever food a man eats in this life, by that food he is eaten in the next." It seems my head my breast will break with my love of you, or I shall be a balloon, I'll float through a grand landscape that shines, yellow pots big as mountains, platters like luminous cities, glasses and crackery like valleys like expressways, as if they were blazing in yellow lights, from below and above, but all arranged in round ranks and balancing as one thing on a broomstick as long as an ocean, and we are in the middle of the ranks of dishware thinking we are becoming insane from too much love, no, it is only these things are harmless—but this morning, I made a little altar in my room. I set incense and flowers on it. This was that I might exhibit, to myself, Twang's grief of your suffering. Each morning I shall put new incense, flowers, until you are next to me. Now you take five dollars even if your last and send a cable. I have telephoned but it will not answer, and shall wire but you will not believe it, but you must go to the air office, and there is the ticket to Italy for you, and I shall this time be waiting at the airport of Rome. There can be no more error, it is no longer in my power, there is no more harm in our mind there is no limit there is no hatred of anything breathing or un-breathing—it is a mind without knowledge of ill will, my Zachary! but you must come. Alone I cannot carry this burden of joy, and doubt

Index

to *The Sinking of the Odradek Stadium*

194 THE SINKING OF THE ODRADEK STADIUM

crab, 9, 62, 68
Crawford, Joan (Lucile Lesueur)
  (Billie Cassin), 14
cross, 3, 91, 163, 167, 168, 169
crow, 9, 23, 27, 79, 80, 93, 125,
  126, 150, 153, 154, 164, 177,
  182, 184, 186

Dalmanutha (Florida), 51
Day, Doris (Doris Keppelhoff),
  98
Dejanira, 8
de Roover, Florence, 78, 108,
  182, 185
———, Raymond, 32, 39, 73, 77,
  78, 79, 82, 83, 84, 104, 105,
  182, 185
Dickens, Charles, 156
dog, 8, 9, 18, 27, 50, 86, 98, 100,
  106, 136, 146, 151, 154, 162,
  178, 191
dolphin, 27, 161
D(oolittle), H(ilda), 165
dragon, 71, 96, 154, 182
Dubillard, Roland, 82
Duccio di Buoninsegna, 104

Egk, Werner, 98
Eire, 190
Eliot, Thomas Stearns, 88, 90, 92

Farah, -Sahi, Mahjubah, 63ff.
Favell, Ayer, 62, 65ff., 134, 136,
  156, 159, 160, 161
fish, 19, 23, 24, 26, 27, 30, 33, 38,
  40, 45, 68, 80, 86, 87, 96, 112,
  114, 115, 126, 147, 153, 161,
  177, 183, 184. *See also* remora
Fiumicino (Italy), 140, 141, 192
Florence (Italy), 4, 18, 28, 32, 40,
  47, 50, 51, 55, 84, 104, 111,
  116, 126, 129, 132, 138, 139,
  140, 183, 184, 185, 187, 188,
  190, Palazzo Rucellai, 83
Fontfroide (France), abbey of, 24

Gabritius, 146
Gander (Newfoundland), 135
Gardner, Ava Lavinnia, 14
Gazzara, Ben, 169
Geneva (Switzerland), 47
Genoa (Italy), 47, 48, 185, 190
Gershwin, George, 98
Gherucci, Bartolommeo, 22ff.
Gibran, Kahlil, 162

Glinka, Mikhail Ivanovich, 5
Greek, Lester, P., 18, 22, 85, 86,
  99, 103, 107
Griffith, David Wark, 161
Groffsky, Maxine, 139
Guardia, Otto di, 32, 33, 73, 183
Gutkind, Curt S., 79

Händel, Georg Friedrich, 114
Hannibal, 67
Hanover (Germany), 98
Harvard University, 142, 153,
  183
Havana (Cuba), 9
Hawaii, 4
helmet, 57, 95f.
Hercules, 133
Hermes Trismegistus, 133
Hodge, Dexter, 9, 27, 28, 29ff.,
  33ff., 40, 41, 43, 49, 50, 54, 61,
  62, 68, 70, 71, 76, 82, 83, 85,
  86, 88, 91, 93, 94, 95, 96, 99,
  103, 106, 107, 108, 109, 115,
  120, 123, 127f., 145, 146, 147,
  152, 155f., 160, 166f., 169ff.,
  174, 175, 177, 178, 180, 181
Holden, William (William
  Beedle), 139
Hood, Miles, 28f., 62, 68, 85, 88,
  91, 93, 94, 95ff., 98, 99, 100,
  101ff., 106, 108, 109, 112, 115,
  119f., 121f., 123, 124, 125,
  127, 128, 142, 145, 149f.,
  151f., 154, 170ff., 173, 174,
  181, 187, 188
hypoglycemia, 59, 130, 189

imperialism, American, 65
Indonesia, 4

Japan, 21
Jeffers, Robinson, 157
Jeigh, Peter, 45, 62, 85
Jespersen, Otto, 40
Jewcett, Silex, 30, 62
Joan of Arc, 156
Jourdan, Louis (Louis Gendre),
  98
Joyce, James, 18, 86

ka, 33, 36ff., 162
Kabod, E. Peter, 70f.
Kavya, An-natan Slong, 87f.
Keeler, William H. ("Wee
  Willie"), 81

DALKEY ARCHIVE PAPERBACKS

Yuz Aleshkovsky, *Kangaroo.*
Felipe Alfau, *Chromos.*
  Locos.
  Sentimental Songs.
Alan Ansen,
  Contact Highs: Selected Poems 1957-1987.
Djuna Barnes, *Ladies Almanack.*
  Ryder.
John Barth, *LETTERS.*
  Sabbatical.
Andrei Bitov, *Pushkin House.*
Roger Boylan, *Killoyle.*
Christine Brooke-Rose, *Amalgamemnon.*
Gerald Burns, *Shorter Poems.*
Gabrielle Burton, *Heartbreak Hotel.*
Michel Butor,
  Portrait of the Artist as a Young Ape.
Julieta Campos,
  The Fear of Losing Eurydice.
Anne Carson, *Eros the Bittersweet.*
Louis-Ferdinand Céline, *Castle to Castle.*
  London Bridge.
  North.
  Rigadoon.
Hugo Charteris, *The Tide Is Right.*
Jerome Charyn, *The Tar Baby.*
Emily Holmes Coleman,
  The Shutter of Snow.
Robert Coover, *A Night at the Movies.*
Stanley Crawford,
  Some Instructions to My Wife.
René Crevel, *Putting My Foot in It.*
Ralph Cusack, *Cadenza.*
Susan Daitch, *Storytown.*
Peter Dimock,
  A Short Rhetoric for Leaving the Family.
Coleman Dowell, *Island People.*
  Too Much Flesh and Jabez.
Rikki Ducornet, *The Complete Butcher's Tales.*
  The Fountains of Neptune.
  The Jade Cabinet.
  Phosphor in Dreamland.
  The Stain.
William Eastlake, *Castle Keep.*
  Lyric of the Circle Heart.

Stanley Elkin, *Boswell: A Modern Comedy.*
  The Dick Gibson Show.
  The MacGuffin.
Annie Ernaux, *Cleaned Out.*
Lauren Fairbanks, *Muzzle Thyself.*
  Sister Carrie.
Leslie A. Fiedler,
  Love and Death in the American Novel.
Ronald Firbank, *Complete Short Stories.*
Ford Madox Ford, *The March of Literature.*
Janice Galloway, *Foreign Parts.*
  The Trick Is to Keep Breathing.
William H. Gass, *The Tunnel.*
  Willie Masters' Lonesome Wife.
C. S. Giscombe, *Giscome Road.*
  Here.
Karen Elizabeth Gordon, *The Red Shoes.*
Patrick Grainville, *The Cave of Heaven.*
Geoffrey Green, et al, *The Vineland Papers.*
Jiří Gruša, *The Questionnaire.*
John Hawkes, *Whistlejacket.*
Aldous Huxley, *Antic Hay.*
  Point Counter Point.
  Those Barren Leaves.
  Time Must Have a Stop.
Gert Jonke, *Geometric Regional Novel.*
Tadeusz Konwicki, *A Minor Apocalypse.*
  The Polish Complex.
Ewa Kuryluk, *Century 21.*
Deborah Levy, *Billy and Girl.*
José Lezama Lima, *Paradiso.*
Osman Lins, *The Queen of the Prisons of Greece.*
Alf Mac Lochlainn,
  The Corpus in the Library.
  Out of Focus.
D. Keith Mano, *Take Five.*
Ben Marcus, *The Age of Wire and String.*
Wallace Markfield, *Teitlebaum's Window.*
David Markson, *Collected Poems.*
  Reader's Block.
  Springer's Progress.
  Wittgenstein's Mistress.
Carl R. Martin, *Genii Over Salzburg.*
Carole Maso, *AVA.*
Harry Mathews, *Cigarettes.*

Visit our website: www.dalkeyarchive.com

DALKEY ARCHIVE PAPERBACKS

Visit our website: www.dalkeyarchive.com

Dalkey Archive Press
ISU Campus Box 4241, Normal, IL 61790–4241
fax (309) 438–7422